TROUBLE

USA TODAY BESTSELLING AUTHOR

TIA LOUISE

This book is a work of fiction. Names, characters, places, and incidents are products of the author's imagination or are used fictitiously. Any resemblance to actual events or locales or persons, living or dead, is entirely coincidental.

Trouble

Printed in the United States of America.

Cover design by Lori Jackson Design.
Photography by Michelle Lancaster.

This book is for you, my readers. I hope it brings you joy and gives you happiness, hope, and a little escape from your worries.

And for Mr. TL, always.

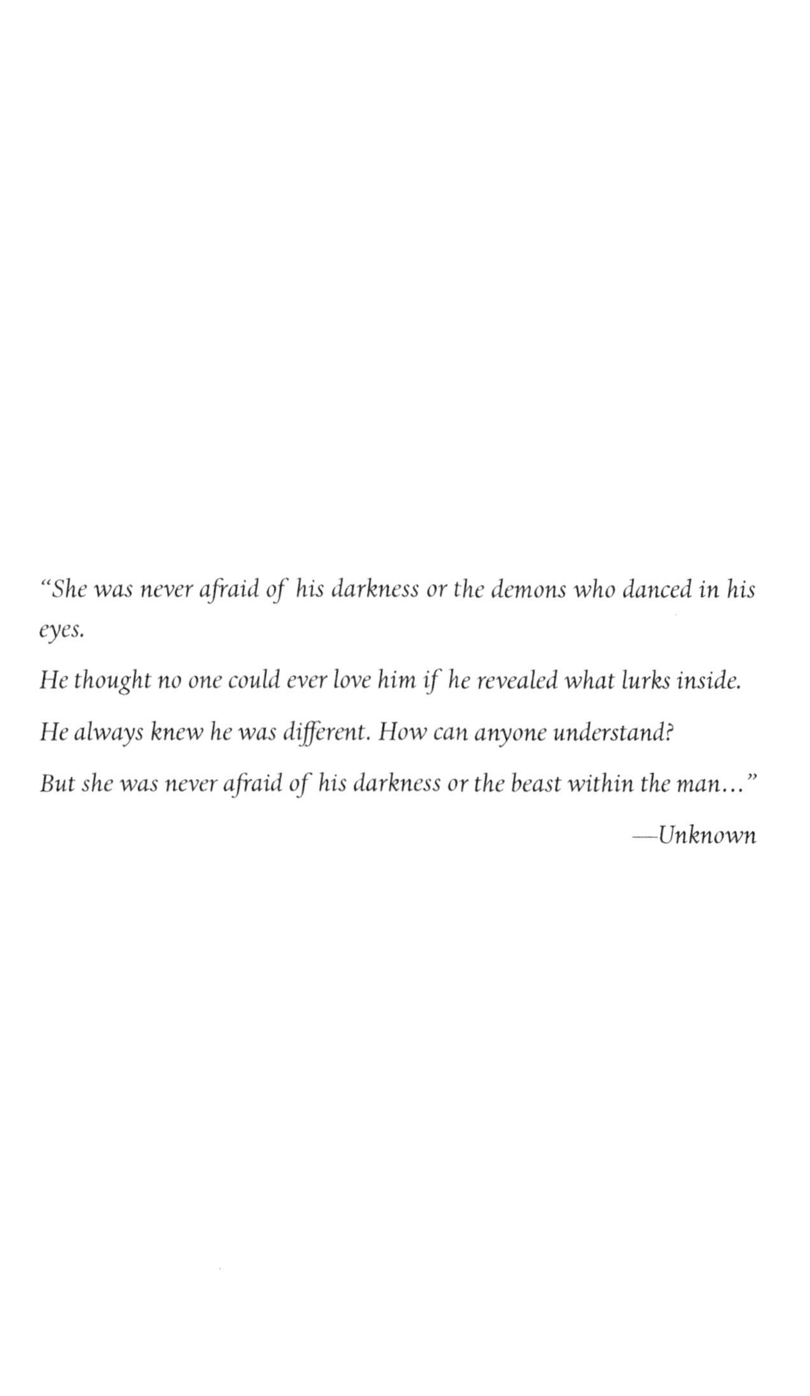

"She was never afraid of his darkness or the demons who danced in his eyes.

He thought no one could ever love him if he revealed what lurks inside.

He always knew he was different. How can anyone understand?

But she was never afraid of his darkness or the beast within the man…"

—Unknown

Prologue

Spencer

"I HAVE ICE. ICE MAKES THE PAIN GO AWAY." MY MOM CROUCHES BESIDE me, her entire body shaking as she presses a cloth to my shoulder.

Her face is so white. I want to say her name, but my throat constricts as searing pain burns through my upper body. My eyes squeeze shut, causing tears to stream down my face.

All around us is chaos.

The kitchen table is against the wall, and a chair is broken in two. Beside me on the floor, a splintered piece of wood lies in what looks like a growing puddle of red paint. Only, it's not paint, and I'm afraid.

"Look what you made me do!" My father yells at us, pacing back and forth. He jerks my mother off of me by her hair. "You made me do this."

Fear squeezes my lungs so hard, I can't breathe, and lights flash in the room through the windows like a rainbow. People in white rush into our house, and a woman with orange-blonde hair and sky-blue eyes leans over me.

She puts her hand on my forehead and smiles gently while another person in white lifts me off the floor. She speaks softly, but I can't understand her.

Is she an angel? Did I die?

It's my last thought before the darkness closes my eyes...

"This is your room now." The old man opens a door and gestures me into a space the size of a small house.

My eyes are wide as I step carefully on the highly polished wood floor. It's made of small pieces of wood arranged in a diamond pattern, and a thin rug with a large, oval-shaped design covers the floor.

Driving up to this place, I gazed up at the soaring white columns topped with curling leaves and scrolls. Above them, so high I could barely see from the car, the roof had a railing, like you could walk around up there.

I've never seen a house like this outside of a movie or a storybook.

It's a castle.

It's also dark and empty.

"I hope you find it comfortable here."

I look up at him, unsure what to say.

He's tall with lots of gray hair that swooshes around his head like that scientist in the picture at my school. He's wearing a scratchy brown jacket and dark pants, and he has a beard. His dark eyes are intense like a bird or a reptile, watching me.

"Are you a king?" My voice is small.

"I'm your new father. You may call me Drake." His voice is low and measured, like he carefully chooses the exact word to say before he speaks.

"Where's my mom?" Sadness pinches my chest when I remember the last time I saw her.

His eyes blink away, into the hall. "She can't take care of you anymore. You're going to live with me now."

I'm not sure what he means. "Did she die?"

"Not as far as I know." His tone is grave like he doesn't want to dwell on this subject. "If you're all settled, I'll leave you to your thoughts."

I follow him quickly into the massive hallway covered in paintings bigger than me. It's as wide as a dining room, and long rugs cover the floors that go on for miles.

My footsteps echo off the polished wood as I scuffle after him. "Are we the only ones here?"

He pauses and turns, looking down at me slowly as if I'm an insect he's considering gobbling up. I shrink back, wishing I hadn't asked.

"Are you afraid of being alone, Spencer?"

My eyes are wide, and I want my mom. The expression on his face tells me that would be the wrong answer.

"No, sir."

"Good. Only a weak man is bothered by being alone. Are you weak?"

I'm not sure if I'm weak or if I'm even a man yet, but I know how to survive.

"No, sir."

His eyes flinch almost like he would smile if that were possible. "Never fall for the lie that you need other people. Only when you are completely independent are you truly strong."

He starts to go, but I hold out my hand. "But… Why do you need me?"

The spark of approval evaporates like smoke. "I don't."

His gaze travels up and around the hall, pausing at a window twice as tall as he is. "When I am gone, I will leave my estate to you, then you will be like me." Cold eyes return to mine. "Now get some rest. I'll begin your education tomorrow."

Dread filters through my stomach, but I don't dare argue. My shoulder hurts, and I'm sleepy. I don't know why I'm here, but I remember my mom saying it would be okay.

Returning quietly to my room, I notice a sweaty glass of ice water on my bedside table. Going to it, I lift a cube from the top and put it in my mouth, sliding to sit on the scratchy wool rug covering my floor.

My eyes close, and I focus on the cold as it slowly melts away.

Then I do it again.

CHAPTER One

Joselyn

Present day

"Fuck you, Elliot." I exhale a growl as I shove my phone in the hidden pocket of my knee-length, chartreuse-silk bridesmaid's dress.

Anger burns in my throat, but I will not cry.

Again.

I won't ruin my professionally applied makeup.

"Not what I want to hear from my maid of honor!" My cousin Daisy pushes past me into the dressing room suite on the second floor of the Oceanside Hotel. Her vintage Givenchy wedding dress swishes around her knees, and she's moving fast towards the bathroom. "What happened now?"

I follow her, leaning against the outside wall with a long sigh as she shuts the louvered door. "You know what happened."

"Idiot Flick again?"

I chew my bottom lip. "He's not an idiot. He's just…"

"Controlling, manipulative, unreliable—"

"He's not coming tonight. He says something came up at work."

The toilet flushes, and she steps out, washing her hands at the sink. Her brown eyes are narrowed at me in the mirror.

Shame flashes in my chest. "Don't squinch your little pixie face at me."

She shakes her blonde head as she dries her hands on the monogrammed towel. "Not my business."

"Just say it."

Our eyes meet in the mirror as she taps powder on her forehead and nose. "He pulls a stunt like this at least once a week."

"You're saying he doesn't have to work?" I'm tense, waiting for her to confirm my own fears.

"On a Sunday, at six pm?"

"He has a very demanding job."

"In garbage?"

"It's waste management." I step beside her, fluffing my red hair in the mirror. It falls in large waves around my shoulders. "It's very lucrative. How do you think he can afford a penthouse apartment in Columbia? Anyway, it's a far drive, and he just had the Mercedes detailed."

"The black Mercedes?" She tosses the makeup on the counter and starts for the door. "Don't the bad guys always drive black Mercedes?"

"It's a nice car." My voice is soft, and I'm not even convincing myself.

Hesitating, she returns to where I'm standing, taking both my hands in hers. "Does he make you happy?"

My throat aches, and I hate this question. "I should never have moved in with him. Now all my stuff is at his place."

"I know two guys who will be happy to help you move."

Even in heels, her head only reaches my nose. If I leaned forward, I could rest my chin on the top of her head.

"This is not something to worry about on your wedding day. Let's get back to the party. All that champagne won't drink itself."

"Would you do one thing for me? As a wedding gift?"

"I gave you that expensive fondue set you wanted for a wedding gift."

"And it's very nice." She squeezes my hands.

I force a teasing smile. "You want more, Britney Spears?"

"I want you to come back to the reception and just look at all the handsome, eligible bachelors waiting to sweep you off your feet."

"Who says I need a man to be happy?" Lifting my chin, my stubborn streak is fierce. Ma says it's because of my red hair.

Daisy shrugs and heads for the door. "Not me."

I'm behind her, doing my best to shrug off my dark mood. "Maybe I'll turn over a new leaf. Start dating nice men."

"You hate nice men. Now I've got to get back to my guests. Drink all the champagne and have *fun*."

She's out the door, and I look at the text again. ***Work comes first, CM.***

CM. Country Mouse.

I'm the country mouse and he's the city mouse because I'm from Fireside, one of the smallest towns in South Carolina, and he's from Columbia, which trust me, is no booming metropolis.

"Fuck you, Elliot." I shove the phone in my pocket again and head out to the party.

Lifting my fourth glass of champagne off a passing server's tray, I trace my finger along one of the shiny green leaves that make up the skirt on the oversized floral Tinkerbell statue.

Ma took me to Walt Disney World and Epcot Center one

year for spring break—just in time for the massive Epcot Flower and Garden Festival—and I was blown away.

Walking around the giant, floral topiaries of Disney princesses, Mickey Mouse, lions, and everything imaginable from the Disney movies, I got it in my head I wanted to be a part of this. I wanted to build the statues and thread the flowers and have them all over our town.

It's pretty much all I did in high school. For every homecoming game, wedding, and civic event, one of my oversized floral statues was the centerpiece. Eventually, I gave it up to study massage therapy and sports medicine, but Daisy asked me to make something for her.

Tinkerbell, the brave knight, and a quarterback princess was my mash-up tribute to my cousin and her new family.

Leaning forward, I take a long inhale of the green roses I used for the bodice, but I'm not paying attention. My hair slides across my shoulder and loops around an outstretched hand. When I pull back, the entire statue comes with me, and my arm flails, slinging wine into the air.

"No… Nooo!" My voice modulates like a cartoon character's, but a firm grip closes around my upper arm, sweeping me up against a hard chest.

"Hang on. I've got you."

"Sorry, I'm…" I'm surrounded by a delicious scent of leather and sandalwood and a touch of patchouli. It smells like *money*.

"No need to apologize. I figured you didn't want to end up on your bottom in the middle of the garden."

As I regain my balance, my eyes slide up a square jaw covered in dark scruff past a perfectly straight nose to a bewitching, smoky blend of green-brown hazel eyes leveled on mine in a way that heats my lower stomach.

"Oh no." Clearing my throat, I relax my grip on his expensive-feeling, charcoal suit jacket. "I hope I didn't spill on you."

"You didn't." His dark brow lowers, and I can't tell if he's smiling or mentally undressing me. Or both.

I release his forearm and take a step back as his grip on my bicep slowly lessens.

"I made that garden as you call it." Nodding toward the statue, I polish off the last bit of champagne in my now-empty glass.

"Is that why you watered it?"

"I got caught." I push a heavy lock of auburn hair behind my shoulder, and his eyes track my every move. "I leaned in too far."

"It's beautiful."

The way he says it and the location of his gaze makes me wonder if he means the statue or my hair. Either way, I feel pink rising in my cheeks.

"Thank you."

"Are you embarrassed? I would think you'd be accustomed to such praise. It's a stunning creation. I'm not sure I recognize some of these flowers."

"Oh." I exhale a laugh, unsure how to respond. I suck at compliments. "They're mostly tropicals. Nothing special."

"I disagree. They're very special." He looks at me, and the arrogant clip in his voice sparks my memory.

"I know you. You were in Daisy's store that day in Oceanside. You're the antiques guy. Stuart… No…"

"Spencer." Another tray glides past us, and I lift a flute off it to replace the one I tossed. He watches me. "Don't you think you've had enough?"

"No." I take a sip to spite him. "And I don't like men telling me what to do."

His eyes darken, and I feel it in all the right places. "I didn't mean to overstep, Joselyn."

"You have a good memory."

"I never forget a face. Definitely not a redhead."

"Redheads are trouble, don't you know?"

"I'm not afraid of trouble." He grins, and his eyes trace the side of my face, down my neck, like a caress. "Daisy calls you something different. A nickname..."

"Sly."

"I'm sure there's a story there." His deep voice does tingly things to my insides. "I prefer Joselyn."

I know about this guy. He's the super-arrogant billionaire who was Daisy's mentor when she worked at *Antiques Today*. It's this big media company that has a magazine and a TV show where they do appraisals, kind of like *Antiques Roadshow*.

He has a reputation for being cold and distant, and he's clearly used to bossing people around. He wants to boss me around, and I feel a hostile horniness at the prospect.

I want to rip his clothes off or pick a fight with him or pick a fight with him and then rip his clothes off and have rough, sweaty, angry sex...

I have *definitely* had enough to drink.

Setting my flute on a nearby table, I spot a familiar face holding a tray of finger foods. "Excuse me just a second."

I leave Mr. Bossy Sex-god to grab some alcohol-absorbing munchies.

"Hey, Sly." The friendly guy holding the tray slides a lock of floppy blond hair behind his ear.

"Hey, Max. I didn't know you were working tonight." I shove a ham and cheese rollup in my mouth and take another off his tray.

Max is unfazed by me stuffing my face. "Yeah, need the cash mon-ay. I'm heading to Melbourne Beach next week."

"Surf competition?" I stuff the second appetizer in my mouth and wrap one in a napkin. I wonder if I could put it in my hidden pocket or if it would leave a stain.

"First of the Prime East competitions."

"Cool," I nod, and the heat of a body warms my back.

"Have you made a friend?" Spencer sounds annoyed, and I decide to forego the third appetizer.

"Mm." I swallow quickly motioning between the two. "Max, this is Spencer. Spencer, Max. We used to work together." I give Max's arm a squeeze. "Good luck."

Spencer's brow is arched as we stroll towards the dance floor. "Where did you work together?"

"I was a cater-waiter in college. I actually hired these guys for the reception."

"You're a Jill of all trades."

"Master of none," I mutter, as he takes my hand.

"Let's dance."

"You're not here with anyone?"

"I would never take a date to a wedding." He acts as if it's so obvious.

"And why not?" My tone is defiant, and he pauses, studying me with a grin, like I'm one of those rare finds he and Daisy like to talk about. It tingles low in my stomach.

"I have my reasons."

I allow him to lead me onto the dance floor. A slow Olivia Newton-John song I don't recognize is playing, and the crowd has cleared after a boisterous round of Sir Mix-A-Lot's "Baby Got Back."

Spencer slides his hand to the middle of my waist, and our hands clasp. I lean closer, placing my eye at the level of his lips. He must be six-two, and I kind of love that he's taller than me. I'm five-eleven, which means I've always been the same height or taller than my dates. I haven't worn heels in years.

I close my eyes, listening to the song lyrics as I inhale his luscious scent. *Fuck you, Elliot* drifts through my mind.

"I hope you don't take this the wrong way..." His mouth is at my temple.

"You secretly hate flowers?"

A chuckle rumbles from his throat. "You have the perfect body for that dress."

My insides shimmer, and again, I'm at a loss. "You don't think I need to lose a few pounds?" Elliot's always commenting on portion size.

"Don't you dare. You're a perfect hourglass, a vintage beauty." He steps back, and gives me an appreciative glance. "I'm sure that's why Daisy picked it for you. She has a great eye."

"Right." We sway side to side, and I'm quiet.

"I'm sorry if I offended you."

"No. You didn't." I lean back, squinting an eye as I study his perfectly straight nose and wicked gaze. He's more like a model or an actor than how I've always pictured an antiques dealer. "How does a man like you get interested in antiques?"

"A man like me?"

"Yeah. You're not an old professor in a moth-eaten coat with crumbs in your beard."

"Thank God." He exhales a scoff.

"So what's your story?"

"I was born into it. My father had the largest, best-curated collection of priceless antiques in Newport. Drake Carrollton was the best in the business. A legend."

"Are you a legend?"

"I'm an asshole."

His frankness makes me laugh. "I've heard that about you. Daisy says you're Mr. Freeze."

"I don't waste time on sentimentality. We deal with junk found in attics or sorted after the death of a relative. Your cousin gets too emotionally involved. It's a waste of energy."

"Right." I move my nose to his shoulder again so he doesn't see me grinning at his arrogance. "She told me."

The song ends, and he gives me a little squeeze before

releasing me. I miss the warmth of his body, but he slips my hand into the crook of his arm and leads me to the balcony.

Guests shriek and funnel past us as the DJ launches into another banger. Their laughter and the noise of the music fade to a low roar as we step outside.

It's a warm, breezy night, and the scent of brine and salt air surrounds us.

The lights of the beach houses and mansions lining the shore reflect off the water, and I remember how much I miss this when I'm in Columbia. Maybe Daisy's right, and I need to ditch the idiot and move home.

"How does a pinup like you get involved in flowers?" Spencer's deep voice breaks my reverie.

Lowering my chin, I exhale a smile. "Disney?" His brow furrows, and I continue. "I always loved watching those old parades, the Rose Bowl and Mardi Gras. Then my mom took me to Epcot once, and when I saw all the gardens, I realized people actually did this for a living. I couldn't believe it."

The slightest grin lifts the corner of his mouth, and my bottom lip slides between my teeth. Spencer Carrollton is not a nice man. He's an asshole my cousin also playfully refers to as *Lucifer*, which is a more fitting description from what I can tell at this point.

Naturally, I'm wildly attracted to him.

"Well, I can't speak to your work as a waitress," He leans against the balcony railing, crossing his arms. "But your skill as a florist is quite masterful."

I blink a few times, fighting a grin.

His brows lower, and his frown returns so fast. *Mercurial.* "What?"

"The way you talk."

"What about it?"

"Do you always speak like you're reading from an encyclopedia?"

"I don't know what you mean." He straightens as if I've offended him.

"Your skill as an artist is quite masterful." I imitate his voice in an affected, snooty-nasally way.

"I sound nothing like that."

I can't resist. "I sound nothing like that."

"Stop it."

"Stop it."

His eyes flash with fire, and I wonder if I make him hostile and horny too. I press my lips together hard, but a laugh snorts through my nose anyway.

Yep, I'm definitely a little drunk.

He places both hands on the balcony rail on either side of me, caging me against his chest. "Don't mock me, Joselyn." His nostrils flare and his voice is low with a bit of a snarl.

He might be Lucifer, but I'm a witch. "Or what?"

The salt air stills around us. Everything stills, as if our chemistry has created a bubble just for us. The party noise is gone, and it's him and me and electricity and this moment. His eyes darken and flicker to my lips as if he's trying to decide.

I'm not.

I reach out and thread my fingers in the dark waves touching the back of his collar. His hair is soft, but his lips are softer. As soon as I press mine to his, he takes charge, pushing my mouth open and sliding his tongue inside.

My knees melt. One large hand moves to my lower back, palm flat, radiating heat through the thin silk of my dress as he pulls me closer. His other hand grasps my face, two fingers against my cheek, his thumb under my chin, tilting my head so he can kiss me deeper.

The way he kisses me... It's like being devoured, yet savored.

He slides his tongue along mine like he's tasting delicious fruit. He's minty and luscious, parting my lips with his and guiding them. My eyes roll back, and my panties drench when I feel his erection against my stomach.

I exhale a moan, one hand still threaded in the back of his hair while the other grips his coat tighter, pulling him closer. *Devour me...*

This. Is. Insane.

The hand on my back slides lower, gripping the silk of my skirt, drawing it higher until his fingers slide against the bare skin of my ass.

"You are so gorgeous." It's a low growl rumbling in his throat as his lips move to my jaw. "I have a room in this hotel. Let me fuck you all night."

Fuck me.

All night.

Yes.

No.

God, what am I doing?

I struggle through the fog, the heat of what he's doing to me, the gnawing ache between my thighs I know for certain he can satisfy. I'm breathing fast, my breasts rising and falling, and I flatten my palm against his chest and step away from the inferno of us.

"I'm sorry. I can't." My chin drops, and I don't meet his eyes. "I have a boyfriend."

"Dump him."

"I can't do that."

He studies me, not smiling. He's gorgeous in this moonlight, hazel eyes full of lust, lips even fuller, pinker from consuming me. *Fuck me all night...*

He doesn't move, and I'm sure he's waiting to see what I'll do next.

I know what I'll do next.

I'm doing it. "Goodnight, Spencer."

I turn on my heel, ready to run all the way home. I might be stubborn and impulsive, but I always do the right thing. No wickedly handsome CEO will change that. No matter how fantastic of a kisser he is. No matter how much I want what he could do to me. No matter how much of a douche my boyfriend is.

I don't do trouble.

CHAPTER Two

Spencer

"ANTIQUES NOW." MY PARTNER MILES SNAPS FROM WHERE HE STANDS behind his polished mahogany desk.

I'm standing in his well-appointed, corner-office at *Antiques Today*, and he's holding an oversized iPad, swiping repeatedly. "He has an exclamation point in the title. It's like a disaster film. *Earthquake!*"

"It's Zoomer nonsense." I take a seat in the leather chair across from him, unimpressed. "Is this why you called me in here? To discuss an unaffiliated scrub on the Internet talking about antiques?"

"What are we going to do about this, Spencer?"

"About what?" I straighten the cuff of my crisp white shirt inside my suit coat, and he turns the screen to face me.

"Link Sherlock. He practically stole our name."

"Please tell me you're joking." I study the shaggy-haired

man-child with a beard in desperate need of shaping, dressed in sloppy jeans and a tee. He's the disaster. "Ignore him."

Miles's brown eyes narrow. At five-seven, what he lacks in stature he makes up for in theatrics. "He's got this... YouTube and TikTok. The man has more than a million followers."

"He is not a man." I find it difficult to take anyone seriously who can't be bothered to wash themselves.

It brings to mind a gorgeous redhead I know, who recently described antiques dealers as old men with crumbs in their beards and moth-eaten wool coats. Nothing like me, she'd said, swiping a silky wave of fiery hair off her ivory shoulder. She was gorgeous, full breasts, hips, tiny waist.

I'd occasionally thought of her since the day we met in Daisy's store, but that night at the wedding. That kiss... I'd wanted to explore every inch of her perfect figure with my mouth, learn her sweet spots, make her moan, but she ran.

She said she had a boyfriend, but what man in his right mind would let her out of his sight? I'd expect her to demand better of a man. She's fully capable. Is it possible she lied? Either way, she seems to have taken up residence in my mind ever since that night, like some unwelcome, redheaded Cinderella. *Sin*...

"He's courting Brimfield and Skinner." Miles is still going on about the kid, and I file away my lusty thoughts. "Grafton was on his last episode."

"What does it matter?"

"It matters because when he puts them in front of millions of viewers, they'll go to him first with their acquisitions. He'll have first look at their catalogs." My diminutive partner is apoplectic over this guy, and I try not to antagonize Miles when he's having a moment.

Inhaling slowly, I hope someone in heaven takes note of this. It proves I can be kind—when I have to be, which thankfully isn't very often.

"Let's look at this from another angle." I lean forward and place my forearms on my knees, clasping my hands. "This... Link Sherlock, despite the ridiculous name, is presenting the world of antiques to a new generation of buyers and collectors. They're taking their first sip of coffee milk or venturing into the livestock shows in Branson."

Miles lowers his shaggy brow. "I'm not sure I follow..."

"Mr. Sherlock will whet their appetite, but we own this field. We've made collecting antiquities an art. He's a barker at the county fair. We're the auctioneers at Southeby's. They'll come to us when they're ready for class."

Miles leans back, stroking his short beard. "Class..." He lowers himself slowly into his leather desk chair and his lips pucker as he contemplates my words. "I like it, but how will they find us?"

"The same way anyone finds anything of value. Word of mouth." Pushing off my knees, I stand, ready to get back to my office and set up my next trip to Manhattan.

"And Brimfield? Skinner?"

"They're smart to court his attention. He'll bring a new audience, freshen the market."

"I think we need to remind them we're here. Remind them we're still top of the line, ready when they need us."

I'm not sure I like the sound of this. "How will we do that?"

"A gala."

"Gala." My lip curls. Large social events are not my cup of tea, and I despise party planners. They're usually pushy, loud women with ideas I don't like. "I don't think that's necessary. I'll do my usual rounds, pay them all a visit—"

"Don't get me wrong, friend, but you're hardly the warmest cookie on the platter."

"I'm not sure I follow that metaphor. Still, I have established relationships. It'll be fine."

"It'll be old-fashioned. People want new things." He's on his feet, pacing the large, oak-paneled office. "We can go all out, maybe something outdoors, on Lake Murray. Luxury accommodations, a video montage of us through the years, SWAG bags…"

"SWAG bags?"

"Stuff We All Get. You know, robes and iPads."

"I'm aware of what SWAG is. How will robes and gadgets sell antiques?"

"They'll show we care."

"Here's how we show we care. I have a meeting with Grafton in a few weeks. I'll do a quick tour of our Vermont and Pennsylvania locations—"

"I'll save you the trip. We're bringing them to us." He smiles, and I can tell there's no talking him out of this idea.

Miles is five minutes older than me in this company, and even though we're partners now, he still likes to pull rank when he gets an idea I hate. Sometimes it's easier to let him win. With a sigh, I sit in the chair again.

"So you're thinking Lake Murray?"

"You're right." He points at me across the desk. "The coast is better. Daisy's there now. We can bring her onboard to help us. It'll benefit her business as well. Win-win!"

His suggestion eases my irritation slightly. Daisy is not an obnoxious party planner, and she's connected to someone I'm very interested in seeing again. "It might be worth a try."

He pauses and studies me from across the desk. "That's a sudden switch."

I'm on my feet again, straightening my suit. "Daisy's wedding reception last month was quite elegant. She has good taste, and she knows our clients."

"Excellent. Set up a time for us to meet here in the office. We can hash out all the details, set a date, and get the ball rolling." He returns to his chair, smiling with satisfaction. "Glad you discovered that girl."

At the moment, I tend to agree.

Heading back to my office, I slide my phone out of my pocket and send a quick text to Daisy. ***Need to chat. Miles wants to host a gala in Oceanside. Hoping you'll join forces.***

It doesn't take long for her to reply. ***Ooo... a gala. I'm sure you're thrilled.*** She includes a string of those small yellow faces that are either laughing or crying.

I ignore her sarcasm. ***Would your cousin be available? Her floral work is stunning.***

As is she.

Gray dots float on the screen, and I'm annoyed by the tension in my shoulders. It's unprofessional, and I never pursue women I can't predict.

Perhaps this is a bad idea.

Daisy's reply pops up on my screen. ***I'll ask her. If it's a yes, I'll give you her number.***

The tension in my shoulders releases at once, which should be another red flag. I ignore it. ***Thanks. Let me know. Miles would like you to come to the office.***

Another pause. More gray dots. ***I'll stop by tomorrow afternoon. Should know about Sly then as well.***

Sly. I prefer the name Joselyn, but I'm intrigued by her nickname. I want to know how she got it. Maybe she can tell me as I trace my tongue along the curve of her full breasts, as I cup them in my hands and roll her tight nipples between my fingers. The fantasy rouses my cock, and I slide a hand down the front of my pants.

One way to handle this. I'll ask her to dinner, take her home, and fuck this itch out of my system. Then we can take care of the gala and my life can return to normal.

I don't do trouble, and I don't do relationships.

Passing the gold-framed antique mirror in the long hallway, I inspect my designer suit and straighten my silk tie. My beard is close and my hair is artfully messy. Everything in my life is controlled, including the females with whom I choose to interact.

It's a good plan. Balance restored.

CHAPTER Three

Joselyn

"It's happening." My throat is tight as I clutch my phone to my ear. I'm breathless, and I tell myself it's anticipation, not dread. "He's going to propose."

"Is that really what you want?" Daisy's hesitant tone frustrates me.

"God, is it so hard for you to just be happy for me?"

"Is it so hard for you not to act like a fifteen-year-old on her period?"

My cousin is one of the few people in my life not bothered by my strong personality. She'll also call me on my shit.

"It's what I've been waiting for, Daisy. Yes, it's what I want."

"Well, he's definitely got you where he wants you." She still doesn't sound happy for me. "You've given up half your clients, moved in with him—"

"I wanted to move in with him. His place is gorgeous, and I'm there if he has a spasm in the night."

"You were just building your client list. Now you're his personal nurse. Next, you'll be his wife. Then you'll have nothing of your own at all."

I'm quiet, because she's right. Elliot made me give up all my male clients when we got together. He said I could only work with females if he and I were to be a couple.

Daisy went off when she found out, and while I agree it's silly for him to be jealous, I can see his side of it.

Massage therapy requires the utmost professionalism, and while I never, ever give any hint of impropriety, I know a few of my old male clients wouldn't have minded a bonus cock-rub.

"Elliot is my primary client because it helps him. He takes good care of me."

"He's your only client."

"That's not true. I have others."

I hope she doesn't ask how many, because she's right. I've got Elliot and about two other women who call me occasionally.

I met Elliot when I was just getting started. I finished my training in sports medicine and massage therapy at Palmetto college, went around to all the offices downtown and left my card, set up some Groupons. He messaged me back in a day.

Then I met him, and he was so fine. Golden-brown hair, blue eyes… He's not tall, but his body is amazing—all hard muscles and a tight ass honed by years on the baseball field.

A back injury forced him into retirement early, and he went to work with his dad in waste management. Sitting behind a desk all day aggravated his injury, which is how I got my hands on that body. He asked me to dinner, and *yadda yadda yadda*… three weeks later, I moved in with him.

It was pretty great at first, but now, that same old injury is the excuse he gives for why we haven't had sex in three months.

Three months is a long, damn time.

I haven't dared tell Daisy.

"Weren't you just fighting last week? What makes you think he's going to propose?"

I swallow the tightness in my throat. "I accidentally opened his credit card bill, and I saw a huge charge at Jared's."

"Hold the phone. Snooping in his mail is a big red flag. Also, seriously? What kind of engagement rings do they have at Jared's?"

Damn Daisy.

"Nice ones!" I match her tone, and she blows air into my ear. I shake my head. "I'm hanging up now. I'll call you after he proposes. Or better yet, I'll send you a photo of my gorgeous new ring. Then I'll accept your apology."

"Hang on, don't hang up." Her tone softens. "I'm worried about you, cuz. I want you to be with someone who deserves you. Someone who's going to make you happy."

"Elliot makes me happy." My voice cracks, and anxiety flashes in my chest. I choose to ignore it. "I'll call you later."

"Love you, bitch."

"Love you more."

The sun is setting through the high-rises, and I shove my phone in the side pocket of my black yoga pants. I'm wearing a sports bra and tank, because I did a mini spa day in anticipation of tonight. I got a body scrub, bikini wax, facial, and of course, a fresh mani-pedi so when I post pictures on social media, my hands will look perfect.

Pushing through the glass doors, I smile and wave at Eric the doorman. He's on the phone, and he seems startled to see me.

I hope I'm not spoiling any surprises as I skip into the gleaming elevator and hit the PH button, swiping my door card over the keypad.

The elevator shoots upwards, heading to the top floor, and I gaze out over downtown Columbia.

It's not the biggest city in South Carolina, but it's bigger than

Fireside. I love being a cosmopolitan girl living in a penthouse apartment with a sexy, rich boyfriend. I'm like *Gossip Girl* or *Sex and the City* light. Or something.

The bell dings and the doors open to the small foyer. I cross the space to open the door, and I'm surprised when Elliot meets me on the landing. He's wearing his suit pants, but his jacket is gone. His white dress shirt is crumpled and buttoned awkwardly.

"Hey, babe. You're back early." Sweat glistens on his upper lip, and his hair is messy and damp at the temples.

"I've been gone three hours." I glance at the clock hanging in the kitchen and back to my slightly pale boyfriend. "Are you okay? Is your back hurting?"

"No, no." He forces a laugh, but it's off. Something's wrong. "I'm good. I was just getting changed. Thought I might go for a jog."

"Really?" I can't hide the disappointment in my tone. "It's after six."

"On a Thursday. Did you want to go to dinner or something? We can make a reservation for tomorrow. Tell you what, why don't you run down and ask Eric if he'll set that up for us?"

"Run down? I can call him from here." My chest tightens, and I push past my sweaty boyfriend into our shared apartment. "What's going on?"

My eyes travel around the living room. Everything is in place—the rich leather sofa is pristine. The polished oak furniture is in order, and a low fire burns in the wall fireplace.

I see no signs of anything unusual, but I can't deny the sneaking suspicion someone is here.

"What the hell would be going on?" Elliot's voice goes high, and he clears it. "You're being silly."

"Am I?"

"Tell you what, I'll skip the run, and we can take our chances. Let's go out to dinner. I'm sure we can get a table somewhere."

I don't answer him.

I walk to the bathroom, sensing a trail. It's like a scent hanging in the air. I'm following the lure of suspicion about the truth I've wanted to ignore for so long.

Anxiety is back in my chest, and my stomach trembles. My shoulders are tight when I realize it's happening. His lies are about to be exposed, and I'm not looking away anymore.

"Who's here, Elliot?" My voice is even, and I glance from the bedroom to the living room, where he stands watching me.

"I don't know what you mean, babe." He smiles, but it's not his usual, disinterested smile. He's very interested in what's happening right now. "I'm here. You're here."

"Who else is here?"

I don't wait for his answer. I continue into our bedroom, where the California king is made perfectly. Hospital corners, not a wrinkle in sight. Only…

"I never make the bed this well."

"I didn't want to say anything…" He exhales a heavy chuckle, and I go straight to his walk-in closet.

I used to joke it was as big as my first apartment in Columbia. He's on my heels, but I beat him to it, jerking the door open.

It's what I knew I'd find, but still, the blood drains from my face. I feel light-headed.

Sitting on the divan in the middle of the closet with her legs crossed under the yellow spotlight is Nadine.

Her only clothing is a push-up bra and beige silk skirt, and her inky-brown hair is styled in a shoulder-length swooshy bob.

"Your secretary?" I'm shocked by how calm my voice sounds.

"Surprise…" Nadine does a little wave, smiling as her foot bobs in my slip-on pink feathered heels. They were a gift from Daisy, vintage Chanel. She told me to wear them when I felt sexy.

Nadine's lips are swollen and her red lipstick is smeared. My eyes go to Elliot's clean face, and I taste bile when I realize she was probably sucking his cock.

"I can explain." He's at my side, but I push past him, crossing the bedroom to my smaller closet.

I moved in here with one suitcase. It'll take exactly one suitcase for me to gather the few things I care about in this world. Sadly, the vintage Chanel slippers will have to stay behind.

"Joselyn, what are you doing?" Elliot grabs my arm, and it takes all my strength to keep from slapping him across his stupid face.

"Even an idiot like you can see what I'm doing."

"Don't do this." His grip tightens, and fire burns up the anxiety in my chest.

"Take your hand off me, or I'll rip your head off."

His grip loosens, falling away from my arm, and I jerk open the dresser, shoving everything into my bag as fast as I can. My panties, my *Unsolved Mysteries* PJs, my fluffy socks. Running to the bathroom, I scoop up my toothbrush and my face creams.

Making my way to the door, I grab my one Armani suit from the closet. I sacrificed and bought it for when I made executive visits… It still has the tags on it.

God, I'm so ashamed.

I hate that Daisy was right.

I hate I stayed here three months longer than I ever should have.

"I wish you would slow down and let me explain." Idiot Flick is still speaking like I have any interest in hearing his excuses.

Nadine has pulled on a shirt, at least. She's fastening the buttons over her push-up bra when I see a diamond tennis bracelet sparkling on her wrist.

"Is that…" My eyes squeeze briefly, and *I will not cry.*

Dammit, I will never cry over this loser again.

"What?" Elliot looks all around the bedroom, and I spy the fucking Jared's box on the desk.

I almost lose my battle with the tears, but I steel myself. I'm almost out the door.

Stay strong, Sly…

"I'll leave my key card with Eric." My voice is so controlled, I wish they gave awards for best actress to regular people.

"Sly…" He touches me again, and my expression must warn him. He quickly holds up both hands like I've pulled a gun. "I never meant to hurt you."

"I hope your dick falls off."

With a slam, I'm in the elevator, hurtling to the ground below.

"I knew. That's the whole problem. I always knew." My nose is hot from crying, and I'm curled up on a plush sofa with my head in Courtney's lap.

I couldn't drive all the way home, and I couldn't call Daisy tonight. Instead, I went to the grocery store and bought several pints of ice cream before calling my friend Courtney.

She told me to come straight to her tiny apartment in Belmont. She's a true friend.

"It's not your fault." She traces her fingers through my hair. "If you'd known, you wouldn't have stayed with him."

Pushing up into a sitting position, I wipe my nose again. "I kept holding on to the memories of when we met, how things were those first months. I couldn't believe he would let that go… God, I'm such a fool."

"You're an amazing person." She holds the pint of Ben & Jerry's Cherry Garcia to me, and I stab the fork in and take another bite.

Courtney and I met in massage therapy school, and we've been there for each other through the pain of getting established in a new town. I've kept her son Oliver when Ozzy, her ex, started harassing her…

"If he would throw what you had away for a bimbo secretary, he deserves whatever he gets."

I wipe a fresh tear away. "We hadn't had sex in three months. I knew he was sleeping with someone else. I just couldn't let everyone be right." Shaking my head, I look down at my lap. "I'm the idiot."

"You loved him. I remember how giddy you were the day he asked you to move in with him." She gives my hand a squeeze. "You're not an idiot for loving someone. He's a loser for not valuing what you had."

"It was too fast. I'm so impulsive. I moved in with him after only three weeks. Who does that?" Falling back on the couch, I curl my legs under me. "That's it. No men for a year."

She starts to laugh. "You'll find somebody new tomorrow."

"Nope. This chick is off the market."

Courtney gives me a wink. "He doesn't deserve you."

I sit up and hug my friend. "Men are rats. They're fleas on rats."

"He's probably a Clemson fan." That makes me laugh, and I squeeze my eyes shut. "Two of my best friends went to Clemson."

"Oh, well. He's a USC fan, then."

We laugh more, and fresh tears fill my eyes until we spot a little visitor standing in the hallway watching us.

His mother gives him a gentle frown. "Aren't you supposed to be sleeping?"

Courtney holds out her hands and seven-year-old Oliver closes the space between us, crawling into her lap.

I pass him the pint of ice cream and grab a tissue, quickly blotting my eyes and pasting on a smile. "Hey, buddy. Are we being too loud?"

He takes a big bite of vanilla with chunky cherries. "Why are you crying?"

Taking a deep breath, I try to conjure a reason he can understand. "I thought I was getting a present, but I got a kick in the pants instead."

He scoops more ice cream, eyes wide. "Mom says kicking is bad."

"Your mom's right. I should've known better."

"Somebody kicked you?"

"No…" My eyes meet Court's, and she rolls hers. "It's a figure of speech. Like an unpleasant surprise. I found out somebody wasn't who I thought he was. Or he was who I thought he was, and I didn't want to admit it."

Oliver's little brow furrows, and I'm pretty sure I've only succeeded in confusing the shit out of him.

Court jumps in and saves me. "Aunt Sly is going to stay with us a few days. Isn't that fun?"

His confusion disappears, and he hops onto his feet between us. "Can she sleep in my room?"

"You've got the twin beds, so I guess I will."

He bounces again, throwing up both hands. "We can build a fort and tell ghost stories and I'll let you hold Chartreuse and—"

"Tonight, you need to go to sleep." Court stands, putting him on the floor, and I stand, too. "Aunt Sly will be along later. You've got school tomorrow."

And I've got to find a place to live. "I wonder if I could afford a place in The Vista?"

She shrugs. "It's pretty expensive."

"Yeah, and I'm down to three clients now." Shame squeezes my chest. I hate when Daisy is right. "I'll probably have to move back to Fireside. Live with Ma."

"You're staying right here until you're back on your feet. You can't build a client list from three hours away."

"Two and a half hours." She narrows her eyes, and I concede. "You're right. If I want to work here, I have to live here. Just promise me one thing."

"What?"

"When you've had enough, you'll kick me out."

She laughs, giving me another hug. "Shut up. I'm not kicking you out. Free babysitting!"

That makes me smile. "You know it. What else will I be doing all year?"

I never got a photo of your gorgeous new ring. Daisy's text glows in the darkness, and I roll onto my side so it doesn't wake Elliot.

I moved out of Elliot's place. You were right. My phone starts to ring, but I silence it quickly. ***Can't talk. Sharing a room with Oliver.***

Want a job? I'm meeting Miles and Spence tomorrow about a gala. I need a florist.

Chewing my lip, I think about it. ***I quit doing flowers so long ago. I don't have any contacts here.***

They want to do it in Oceanside. You know everybody there.

I do need the money…

Real anticipation tickles my stomach at the prospect of seeing Spencer again. I actually turned him down because of Elliot—and after that kiss.

Heat replaces anticipation as I remember his smoky eyes, the scruff on his square jaw… His angry square jaw that moves when his teeth clench.

No.

No men.

Two tomorrow. I'll pick you up. Text me the address.

Chewing my lip, I hesitate. I should say no. I should tell her it's not a good idea… Only, it's a job, and God knows, I'm broke. Tamping down my libido, I send her Courtney's address.

I'm a mature, professional woman. I never get involved with clients.

Besides, I'll be working with my cousin. It's perfectly safe.

CHAPTER Four

Spencer

"ELEVEN-TEN." MILES GLOATS, AND I SHAKE MY HEAD, RUBBING THE towel through my damp hair.

"I tweaked my back."

We're in the luxury locker room of the Palmetto Lake Club downtown, where I've been kicking his ass at our weekly game of racquetball—until today.

"I beat you fair and square. Admit it." He closes the pine door of his locker, securing it with a thumbprint.

"I have no problem admitting if you beat me fair and square." I pull my suit coat over one shoulder and toss my tie around my neck while doing the same. "I tweaked my back when I hit the wall in our second match."

"Tweaked your back," he scoffs, tossing his racket under his arm. "Don't be a poor loser, Freeze."

Exhaling a laugh, I drop the thick white towel in the bin and grab my racket. Winning is so commonplace to me, I let it go—even though my right side is hurting like a mother. "Congrats on your win."

His elfin face pinches. "You're patronizing me."

"Good God, Miles." I stretch to the side as I flip my tie around, fastening a small Windsor knot. "Don't be a poor winner."

"Fuck, look at the time." He slaps his Rolex. "We've got to meet Daisy in twenty minutes."

I give myself one last check in the mirror. I don't tell Miles I couldn't give a shit about winning or losing today. Daisy texted me she's bringing her cousin to the meeting this afternoon, and that old itch is driving me mad.

I pop an ibuprofen and follow him out of the ancient, red-brick edifice to where a black Lincoln waits to return us to the office.

The conference room at *Antiques Today* has a brilliant view of downtown Columbia. A massive mahogany table is situated in the center, surrounded by butter-soft black leather chairs, and a projector hangs from the ceiling, pointed to a fifty-inch flatscreen television.

In the center is sparkling and still water, coffee, and tea, and a pair of servers have arranged platters of finger sandwiches and fruit on the credenza.

"Good afternoon, Miles. Spencer." Daisy breezes into the room in jeans and a flowing white top, pausing to kiss my cheek. "Can you believe I've never been in this room?"

I glance around the austere space. "We rarely use it."

"Why have it?" She picks up a tiny sandwich and takes a bite. "Mmm... Chicken salad."

"For moments such as this." Miles holds out a hand. "Would you like a snack, Miss..."

"Winthrop. Joselyn. I'm good, thank you."

My eyes snap up, and she's here.

She's dressed in a charcoal suit perfectly tailored to her tall, statuesque frame. It's expensive, Armani, I'd guess, with a white silk blouse under the jacket. The top button in the center of her chest gives me a peek at her soft cleavage, and her glossy red hair is brushed over one shoulder in smooth waves.

She looks amazing.

"Sorry, Miles," Daisy covers her mouth as she swallows her bite. "I forgot you haven't met my cousin. Sly, this is Miles Klaut, founder of *Antiques Today*. He's a legend in the business and not at all as scary as he seems at first."

"Do I seem scary?" Miles puts a hand on his chest and winks up at her. "It's nice to meet you, Miss Winthrop."

I step around the table, and her eyes flare when she sees me in a most satisfying way. "It's nice to see you again, Joselyn."

"Spencer." Her voice is quiet, slightly husky, pure sex. "How are you?"

"Much better now." I give her a rare smile, and she blinks away quickly, cheeks flushing.

Don't be afraid, Sin.

"Spencer said you're an artist when it comes to flowers." Miles motions to the chairs, and she and Daisy sit.

"An artist?" She arches an eyebrow at me, and I lightly shrug.

"I described what I saw. Would you like something to drink?"

"I'll have a water, thanks." She takes a chair, and I hand her a bottle of Pellegrino before rounding the table to sit across from her.

From this angle, I can study her beautiful face as we chat. Miles leads the discussion, explaining his ideas, and Daisy is quick to catch up with him. She lists potential venues and themes and the pros and cons of each.

Leaning back in my chair, I let the two of them run with it, preferring instead to memorize the flicker of dark lashes over ocean eyes. The afternoon sun highlights the red streaks in her hair like fire, and I notice a faint sprinkling of freckles across the top of her cheeks. Her skin is like ivory. She's a rare beauty.

"Sly has connections with one of the best caterers in the area, and of course, she'll handle all the floral arrangements."

"Did you have anything in particular in mind?" Her voice is smooth like whiskey, with a hint of smokiness. "We're lucky that we can get almost anything here."

"I think the New Englanders would be most impressed by tropicals." I lean forward, joining the conversation.

Daisy lights up in her unique way, nodding quickly. "Did you bring your portfolio, Sly? Show Miles the one you did with the tiger lilies."

"I didn't..." Joselyn looks worried, glancing from her cousin to Miles to me. "It's in Fireside. I-I wasn't planning to do this anymore."

"No need to apologize, Miss Winthrop." Miles smiles at her, giving me a knowing glance. "Anyone who can make an impression on Mr. Freeze here must be worth her salt."

Her pink lips part, and a wicked image flashes across my mind.

"Who's on the guest list?" Daisy climbs onto her knees in the chair, leaning on her elbows, and with her hair in a ponytail, she's like a kid planning a birthday party.

Miles eats it up. Nothing makes him happier than people jumping onboard his unnecessarily elaborate plans. "I've got Brimfield and Skinner. Grafton—"

"Oh! I hope they send Heather. She's so fun. I'd love to show her my store."

"I'll put in a special request for Ms. Olsen to attend."

Joselyn sits quietly in her chair, chewing on her bottom lip. She's different today, quieter, and I don't like it. She can't be intimidated by all this. She's far too talented to be insecure. Something else is troubling her, and I want to know what it is.

At the wedding reception, she had the nerve to mock me, and it was annoying as fuck and ridiculously adorable.

I want her to do it again so I can pull her across my lap and spank her creamy, white ass. Then I'll smooth my palm over her soft, pink cheeks. Then I'll follow with my lips…

Her eyes are on me, and I try another smile. She blinks hesitantly before finally returning my greeting with a small smile of her own. *That's better.*

"I think we've got a great start." Daisy is on her feet.

"How soon can we make it happen?" Miles stands as well, and they're eye to eye.

"Two weeks?" She glances to her cousin. "What do you think, Sly? Will that give you enough time?"

"I think so." Joselyn is still distracted.

Daisy glances to Miles, "Yes?"

He's beaming. "I'll send invitations as soon as you verify the venue."

"I'll make some calls on the drive home." Daisy lifts a small leather bag off her chair. "Now I've got to hit the road. I've got a husband to feed."

The pituitary case.

"Is it after five already?" Miles takes her arm, and they're like a tiny power duo. "I've got a date with my Netflix. I just started the Cecil Hotel doc. Very nice to meet you, Miss Winthrop."

They head for the door, and I wait as Joselyn collects a small clutch, which I assume holds her phone. "She was always his favorite," I tease, as if I care Miles prefers Daisy.

"She's a pixie." Joselyn picks up the empty bottles, placing them in the trash.

"You don't have to clean. Maintenance will take care of it."

Her cheeks flush, and she shakes her head. "I'm used to doing all the jobs."

"Daisy told me you're self-employed."

"Trying to be. I recently had a change in circumstance."

"You fired yourself?" I place a hand on the open doors of the elevator, holding them for her.

"What?" She blinks up at me, then realizes I'm joking. "Oh, no. Just… personal stuff."

I'm intrigued, and I can't let her go. "It's after five on a Friday. Let me buy you a drink."

The elevator dings when we reach the bottom floor, and she hesitates. "I shouldn't."

"Still with the boyfriend?" *If she says yes…*

She doesn't answer immediately, and her eyes flinch with something like anger.

Daisy pops back into the foyer. "Sly, you coming?"

"I'll drop her where she needs to go." I glance at Joselyn. "If that's okay?"

She wavers a bit longer before giving a short answer. "Sure."

An edge is in her voice, and I finally catch a glimpse of my feisty redhead.

Her cousin skips over and gives me a hug. "Night, Spence." She turns to Joselyn and kisses her cheek. "I'll call you."

Daisy and Miles are gone, and I'm still waiting to see what Joselyn will say. She glances up at me and presses her lips into a decided smile. "No boyfriend."

"In that case, I know where to get the best martini in town."

"Lead the way."

With pleasure.

"So what makes this the best martini in town?" Sly's jacket is off, and her hair is soft over her broad shoulders.

She's gorgeous, perched on a leather barstool in Nightcaps with that silk blouse giving me a teasing glimpse of her lace bra underneath.

Standing in front of her, I pass one of the two cone-shaped cocktail glasses to her. "For starters, they're ice cold." She takes the drink in both hands and gives it a little sip. Her eyebrows rise as I continue. "They use the precise amount of vermouth, and just a dash of olive juice."

She takes another, bigger gulp, blue eyes wide. "Mm—I agree."

Tilting her head back, she polishes off the entire thing then lifts the toothpick and pops the green olive in her mouth, chewing like it's a piece of gum. "You're right. That was a damn good martini."

I almost laugh, but I narrow my eyes instead. "You're supposed to savor it."

"Can I have another?" Her eyes dance. "To savor?"

"Are you used to shooting straight vodka?"

"No."

"I'll get you another one, but only if you sip it this time."

"I told you, I don't like being bossed around." The fire in her eyes heats my already simmering blood.

Stepping closer, I slide my hand along her narrow waist. "I don't want you drunk tonight."

She considers this before nodding. "Okay."

Signaling the waitress, I order another then turn to study the creamy skin of her neck leading down to the luscious curve of her full breast taunting me from the V in her shirt. God, she's gorgeous. I want to spend the night getting to know her so much better.

But first… "What happened to the boyfriend?"

Her eyes follow the olive as she traces it around the edge of her glass. "We broke up."

"Good. He didn't deserve you."

A gorgeous smile spreads her full lips, and she shakes her head. "You never even saw him."

"But I saw you. Any man who would leave you alone looking the way you did is a fucking idiot."

She snorts into her glass, taking another small sip. "Fucking Elliot."

"I rest my case."

Her lips press together, and she peeks up at me from under full lashes. "That was very nice what you said about my work today."

"I'm not nice. I'm honest."

"So you're not a nice man?" She leans closer on the barstool, and I'm ready to take her home.

"Haven't you heard?" She shakes her head, and her eyes fix on my lips. Yep, time to take this vixen to my bed. "I can be nice when I want to be."

"I don't believe you. You're naughty."

"I am. Just like you."

"At least we know it." She slips the olive between her teeth, chewing as she gives me a sly wink.

I think I get her nickname now. "Are you hungry?"

She nods, and I take her hand. "I ordered dinner for two. It should be at my place the same time as us."

"You're mighty sure of yourself."

Pulling her hand into the crook of my arm, her body slides closer to mine. "I only hoped."

"Then it's your lucky night."

Fuck, yeah, it is.

CHAPTER *Five*

Joselyn

"IT'S BEAUTIFUL." I'M ON THE BALCONY OF SPENCER'S TWO-STORY brownstone overlooking the Congaree River.

It's in a historic part of downtown with galleries, cute little shops, and restaurants, and as the light breeze moves through my hair, I remember walking through the city on my first visit, dreaming of living in one of these gorgeous homes.

We didn't talk much on the ride back, and I feel a little more sober than when I left the bar. Now I'm here. *What am I doing here?*

"The view sold me on this place." He joins me, two glasses of wine in his hands.

He's gorgeous in a bespoke suit with his dark hair falling in perfectly messy waves. I want to curl my fingers in it, remembering how soft his hair is—contrasted with the dark scruff on his square jaw.

I remember the way he kissed me that night, demanding,

possessive, leaving my cheeks scuffed pink. I want to feel that scruff between my thighs.

He's intense and intimidating, sensual and predatory. He's too smart, but I'm not afraid of him.

"You have impeccable taste." I take the glass and sip the dry, oaky wine.

Steak and fish are plated downstairs on the dining table, but I'm not hungry for food.

I texted Courtney not to wait up. I have no idea what to expect, but it's been a long time since a man seduced me.

I could use a bit of seduction.

"It's my job." He looks at me in a way that makes my insides beg. "What do you like, Sin?"

I take another sip of wine and give him a coy smile. "True crime."

His chin drops, and he laughs. "So I've heard. What do you like so much about true crime?"

Shrugging, I step around the immaculately furnished sitting room. It's all leather and brass and stained-glass Tiffany lamps. "The passion, the fear. It's exciting and terrifying."

"You like being scared?"

"Yes, but I like being in control of my fear."

His hazel eyes darken, and I can't tell what he's thinking. "Do you want to eat something?"

"Not just yet."

I take a step closer, setting my wine glass on the end table. At the bar, we started something I want to continue. My tongue wets my bottom lip.

His dark brow furrows as he watches my mouth. "You probably should. You've had a bit of alcohol."

"I'm not a child, Spencer. I know when I've had too much to drink."

"Do you?" The way he looks at me sometimes is pure lust, like he's stripping me bare in his mind.

I place my hand on his wine glass, taking it and setting it beside mine on the nearby table. He slides his hand along my waist, the warmth of his palm radiating through my silk blouse.

My palm is flat against his chest. "Do you enjoy true crime?"

A hint of a smile, a deep dimple, and his voice is low. "I prefer more sensual entertainment."

"What do you like so much about it?" I imitate him, sliding my palms under the lapels of his coat and easing it off his shoulders.

He catches it and tosses it on the couch. "Pretty much the same thing you like about true crime." His hand is on my waist again, fisting my blouse, tugging it out of my skirt and up my back.

I pause to help him lift it over my head, thankful I wore my pretty lace bra. Doubly thankful I just had the complete spa treatment two days ago… *Fucking Elliot*. Glad I'm not wasting a body scrub, waxing, mani-pedi, and facial on that idiot.

"Hey, beautiful. Did I lose you?" Spencer doesn't miss a beat. He monitors my every response, and I have a feeling it's going to be a very good thing.

"Just an old ghost trying to get me down."

He catches my face in his elegant hand. "Don't let it." Our eyes meet, and he's so focused. "Do you trust me?"

"I hardly know you."

"You can always tell me to stop, and I will."

"What are you planning to do to me?"

He turns my body so my back is to his chest and slides one hand over my bare stomach, pressing us flush. I'm still in my Armani skirt, but glancing down, I can see my hardened nipples through the thin cups of my bra.

"I want to take you from behind," he speaks in my ear, his voice thick, his beard scuffing my cheek. "I want to look down and see those beautiful tits bounce as I thrust into you again and again."

Leaning my head back, I close my eyes as he traces the fingers of his other hand up my arm, to the silk covering my breast and squeezes. I gasp as he continues.

"I want my hands all over them, lifting and squeezing as I kiss the side of your neck." He does it, placing warm lips to my heated skin. "Smell your beautiful hair, memorize every inch of your gorgeous body..."

His teeth graze my neck, up behind my ear as he inhales deeply. My insides are wet and clenching, and when he bites the skin on my neck, I almost meow. Lust and hunger and vodka and wine swirl in my veins, and I'm blazing with need.

"That sounds good..." I manage to say.

He releases me, and I take a shaky step forward, turning to watch as he loosens his tie and lifts it over his head. His eyes never leave me as he quickly unbuttons his white dress shirt.

I want to do something sensual for him, so I reach around behind me and unbutton my skirt, sliding it down my smooth thighs.

I've always been a little self-conscious about my body. I'm not petite. I'm tall and curvy, what some people would call a big girl. My stomach is soft, but Spencer looks at me like I'm a chocolate soufflé. He actually licks his lips.

"Incredible."

"Not too much?" I step closer as his shirt opens.

His skin is a nice olive tan dusted with soft, dark hair, and he's hiding some serious abs under all those layers of expensive fabric.

"So hard..." I trace my fingers along the lines in his torso, curling my nails lightly. His slacks hang nicely on his hips, and I felt his cock against my ass a moment ago.

His lip curls as he pulls me to him again. "Do you know how perfect you are? This gorgeous ass. These breasts." He unfastens my bra as he speaks, and I inhale a little gasp when he pulls me to his chest. "You're a Marilyn. A Jane."

"Spencer..." Our skin slides together, and it's electricity and heat.

"You want me to stop?" His smokey eyes hold mine.

"No... It's just... it's been a long time."

That makes him pause. "How long?"

"Months."

"Criminal." He shakes his head as he resumes his movements, holding me to him and sliding his hands down the small of my back. His lips graze my neck, sending chills through my arms and legs. "We'll take our time."

The small hairs on his chest tickle my hardened nipples, and I reach around his waist, sliding my hands down to squeeze the muscles of his ass. "Not too slow."

He grins wickedly. "There you are."

"What do you mean?"

"My sassy redhead, come with me." Taking my hand, he turns and starts towards the hallway.

I step out of my heels as he takes a glass of ice water off the table.

He leads me deeper into his elegantly furnished home. We enter his bedroom, where a massive king-sized bed is positioned against one wall. It's covered in navy sheets, surrounded by more dark wood and leather. Everything is gleaming brass and polished wood, and it smells like money.

Pausing beside a tall armoire, he places his white shirt on a mahogany valet stand. I admire the ripple of muscles in his arms, the deep line down the center of his back, the definition in his waist.

I take a sip of ice water, and nearly choke when he slides his pants off and turns to face me. Those two lines of muscle drop in a V into his black boxer briefs, and the outline of his erection makes my stomach quiver.

"Come here." It's a low command, and I'm quick to set the water down and obey. "Stop. Bring the glass."

Picking it up again, I do my best sexy walk to where he's waiting in all his broad-shouldered, narrow waist, thick cock straining against dark fabric glory. I want to lick him all over.

"You're amazing, Sin."

"Why do you call me that?"

"Because you're sexy as sin… sinfully tempting."

Okay… I like that answer. It makes me smile, which makes him smile.

He takes my hand and turns me so my back is to his chest. His mouth descends to my shoulder as he lifts my breasts in both hands, squeezing and fondling them. My head drops back when he bites my neck, and I almost drop the glass.

He groans, rolling my nipples in his fingertips. "I want you on my lap."

Heat surges through my core, and my body moves in time with his touch. "Do you remember when you said you wanted to fuck me all night?"

His mouth is at my ear. "How could I forget?"

"Did you ever think about it after that night?"

"Many times." Stepping around, he leads me to the bed. He takes the glass and sets it on the nightstand, fishing an ice cube out of the water. "Lie back."

"What are you doing?"

"Close your eyes."

I do as he says then gasp as the frozen water covers my hard nipple. "Spencer…"

"Be still." It's a low order, and I do my best not to squirm away as the cold becomes painful.

"I don't think I can… Oh…" The ice is gone, replaced by his mouth, which feels obscenely hot by contrast.

My back arches off the bed as I moan, as he moves it to my other breast and repeats the process. It's excruciatingly pleasurable, and he rises up, claiming my mouth in a devouring kiss.

His hand holds the top of my head, and he pushes my lips apart, his tongue invading, finding mine. He's possessive and demanding, circling and caressing, and I rise off the bed with a moan as he slips his hand into my panties, circling the ice over my clit.

I hum against his lips. He bites mine lightly, pulling them with his as he slides the ice lower, dipping it into my core.

"Spencer..." My eyes pop open in time to see him rise up and put the cube in his mouth.

"Good girl." A naughty smile curls his lips. "Would you like some more?"

Chewing my lips, I nod, flickering my eyes to his cock. It points like a steel rod at me from inside his underwear. "I want everything."

He takes another piece of ice from the glass. "Be still, greedy girl."

It's almost impossible to be still as he slides the ice around my navel slowly. He moves down to follow it with his hot tongue.

I squirm in the bed, hissing as he repeats the process, tracing a line of extreme cold followed by hot mouth, lower... lower... *Oh, God...*

This time, when he slides his hands between my legs, he holds the ice a little longer. He holds it until I'm about to cry out in pain, and when his mouth follows, closing over my clit, I do scream. It's so hot. It's so crazy.

He licks the water away, sliding his tongue all around my pussy, then sucking me until my ass bucks against the bed. I'm losing my mind. I've never felt anything like this, and he repeats cold strokes followed by hot licks. He tortures me until I'm clenching, begging for him. Until I orgasm so intensely, I forget where I am.

My toes curl and my legs shake, and I want him to fuck me hard.

"Get on your knees." I'm trembling as I move slowly in the bed, following his orders.

His underwear is gone, and he quickly rolls on a condom. He

climbs onto the bed behind me, holding my waist as he slides his cock up and down my slit until he finds my entrance.

We both moan as he fills me, slamming deep and then holding still. He's big, and I'm full. I arch up, pressing against him and kissing his jaw. I thread my fingers in his soft hair, and his large hands cup and caress my breasts, using my body like a toy.

He hums with satisfaction and starts to thrust. He's moving fast, hitting my ass with his pelvis as he fucks me. He holds me firmly against his body, groaning words of approval, of satisfaction between hard thrusts, rough kisses, and little bites.

"So fucking gorgeous." Each word is punctuated by a fuck, and I'm rising again, faster this time.

His cock hits the place inside me, and with every stroke, sparks shoot brighter behind my closed eyes. I'm overwhelmed with sensation. I'm not sure how much more my body can take.

His beard scuffs my neck as his lips trace into my hair, behind my ear. Hot breath coats my shoulders in shimmering sensation, and when his hand drives roughly between my legs again, his touch, his determined grasps at my clit, send me soaring.

"Oh, God..." My voice breaks with my orgasm.

My body shudders, and I fall forward onto the bed. He follows me, holding me down and continuing to fuck me, two, three more times before groaning and gripping my ass, holding still as he finishes, pulsing deep inside me.

We're breathing so hard, and I'm trying to think... I've never been ravaged before. That was definitely ravaging. He takes a deep breath, coughing a bit before his strong arms circle my waist, and he leans forward, placing his cheek against the back of my neck.

Moments pass, and our breathing slowly returns to normal. My eyes are closed, and I'm so relaxed in his arms.

Then I notice his hand is moving, caressing my breast, and I start to giggle.

"Insatiable." My voice is woozy.

His cheek rises against my skin, and it makes me smile. Lifting his head, warm, hazel eyes meet mine, and something unexpected tightens in my chest. He looks at me like he wants to know more, like he cares… which is silly and childish, and I shake that shit out of my head. We've both had a lot of alcohol.

Rolling back on the bed, his voice is satisfied and lazy. "Are you hungry now?"

"No." I stretch my arms and my body in the soft sheets, and he disposes of the condom. "What do you think about football?"

"I don't." That clipped arrogance is in his voice again, and I laugh.

But when he returns to me, he pulls me gently to his chest. He gathers me in his arms like I'm delicate, and his tone softens. "Rest a bit. I plan to keep my promise and fuck you all night."

"I'd expect no less." My voice is sassy, but when I close my eyes, I'm fast asleep.

CHAPTER Six

Spencer

"Sin?" My hand slides over cold sheets, and I scrub my fingers against my eyes as I sit up.

What time is it?

The sun shines brightly through the crack in my heavy silk curtains, and I've got a hard-on. I want to relieve it in the heat between her thighs, caress those luscious tits, test her limits…

Where the fuck is she, and why isn't she in my bed?

"Joselyn?" I rip the heavy sheets back and my bare feet land on the scratchy pile of the hand-knotted, wool Persian rug surrounding my bed.

She's not in the sitting room or on the balcony. I jog naked to the first floor where the surf and turf I ordered from Rioz last night has gone to waste. Our wine glasses are on the table half-drunk, and the bottle is beside them still open.

Glancing around, I notice her clothes are gone. Her shoes, that small clutch... All gone.

Snatching up my phone, I'm all set to fire off an angry text when I realize I don't even have her contact information.

"God dammit." I exhale an annoyed growl, placing my fists on my hips.

I'd planned to take her to breakfast this morning, get in a little more fucking before we went our separate ways. The point of bringing her here was to get her out of my system. Now that damned itch is stronger than before, and I'm more agitated than yesterday.

Rubbing my hands over my face, I head back upstairs to my bathroom.

Why would she sneak out like some kind of thief? She didn't even leave a note.

"Succubus is more like it," I grumble, switching on my oversized rain shower system and adjusting it to hot and strong as I grab a change of clothes from my bedroom.

Stepping into the glass stall, I close my eyes and place both hands against the wall as the soothing waters cascade down from the ceiling. My semi is not helped by a memory of Joselyn hovering over me at some point in the night. Her gorgeous hair fell over one shoulder, tickling my thighs, and those full lips puckered lusciously around the tip of my dick.

She looked up at me with wicked blue eyes as she licked it like an ice cream cone. I believe she spoke into it like a mic, asking my cock if it liked that, which made me laugh. *Ridiculous*.

Then she went to town, sucking and pulling, taking me deeper as she made little eager, hungry noises.

"Jesus..." I have a full-on erection at the memory of her shameless confidence.

Damn her. She knew I was at her mercy as she took me that

way, my cock hitting the back of her throat. She blew me like a porn star. My ass rose off the bed when I shot down her throat.

Snatching the conditioner up, I put some on my hand before sliding my fist over my erection. As I tug, I think of her beautiful body.

She was just as I imagined she'd be, soft and full with flawless ivory skin. Her breasts were perky handfuls, teardrops bouncing, and her hips matched in exact proportion, round and firm. Auburn hair swept down to her narrow waist.

She said her stomach was soft. Fuck that. She's a painter's dream, an hourglass. Her ass was like a heart waiting for my hands to squeeze it, my teeth to mark it, my mouth to cover it, perhaps even my dick... *Shit.*

The thought of my dick in her ass has me on the edge. I can hear her little cries as I punish her for sneaking out on me. I hear her orgasmic moans, loud and ecstatic. She's responsive and vocal and...

"Fuck..." It's an angry groan as my thighs clench, as my cock pulses.

For a moment, I stand under the shower, wishing the hot water would ease my tension. It's no use. I'd planned to possess every inch of her body, and now I'm jerking off in the shower like a teenager. This is not how my Saturday was supposed to go.

Snatching up the body wash, I quickly clean up and switch off the water, stepping out and wrapping in a thick robe.

Standing in the center of my bedroom, I stare at the bed, thinking of her falling asleep in my arms. Her face relaxed with a little smile. My hand was on her breast, and she laughed softly. She asked me if I liked football, of all things.

My brow relaxes, and something moves in my stomach. She smelled like flowers, creamy magnolia and mimosa.

I push that to the back of my mind, reaching for my shirt when the twinge in my back pulls me up short. "Fucking Miles."

It gives me an idea.

Picking up my phone, I quickly tap out a text as I jog down the stairs. ***We need to see Joselyn's portfolio. Would you ask her to drop it by the office on Monday?***

I quickly hit send and switch on the coffee pot.

Daisy replies fast. ***Sorry, I forgot to send you her number. Here it is.***

A little woosh noise, and just like that, Joselyn's information is on my phone. I stare at it for several seconds. She's here in my hands. I could call her or text her and make her tell me why she left that way. I could order her to come back here now.

That is not who I am. ***I'll let you be the point person. Just tell her to stop by on Monday and drop it off. Any time.***

Gray dots appear as Daisy composes a reply. They disappear and reappear, and I imagine she's changing her mind about what she wants to say. I have to hand it to Daisy, she's pretty good at getting what she wants, but I'm not budging.

At last, she sends, ***Should I tell her to bring it to you or Miles?***

Now that is a good question. I don't give it a moment's thought. ***Either is fine. Thank you.***

She sends a little heart, and I take my coffee.

To be continued, Miss Winthrop.

CHAPTER Seven

Joselyn

"It's official. I am my own worst nightmare." I pace Courtney's apartment with my hands in my hair.

With every step, every movement of fabric over my skin, I feel all the places Spencer kissed me or bit me or froze me with ice before covering me with his mouth… Or fucked me silly.

"Stop being so hard on yourself. You'd been through a dry spell." Court's in the kitchen making coffee, and I cross the short distance from the living room with my arms wrapped around my waist.

"I said no men for a year. A year. I was going to focus on me, get my career back on track, and what do I do? I jump in bed with the first hot guy who looks at me."

"A year is a long time."

"I'm a total slut."

"What's a slut?" Oliver's little voice makes me jump.

"Shit!" Both hands cover my mouth.

"Aunt Sly said a swear word." Ollie snorts a laugh, ducking his head.

His mom cuts her eyes as she carries two mugs of coffee to the table. "Are you auditioning for *SNL*?"

"I'm sorry!"

Court bends down to kiss the top of his head. "Ignore Aunt Sly, sweetie. She's having a hard week."

His hands are cupped under his neck. "She woke me up last night."

"I did?" I kneel in front of him, sliding my fingers across the front of his hair. "I tried to be super quiet."

"I thought you were a monster." He rubs his hands back and forth under his chin.

"What's that? You got something?" I smile, leaning closer.

"It's just Chartreuse." He opens them, and my heart flies to my throat.

"Oh, gross!" I squeal, falling back on my ass and scrambling behind a kitchen chair. "Get it away!"

"Oliver James," Court fusses. "Put that thing back in its cage."

"She's not a thing!" He cries, and I peek from behind his mother's chair at the bright green tree frog with oversized orange eyes watching me from his palm.

"I swear to God, Ollie, if that thing gets on me, I will lose it."

"You already lost it," he grumbles under his breath, and my eyebrows shoot up.

"Rude." I look up at his mom, and she shakes her head.

"That is not how we talk to adults, Olls. Now put Chartreuse in her cage."

"She needs her bugs. She's going to starve to death."

"I'll get her bugs. Put her up now."

He stomps up the short hall leading to our shared bedroom,

and I rise slowly. "I've been sleeping with that thing in the room every night?"

"It's just a tree frog. Don't be such a drama queen."

"I'm loving the attitudes around here."

But when she returns from the kitchen with a plastic cup of what looks like crickets, I notice her eyes have dark circles under them.

"Hey," I catch her hand. "Are you okay? Did I wake you, too? I'll sleep in my van next time."

"It's not that." Her shoulders drop, and she exhales heavily.

"Tell me."

She glances towards Ollie's room before lowering her voice and leaning closer. "Ozzy showed up here last night. I didn't even know he knew where we lived. Thank God, Ollie was already asleep."

"What did he want?" My grip on her hand tightens. "Did he hurt you?"

She shakes her head, but her eyes are worried. "He said he wants his son back. He said I can't keep him away."

I've never met Court's husband, but once when we were doing clinicals, I had to treat her clients for a week because he'd sprained her wrist. I'd also kept Ollie for her so he'd be away from the fighting when his dad was around.

"Didn't the judge give you sole custody?"

Her lips tighten. "Ozzy won't sign the divorce papers. I filed a restraining order a year ago, but I guess it expired. I don't know. I thought he'd finally given up and gone away."

"Do they ever really do that?" She doesn't meet my eyes, and I pull her into a hug. "Don't worry. I'm here now, and I can kick some serious butt."

She exhales a laugh. "Thanks, Sly."

Leaning back, I catch her eyes. "What? You don't believe me?"

"It's not that." She rubs her face with her hands. "I'm just so tired. I stepped in this pile of shit, and no matter what I do, I can't seem to get it off me."

"I'm here for you." She blinks up, and our eyes meet. "I'll do whatever I can—just tell me what you need."

"Thanks, girl. I just wish he'd lose interest." She goes to Ollie's room, and I sit in the chair, studying my warm mug of coffee. All those true crime stories I've watched about abuse situations ending in death push against my mind. I'd do anything to protect my friend.

My phone buzzes, and I lift the face to see a text from Daisy. ***Miles needs to see your portfolio. Spence said to bring it by on Monday.***

Adrenaline flashes in my chest at the sight of his name, and I quickly push it down. Not going there. We're working together. I have to be professional.

My thumbs fly across my phone. ***I wasn't coming home this weekend. How will I get it?***

Tell me where it is, and I'll meet you.

Chewing my lip, I think about this. ***When do they want me to come in?***

Any time. Spencer said he'd be there all day.

Because he's my client now. I'll have to see him, interact with him, probably quite a lot. He hired me… He's practically my fucking boss for the next few weeks, and I slept with him. Boy howdy, did I sleep with him.

After what happened with Elliot, I swore I'd never mix business with personal life again. Exhaling a frustrated growl, I scrub my fingers in my hair. How could I be so careless? That man is bossy, arrogant, trouble, and I ran straight into it.

Yep, I'm my own worst enemy.

"Miss Winthrop, I didn't expect to see you today." Miles holds a stylus over an oversized iPad when I enter his large, corner office. It's a stunning space, with oak paneling and a wall of windows overlooking downtown. "Did I forget to write down a date?"

"Daisy said... Spencer told her you wanted to see my portfolio."

"He did?"

Looking down at the oversized black folder in my hands, I'm starting to think Miles had nothing to do with my being here today.

"No worries." He grins warmly. "I hate you made a special trip, though. Isn't your portfolio online somewhere?"

He says it like it's the most obvious thing, and embarrassment heats my cheeks. "That would probably be a smart idea. The truth is, I thought I was done with this type of work, so I never made time to scan it all—"

"Oh yes, we're pulling you out of retirement." He gives me a wink as he taps a button on his desk phone. "Spencer, can you join Miss Winthrop and me in my office?"

"Be right there." Spencer's rich voice fills the room, and my insides zing.

I squish that zing.

I'm more casual today in a short navy skirt and chambray shirt. Still, I anticipated seeing him, so I styled my hair and spent a little time on my makeup.

It's all so completely ridiculous, because I have no intention of continuing any sort of romantic relationship with Mr. Carrollton.

Miles has the right idea keeping things formal. We should use last names.

The door opens, and my chest squeezes at the sight. He's wearing a thin, black sweater that clings to his muscles and gray pants. He walks past me without a look and pauses at Miles's desk. "Let's see what we've got."

My breath tightens in my throat, and I blink twice before tearing my eyes away from his ass. I remember every detail, every line of muscle on his body, how his skin felt against mine.

"Take a seat and we'll run through it. Or should we go to the conference room? Which would you prefer, Joselyn?" Miles smiles. "Do you mind if I call you Joselyn?"

So much for formalities.

"I don't mind." My voice seems too soft, too delicate, and the muscle in Spencer's jaw moves. "It's your call. We can go through the folder here or we can use one of the large tables to spread them out and look at the pictures all together."

"I'm sure Daisy told you the Oceanside Hotel said yes." Miles rocks back in the chair. "You've worked in their facilities. What would you recommend?"

Spencer's eyes are fixed on my hands, which are now trembling as I turn the plastic-lined pages. Clearing my throat, I steel myself against his unfriendly demeanor.

"I've done so many different events… This is the first time I've done anything for antique dealers."

"They're just as banal and boring as everyone else, I assure you." Miles is a friendly counterbalance to the glacier standing beside me.

"Okay…" I hesitate at a photo of a palm sculpture. "If I at least had an idea of what type of theme you were wanting."

Miles shifts in his chair. "I had hoped you or Daisy could take the lead on that. Themes aren't really my strong suit."

"He's more of an idea guy." Spencer turns, and I jump back, nearly knocking my folder off the desk. He catches it, still not smiling. "Tell you what, I'll take Joselyn to my office, and we can go through this and pull something together."

"Brilliant!" Miles smiles broadly, clapping his hands and rising.

"I don't mind working something up for you on my own—"

"I have some ideas I'd like to discuss." Spencer's voice is firm, and he meets my gaze at last.

His hazel eyes are flat, and I feel very small looking up at him, even though I'm four inches taller than Miles. I feel like I could hide behind him.

"Okay." My voice is subdued.

"I like this plan." Miles motions us to the door. "Spencer has impeccable taste. I can't wait to see what you two come up with."

My portfolio is in Spencer's hands, and I study his broad shoulders as he strides out of the office and down the hall. I can see the muscles rippling through that sweater. He's powerful and arrogant, and what the hell am I doing here?

"Chivalry is dead." Miles chuckles, breaking the spell. "His office is just at the other corner there. The north and the south."

"Warmth versus freezing?"

"Something like that. He won't win Mr. Congeniality, but he's hardly ever wrong."

Squaring my shoulders, I decide I made this bed and had sex in it. I can meet this challenge head-on. Hell, Spencer being cool and professional is exactly the right approach to get things back on track. I have no idea why he summoned me here today, but he said I could always tell him to stop, and he would.

Hopefully he's better at keeping his word than I am.

CHAPTER *Eight*

Spencer

"THESE PIECES SHOULD WORK." I FLIP THE OVERSIZED PAGES, STOPPING at a photo spread of life-sized floral sculptures of a couple dancing in Regency attire. "Since that show on Netflix, everyone is into this royal type of thing. Or maybe it's since that Oprah interview."

"This is actually Belle and Prince Adam."

"I'm not familiar with them."

"*Beauty and the Beast*?" Her blue eyes flicker up at me, and when they meet mine, my stomach tightens in a way I don't like.

She looks amazing, and I'm pissed I still want to fuck her. She's also being very polite and professional—as am I.

"I did this for the high school prom one year, 'Tale as Old as Time.'"

"Was it for your high school prom?"

"No, I was in college at that point. I needed the money."

Clearing my throat, I step away from her hair and its scent of magnolia. It reminds me of how it bounced in soft waves around my arms when I drove my dick into her from behind.

"Go with that. Miles will think he's in a Disney movie. Hell, they all will." *Morons.*

"So Regency romance." She taps on her phone. "Should we tell them to dress in period attire?"

"God, no. It's not a carnival."

Her eyebrows rise, and she cuts me a glance. "You'd be surprised how much people love wearing costumes."

"Nothing surprises me." I walk around my desk as she zips up the folder and takes her clutch. My jaw tightens, and I can't seem to stop myself from going there. "You appear to be well."

She tilts her head, confusion lining her brow. "Why wouldn't I be?"

"Why else would you sneak out in the middle of the night unless you were ill?" Crossing my foot over my knee, I lift an iPad off my desk. "Unless you had some sort of emergency."

In my peripheral, I see her shifting uneasily. Yes, I like seeing her squirm under my cross-examination. I'm not a frat boy, and I'm definitely not a football jock. She's in the real world now.

"I'm sorry." Her voice returns to that soft register that makes me want to wrap her hair around my fist and pull her head back against my shoulder. "Friday was a mistake. I apologize for my unprofessional behavior."

My jaw tightens. Not what I expected her to say.

"You don't have to apologize. We're consenting adults."

"Yes, but I don't sleep with clients. I'd had too much to drink—"

"Stop." My eyes flash to hers, anger tightening in my chest. "I do not sleep with intoxicated women."

"No..." She holds up a hand. "I only meant..."

"I ordered food, which you refused to eat. I believe your exact words were not to tell you what to do."

Her chin drops, and she squeezes her eyes shut. "You're right. I said those things. It was poor judgment. I was dealing with some personal stuff."

Sleeping with me is poor judgment? I don't think so.

I grab the reins on my stinging rebuttal and put it in the box of cool self-control. I'm Mr. Freeze, after all.

Idiotic nickname.

"I see. Is this 'personal stuff' going to impact your ability to do your work? Or is that too invasive of me to ask?"

"It will not." She stares at her shoes like a child.

I want to tell her to look at me, but I don't.

"I'm glad to hear it." Standing, I round my desk and open the door, holding it for her to go.

She looks up at me as if she feels the need to explain. "I caught Elliot having sex with another woman. I was angry. I guess I wanted to prove something to myself… that I was still attractive or whatever. I know how dumb that sounds. I don't expect you to understand. It was reckless and completely unprofessional. It won't happen again."

Her words only toss lighter fluid on the situation. I'm pissed she's labeling our night as revenge sex. We were better than that. I'm pissed she sneaked out without letting me drive her home, like some kind of cheap hooker. I'm pissed she thinks she can decide it won't happen again.

If I want her, I'll have her.

"I'm sorry that happened to you." That's as far as I'll go. "Friday night, we scratched an itch. It's done, and we can put it behind us now."

"Behind us."

"You made the point we don't know each other very well. If we did, you'd know I'm not interested in a relationship. You're quite safe, Miss Winthrop. I have no intention of holding it against you or expecting a repeat performance."

Unless, perhaps, if you get on your knees and beg me…

She blinks several times, pressing her lips together, and I wonder if I've gone too far.

If she starts crying…

Pressure builds in my chest, but she pushes her hair behind her shoulder. "Thank you for that. I'm lucky you're such an understanding guy."

"I'm not a guy." *I swear to God.* "I look forward to seeing your art. In the meantime, I've got work to do."

With a quick turn, she stalks out the door, leaving behind the scent of creamy magnolia, mimosa, and memories.

"Now you own the place." I'm in Fireside, one of the smallest towns in South Carolina, standing in the kitchen of a century-old, red-brick colonial house on the only main street in town. "How long has it been since we renovated it?"

"We?" Daisy cries, then winks. "Let's see… I had just finished college, so five years?"

"I've lost track."

We're all in Oceanside to prep the ballroom and get ready for Saturday night. Joselyn is staying with her mother here in town, and Miles will join us on Saturday.

Some masochistic part of me relishes the idea of spending the next three days with her, even if it's to work, and when Daisy said they needed help or we'd miss our deadline, I found myself agreeing to come here. Miles has been good to all of us, and I try to support him, even if I think it's unnecessary.

Daisy crosses her arms, growing wistful. "Isn't it funny how things come around?"

"I still don't care for grand millennial or country." Walking through the floral-wallpapered space, I lift a red and white checked table cloth. "I'm glad you rethought this blunder."

"Miles said my interior design was inspired."

"Miles thinks you're an angel descended from design heaven, poor man."

She laughs, as we stroll through her living room to the front door. It's decorated in gingham pillows, large churns of dried lavender, and lace doilies. "Don't try to fool me with that icy exterior. I've seen behind the curtain, Mr. Freeze."

"Will I ever shake that nickname?" I don't even know how it got started.

"You could try being a little nicer."

"I value honesty above all."

"I didn't say be dishonest. Remember when you gave Ms. Nelly your prized Fenton art glass to complete her collection? That was very thawed of you."

"It was a loan. You said I'd get it back when she dies." Lifting a photo of a handsome man holding a golden-haired little girl, I pause. "Where are they?"

"Football practice."

"Of course." I lift my chin. *Pituitary case.*

"So a gala? Just like that, out of nowhere? You hate big events. What's behind all this?"

"Link Sherlock." I place the photo down and we step out onto the red-brick front porch. It's expansive and catches the breeze nicely, and Daisy has wicker chairs and rockers at various intervals.

"The YouTuber? He's hilarious!" Her blue eyes crinkle and she mimics the voice of his intro line. "'Finding treasures wherever they may hide…' I love him."

"Miles is very threatened by him. Thinks he's going to steal all our clients."

"Why don't you join forces with him?"

"I can't think of anything worse. I prefer my idea."

"Which was?"

"Ignore him."

"You can't ignore the future." She shakes her head, and I remember a time when she and I were the future in this business.

"Speaking of, what happened to that ambitious young woman who dreamed of traveling and taking over the southeast region?"

She takes my arm as we descend the stairs. "She grew up to be happier than she ever dreamed possible."

One look in Daisy's eyes, and I know she's telling the truth. "Well, good for her."

"You could always tell Miles no. He's not your boss anymore."

"He doesn't have a lot of excitement in his life. I'll let him have his fun if it saves me a trip."

"Good thing, because we've spent the last two weeks busting our asses. We might set a record on fastest gala assembly in recorded history."

"Always the over-achiever."

She snorts, shaking her blonde head. "I'm actually looking forward to it. I haven't been to a big party since I got married."

"There you go."

She rises on tiptoes to kiss my cheek. "You're an old softie, but don't worry, I won't tell anybody. Now get to the hotel. I reserved the executive suite with a view of the water for you. It's coastal chic, not a quilt or a doily in sight."

"I remember it from your wedding. The northeastern crew will adore it. They'll think they're in the Hamptons."

"We'll take them all to the Tuna Tiki to remind them where they really are."

I start to recoil at the low-rent tiki bar on the beach, but I remember one positive. "They have very good sushi."

"Thank you!" Daisy slaps my arm. "One of these days, you're going to stop being such an old fuddy-duddy."

"If you're implying I don't know how to have fun, you know that's wrong. I don't care for places where I'll be vomited on or have draft beer spilled down my back."

"I told you not to wear your best blazer."

"I don't own cheap clothes." We're standing beside my black Tesla parked on the street.

"We'll have to find you some play clothes, Captain Von Trapp. I think I have an old pair of drapes—"

"I'll see you in the ballroom in the morning. In appropriate work attire."

"Thanks for agreeing to help out. I know it's not your thing."

"I don't mind."

"You're a good man, Spence."

Glancing at the sky, I decide this was a mistake. "I'm an asshole. Don't forget it."

CHAPTER
Nine

Joselyn

"HOLD IT RIGHT THERE." I'M ON A LADDER, BLOWTORCH IN HAND. JR is down below, bracing two tall metal rods as I weld them.

"Hurry up," he grunts. "I can't hold it much longer."

Dark glasses are over my eyes, and a cascade of golden sparks flies around us as the pieces melt into one. My high-waisted jeans protect my legs from the fire, and my hair is piled on my head in a bun, covered with a handkerchief tied on top.

I'm Rosie the Riveter, and I applied red lipstick and tied my shirt in a knot at my waist to complete the look. I told myself it has nothing to do with Spencer calling me a vintage pinup.

It's a total lie.

After several seconds of firing, the two beams are finally secure, and I climb down. JR leans to the side wincing, and I take a break to massage his mid-back.

"That feels good," he grunts.

"Why isn't Scout here? You can't help me with that old injury. It's only going to get worse."

"The Quarterback Princess has a daddy-daughter tea." He wipes the back of his hand across his forehead, and a nostalgic smile curls my lips.

I had the biggest crush on John Roth Dunne in high school. He's only a year older than us, but it was enough for him only ever to think of me as a skinned-kneed little kid. I finally grew out of being hopelessly devoted to him when he went away to college and later married, but he's still one of the best-looking guys in town. He's not even taller than me.

"You'll be the same way in a few years, once Sunny is big enough to run and play." I elbow him in the ribs, and it gets me a rare chuckle.

"Yeah."

John has always been quiet, serious, way too old for his age, and now he's happily married with a family of his own. Maybe one day I'll have that, even if it's nowhere in sight. I thought I was getting there, but life sure likes to jerk the rug out from under me.

"Joselyn, would you mind... a moment?" Spencer's deep voice pulls me from my pity party.

Straightening fast, I touch my hair, taking the protective glasses off my head, and smoothing my hands over my knotted blouse. I stand a little taller, subtly arching my back so my breasts lift. I still get slippery inside when I remember how eager he was to touch them. It was so hot.

"What's going on here?" He nods towards JR, who's polishing off a water bottle.

"We're assembling the framework for the sculptures. I need someone to hold the metal beams so I can create a skeleton, then I'll cover it with floral wire and thread the flowers through—"

"Isn't he married?" Spencer's voice is sharp, and my chin pulls back.

"Yes, with two kids. Why do you ask?"

"You were flirting with him."

"I was not!" My voice goes too loud, and I look around fast, lowering it quickly. "I was not flirting with him."

Spencer takes a moment, studying my hot face with a scowl. "I'll help you assemble the frames. He can do something else. Or better yet, send him home."

My jaw drops, and Spencer turns on his heel and walks to where my cousin is sticking star labels on nametags. I watch as he points to where I'm working and hands her a brown manila envelope.

Closing my mouth, I go to where John is chatting with Bruce, who handles security and graduated from Fireside High a few years before us.

"Hey, Sly." Bruce gives me a hug. "It's been a while since you made one of these things. I thought you'd given it up."

"Just when I thought I was out, they pulled me back." I do my best Michael Corleone imitation, and the guys chuckle.

"Can't wait to see the finished product. You always knock my socks off." He does a little wave and strolls to the other side of the large space, leaving me with JR.

"Hey, you're off the hook. You should head home and put a heating pad on your back."

Ice blue eyes blink up to mine. "I can help you a little longer."

"And I really appreciate it, but I don't want to be in the doghouse for breaking your back. You've got babies to carry now. Spencer will help me."

That deep dimple appears, and I sigh, wondering if it's a sin to acknowledge how handsome he is.

"You're still a badass with a blowtorch." He holds up a hand, and I high-five it feeling proud.

"Thanks, babe." He gives Daisy a wave before heading out the door, and I turn to see Spencer watching me with his dark brow lowered. Such a deep frown for someone who has no interest in me anymore.

Stalking back to the beginnings of my sculpture, I pull my glasses over my eyes again. "I don't know why you're frowning. I did what you said."

"Good girl. Now, what do you need me to hold?" I'm annoyed at him speaking to me like a child. At the same time, his possessive tone tingles my stomach.

I have two things he can hold… and fondle… and nuzzle…

"Aunt Sly! Aunt Sly!" Ollie charges into the empty ballroom waving a plastic cup over his head. "Look at all the crickets I found!"

Spencer exhales impatiently. "How do you get anything done?"

"Magic." I do a little starburst with my fingers, and he shakes his head, turning away.

Pretty sure I see the smallest hint of a grin trying to break that ice, and it reminds me of the time I heard him laugh—another dirty memory of his dick at my lips.

"Chartreuse is going to be so fat!" Oliver turns the cup side to side. "Just look at them."

"That is really gross, Olls. Let me check that thing."

The lid has tiny holes punched in it, but they're not too big for anything to escape. I double-check it's sealed tight, shuddering at the pile of crickets inside climbing over each other to get to the top.

"Don't let those get loose in the house." I hug his little shoulders. "Mom will have a cow, and I'll have to sleep in my van."

"Ms. Regina said she likes Chartreuse. She held her and let her climb onto her shoulder and everything! We almost lost her in her hair!"

He's talking loud because he's excited. I have a full-body shiver at the thought of that slimy thing in my mom's hair. "You should be a props master for Indiana Jones movies when you get big."

"What's a props master?" Ollie's face scrunches. "It sounds cool!"

"It's right up your alley, froggy boy. Tons of bugs and snakes and alligators. Have you finished your homework?"

"Yes, Aunt Sly," he grouses, and I goose his side, making him shout with a laugh.

When I told Courtney I had to be here until Sunday, she asked if I'd bring Ollie with me just in case his dad showed up again. Naturally, I said yes. I didn't like leaving her in Columbia alone, but she said she couldn't ditch out on her clients. Still, I call her every night, and she's joining us this weekend.

"What if you traded in your frog for a dog?"

"Mom said we can't afford a dog." He reaches into his pocket and pulls out the vivid green frog with enormous, red-orange eyes.

My throat knots. I'm a little less creeped out by her now, but not much. "I can't look at those eyes. They're too big."

"They help her eat." Ollie smooths a finger down her slippery head. "She pulls them in to swallow, and they shove the food down her neck."

"That's disgusting."

"Did you know the males ride on the females' backs during mating season? That way they can fertilize the eggs as soon as they're laid."

"That sounds about right." I look up at my sculpture and then over to Spencer, who's sliding his phone into the pocket of his dark brown pants—no jeans for him. Still, his ass looks so fine in those pants.

"I need to get back to work. Stay out of trouble, okay?"

"I'm going to feed Chartreuse."

"Don't lose her. Or her eyes." I point sternly before walking to where Spencer is standing with his hands on his hips. "Sorry. Feeding time at the zoo. Did you know that species of tree frog has been around ten million years?"

"Fascinating." He follows me to the pile of scrap metal sounding the exact opposite of fascinated. "Why isn't he in school?"

"That's not really your business, is it?" I separate out a few smaller pieces I can use for the arms and joined hands.

His expression darkens at my sass. "You're my business as long as you work for me."

Chewing my lip, I wonder why that statement is perversely thrilling.

Either way, I swallow my snappy comeback. "His dad's kind of a rough guy. He's been threatening to take Ollie from his mother, so I told her I'd keep him with me—in case he shows up again. She'll be here Friday night."

"That sounds dangerous. Is she okay?"

"I think so. I call her every day to be sure. She said she's got it under control."

"I hope so."

His sudden concern surprises me, but I'm glad for it. I didn't make arrangements for Ollie while I'm here working, and I don't want to let Courtney down.

We carry the pieces back to the half-finished structure, and I pass the spare set of safety goggles to him.

"I like this look you're doing here." He motions towards my outfit, and I scrub my forehead to keep from beaming like I've never gotten a compliment before.

"Thanks. I was feeling playful this morning."

"It's cute, Rosie."

"Puppies are cute."

My quip almost gets me a grin, but at the last minute, he turns away as if he's sorry he complimented me. I'm not sure what to make of it. One moment he's trying to rebuild our friendship, then just as fast he's back to angry and distant.

Shaking my head, I pull on my gloves and position the small

pieces of metal, sparking the blowtorch. Muscle memory takes over, and it doesn't take long to finish this assembly.

Spencer holds the pieces with gloved hands, looking down as burning sparks fly around us. The joints glow white-orange for a second before fading to gray metal as they quickly cool. Since I'm covering them with mesh and flowers, I don't have to worry about making them pretty.

We're back and forth, selecting the pieces and attaching them, and less than an hour later, we're done.

"This gives new meaning to the phrase 'fiery redhead.'" He almost sounds impressed as he helps me clean up the scraps. "Who taught you to do all of this?"

"Shop teacher at school. I'm the only girl who took welding."

"You're a welder. Daisy's daughter plays football." He places the metal pieces in the box I'm filling to take to the recycling plant. "I take it your family enjoys busting stereotypes."

"We're descended from a long line of witches. Don't piss me off or I'll turn you into a frog and give you to Ollie."

"I was wondering where he got his little pet." He straightens, and we're so close, I can feel the warmth of his body. "Must be nice to dispose of your enemies so cleanly."

"It has its moments." I lift my chin, and he takes a step back, lifting the floral mesh off the pile of supplies.

"Up next is this stuff?"

"Yep. I'll drape it over the frames and fasten it with the clear zip ties. Then I'll smooth the flower food and dirt and moss paste on the outside. Once that's done, I'll thread the flowers through the netting. I'll wait until Friday morning so it'll be as fresh as possible on Saturday night."

"How long does it last?"

"As long as they water it. The paste keeps the flowers hydrated, and I try to select ones that hold up well after cutting. Roses are the worst, but we have to have roses for Beauty and the Beast."

"Why is that?"

"The rose is Beast's countdown clock. As each petal falls, the time runs out for him to learn to love Belle and earn her love in return. If he doesn't before the last one falls, he'll be a beast forever."

Hazel eyes meet mine, and the pull between us is real. I'm the magnet and he's the steel. I'm fire to his ice.

I want to thread my fingers in the back of his hair and kiss him. I want to slide my nose along his jaw and inhale his rich scent of sandalwood and leather. I want to see the energy swirl around us like the cascades from my torch. *We had something…*

"Does he make it?"

Blinking quickly, I shake my head. "In the movie he does. Just barely, though. Belle shows up in time to save him."

His full lips press together, and he frowns up at the sculpture. "What about the non-Disney version?"

"I don't know. I like the Disney version of the story."

"Probably best to get the whole truth before believing in fairy tales." He lowers the netting, dusting his hands together. "I think you've got it from here. Let me know if you need any more help."

"Scout's coming to help me tomorrow. Thanks, though." The muscle in his jaw moves, and he seems annoyed by my answer.

I want to ask why. I want to ask what his true story is, but if he said it's not my business, he'd be right. No more going down that road, no matter how orgasmic it promises to be. We're keeping this professional.

CHAPTER Ten

Spencer

"THREE LOVE BOAT PLATTERS AND TWO PITCHERS OF NATTY LIGHT." Daisy's high voice rings out over the live reggae band.

It's Thursday night, and we're treating the crew to dinner at the Tuna Tiki before our guests roll in tomorrow evening. I lean to the side, speaking in Joselyn's ear.

"I'm going to the bar. Want a martini?"

Her blue eyes widen, and she grips my arm. "Please. I can't drink Natural Light."

Working with Joselyn these last few days has been unexpectedly challenging. Wednesday, she showed up looking like my every pinup fantasy come to life.

Tight jeans cinched her narrow waist, and her red blouse was knotted right under those amazing tits. Every time she moved, I got a teasing glimpse of creamy white skin. Her lips were red velvet, and perched on that ladder, wielding a blowtorch, I almost had to toss her over my shoulder.

Standing beneath a cascade of sparks raining all around us, it was like I'd been snatched into some ancient Greek myth where the gods had decided to have their fun with my resolve.

Today was a different kind of test with Daisy's husband in the mix.

Unlike his quiet, irascible brother, Scout Dunne is the classic, all-American football golden boy. He oozes charm, which is irritating in its own way, and he and Joselyn spent the day pranking each other and laughing.

From ice down her shirt and his pants—one after the other, I was ready to punch that guy in the nuts, and when I offhandedly noted our guests would be arriving tomorrow afternoon, I'm pretty sure, Joselyn mimicked me behind my back.

If she thinks she's getting under my skin with these antics…

My confidence in Daisy's marriage kept me from suggesting he was too much of a distraction. They claimed to be working, and by 6 p.m., the sculptures were ready to be flowered.

At least it's over now.

Standing at the bar, I study the group as the bartender mixes two pretty decent martinis. Scout says something, Joselyn seconds it, and Daisy shakes her head, laughing. Then he puts his muscled arm around his wife and kisses her head.

It's unsettling in a way I don't expect, like a glimpse of something I've never had and never particularly worried about not having.

This is why I don't spend time in the country. All this quiet starts messing with my priorities.

I'm walking to the table with two martinis at the same time the servers deliver three large platters of raw fish.

"Sly, remember when we were shearing that topiary back in high school, and you sliced the top layer off your finger?" Scout points to a strip of Ahi tuna. "There it is."

"Stop it!" Joselyn cries, throwing a balled-up napkin at him. "You're ruining my tuna nigiri!"

"Who knew there was so much blood in the old girl?" He misquotes Macbeth in a pretty decent Shakespearean accent, and I realize he's not as dumb as a box of rocks like I'd originally assumed.

Asshole.

"No blood talk at the table." Daisy pushes his shoulder, and he gives her a wink.

I turn away from their easy familiarity placing one of the martinis in front of Joselyn.

Her eyes light. "Yes!" She lifts it, taking a delicate sip before putting it down again. "It's delicious. I'm going to savor it."

She gives me a deferential smile, and fuck, if my dick doesn't twitch.

Clearing my throat, I pick up the thread. "What's this about your finger?" I figure gore is a good boner-killer.

She tilts her hand to the side, studying her digit before extending it to me. "This one. Almost sliced it right off with my pruning shears. It must've bled for an hour. I thought I was going to pass out. Ten stitches later..."

I hold her hand, turning it so I can see the silver scar running along the inside of her slim finger. "So these sculptures have always been hazardous to your health?"

She shakes her head, lifting a piece of fish to her mouth. "I knew I stopped doing this for a reason."

After watching her work, I'm not sure I agree with that decision. "Brushes with death and dismemberment aside, you're an artist."

Her cheeks pink attractively, and she covers her mouth blinking away from my eyes. "Thank you, Spencer."

"Where's your little charge this evening? No sushi for him?"

"He's actually hanging out with JR's son this evening. They

played on a little football team together one summer, and they've been friends ever since."

"And his mother?"

"Courtney should be here tomorrow afternoon. She said it's been a pretty quiet week, so that's good news. It's really nice of you to ask… and a little surprising. Most people don't want to talk about that kind of thing."

I don't say I'm aware. I push those dark memories away and give her a tight smile. "I try to know my employees' situations. Especially if it might impact your performance."

"I told you it wouldn't."

Glancing at the table, I see we've eaten most of the fish. I'm about to say I'll call it a night when an electronic drum beat echoes over the crowd, and the singer launches into "Red, Red Wine."

Joselyn's hands fly to her face in surprise, and Daisy cuts her husband a disgusted look.

"I didn't do it," Scout insists, holding up three fingers. "Scout's honor."

"You did not just say that," Joselyn cackles, and my stomach tightens. Why is she so damn intriguing to me?

Daisy is not impressed, but I notice Miles approaching from behind her.

"Hello, friends!" he calls. "Hello, Spencer! Daisy, I played this song just for you. I heard it's your favorite."

Her eyes widen, and Scout gives her a smug look.

With a groan, she stands and hugs our former boss. "Miles, I'm so glad you made it. Did you just get in town? Have some sushi. There's plenty."

"We have to dance." Scout is on his feet, catching her hand. "Miles played this song just for you, Tink."

"Miles has impeccable timing," I mutter to Joselyn.

She snorts a laugh, covering her mouth. "I don't know why Daisy hates this song so much. It's not that bad."

"It's that bad."

"What's funny is the way she gets so bent out of shape about it." Her voice is so light, compared to how she was in Columbia. I can't resist.

"Want to dance?"

She leans back like she's stunned, but her eyebrows rise with a nod. "Sure."

Taking her hand, I lead her to the floor, ignoring the surge in my chest, the fact of how much I've wanted to hold her in my arms again.

Moving through the press of dancers, she puts a hand on my waist. Her cheek is at my shoulder, and I hold her other hand close.

Her body is soft against mine, soft breasts against the hardness of my chest. It's a tantalizing memory of how our bodies feel bare against each other's, how gorgeous her tits are, how she sounds coming on my mouth.

She's not wearing heels, so the top of her head is right under my nose. I only have to tilt my chin down to inhale creamy magnolia...

She weakens my defenses, but my instinct pushes back. Clearing my throat, I refocus. "You seem to make a habit of flirting with married men."

Her body stiffens. "I'm sorry? What did you just say?"

"Yesterday it was John. Today, it's Scout..."

She tries to pull away, but I tighten my hold. Her nose is slightly upturned, and her blue eyes flash in the yellow lights.

"I'm not flirting with married men." Her teeth are gritted, and fuck me, her feistiness makes me hard.

"That's not how it appears."

We move side to side in silence, and I think I have her until her lips relax into a smile. Her wicked sass emerges. "I see," she nods. "You're jealous."

"Jealousy is never a good look on anyone. You won't see it on me. I just think as someone who has experienced the pain of infidelity, you wouldn't want to inflict it on others."

The fire is back in her eyes. "You are such an ass—"

"Yes, I've been told."

"For your information, Scout and I grew up together. He's like a brother to me. I introduced him to Daisy when we were in high school, because they're perfect for each other. I practically shoved them into each other's arms. I have no interest in him romantically."

"Or JR?" I don't like that guy. He's an asshole just like me, and she's drawn to him—just like she is to me.

"I stopped crushing on JR years ago."

"Are you sure?"

"Why do you care?"

"I don't."

Her eyes narrow, then she looks away. "When he got married, those feelings went away. I'm not a cheater. I never have been. I'm honest, and I respect other people's feelings."

I'm glad to hear it, but I don't say it out loud. I've shown enough of my cards for one night, and either way, her dating life is none of my concern. I don't know why I even asked. I need to re-establish the space between us.

The song has changed, and now they're playing slow-assed Clapton like every beach band on the planet. I preferred him when he was on drugs.

The rest of our party has returned to the table, where they're laughing and joking as usual.

I glance down at her secure in my arms. I don't know what to make of her—or me. "You're different here."

"Am I?"

"You laugh more."

Her head tilts to the side, and I watch her consider this. "It's my home. I'm with people I've known all my life. It's familiar, I guess."

"So why don't you move back?"

"You sound like Daisy." Her tone grows impatient. "I have no interest in moving back to the low-key, 'What are you going to do with your life?' all the time. No thanks, I'd rather have a root canal."

"Is this coming from your mother?"

"It comes from everybody. They're all wonderful when I'm here for a visit, but if I stay too long, it turns into nonstop pressure to either get married and have kids or to be the best whatever at whatever. No resting on your laurels in Fireside. It's much easier to leave and be a failure than to stay and simply exist."

Unexpected. "How old are you, Joselyn?"

She hesitates a moment, as if her age is something to hide. "I'm twenty-five."

"You're hardly old enough to be a failure at anything. Maybe they're excited for your potential."

"You couldn't possibly understand. You've never had to work to prove yourself."

A laugh breaks from my throat. "You have no idea what my life has been like. No one gets a free ride."

Her chin drops, and she studies my shirt. "I keep forgetting I don't know anything about you. I'm sorry."

The song is coming to an end, and I slide a lock of bright red hair off her cheek. "No harm done."

She glances up at me. "After Saturday, you won't be my boss anymore."

"It's true. It will be the end of our professional relationship." Grazing my eyes along her cheekbone, I confess, I'll miss her. "What will you do then?"

"Back to building my client list, pounding the pavement."

"If you need help, I write a pretty decent letter of recommendation."

"I don't know if a florist rec will help me, but if you know anyone who needs massage therapy or sports medicine, be sure to send them my way. Or if you ever need it yourself."

"Done. I like having you under me."

She gives me a naughty grin. "That's not how I remember it."

My eyes are drawn to her full lips, which are glossy pink tonight. Her cheeks are flushed, and I don't miss the gentle rise and fall of her breasts.

Her ocean eyes are clear and curious. This little ember wants to melt her way through my walls, but it's not an option.

Time to pour some freezing water on this fire.

"You're right. We don't know each other well, but I believe you're an intelligent person. At least, it appears your memory functions properly. In my office I told you I don't do relationships. To be completely clear going forward, what I meant is I don't sleep with the same woman more than once. I do fucking. Nothing more."

Her blue eyes slide to the side. "You do fucking. Now, where have I heard that line before?"

"I'm sure you've seen it in a movie or you've read it in a book, and you think I'm not serious or it's just a line. Or somehow your magic pussy will change my mind and make me grow a heart or some other form of attachment. It won't."

"That sounds both very lonely and very risky to me."

"I don't take risks, and I'm never alone unless I want to be."

"I see. Just out of curiosity, why do you find it necessary to have such a rule? I'm open to a little no-strings-attached sex every now and then."

"Ah, but you see, if I ever break my rule, if I ever fuck the same woman twice, suddenly she forgets what I just said. She thinks it happened—her magic pussy has broken the spell, and I've changed my evil ways. That's when it all becomes very messy. I also don't do messes."

"You almost sound proud of yourself." She gives me that sassy grin, and I'm annoyed her defiance is such a turn-on to me.

"I also told you before, I'm honest."

"Then it sounds like I'm wasting your time." The sarcastic edge in her voice tells me she's angry.

I tell myself it's good. It's how it should be.

Lowering my hands, I give her a slight bow. "Thank you for the dance, Joselyn. Have a good evening."

Then I step back and let her walk away.

CHAPTER Eleven

Joselyn

"I'VE GOT TO SAY, I'M IMPRESSED." COURTNEY WALKS SLOWLY AROUND, gazing up at the larger-than-life topiary statues of Belle and Prince Adam.

"Aunt Sly used a blowtorch!" Ollie hops in front of her holding his hands up like he has a rocket. I can tell he's missed her by how excited he is. "She'd put it on the metal and *Boosh*! Sparks flew everywhere!"

"I told him not to look at the flame. You did what I said, right Olls?" I'm perched on a ladder, threading the final roses in Belle's bodice.

He nods dutifully, but Courtney is still staring up in wonder. "How did you ever learn to do all of this?"

Sitting back on the ladder, I study the massive arrangement. "I mostly taught myself. You'd be surprised what you can learn on YouTube. Then I took some welding classes at school, and I talked to different florists to get advice on which flowers work best in topiaries."

She shakes her head. "I can't believe you did it all by yourself. And so fast!"

"JR and Scout helped me with the framing—and Spencer, I guess." *The asshole.* I'm still trying to decide how pissed I am about last night. "I'm nowhere near done. Once I'm finished with these final roses, I have to make all the arrangements for the tables. Being a florist is work."

"Hold up, back it up." Court lifts both hands along with her eyebrows. "Did I hear you say *Spencer* helped you? Mr. Brown Chicken Brown Cow?"

Ollie rolls his eyes and takes off across the glossy wooden ballroom floor towards the exit. "I'm out of here."

I make a face, but his mother only laughs. "I guess he knows about everything by now."

"To answer your question, yes. Spencer helped me, and we've been very professional. No funny business at all. In fact, I have it straight from the horse's mouth we will not be revisiting his bedroom."

"Eh, so you'll visit yours," she deadpans.

"Mr. Carrollton says he never sleeps with the same woman twice."

My friend's forehead crinkles, and she looks as confused as I felt last night when he said it. "That's strangely sucky."

It absolutely is, but let him have his silly rules. Spencer Carrollton has lived up to his nickname one hundred percent on this trip. He has completely frozen me out.

When Scout was helping me yesterday, I caught him glaring at us a few times in a way that I wanted to believe was jealousy. I tried to poke that bear, but he only went home early.

Now, after what he said last night, I'll be damned if I'm going to chase after him, no matter how magnetic it feels when I'm in his arms or how my eyes slide closed when he inhales deeply at the top of my head...

Which makes absolutely no sense. I should have told him he was full of shit. He wants me as much as I want him. It's not my job to tell him to get his head out of his ass.

Anger tingles in my throat, and I grit my teeth. "Fuck Spencer Carrollton. This will all be over tomorrow night, and I can get on with my life. I'm not wasting any more time running down dead-end roads."

"That's the spirit." Courtney's such a great friend.

"How about you? Any word from Ozzy this week?"

"Not a peep. Maybe he's decided to leave us alone finally. I can hope, right?"

A pinch of dread is in the pit of my stomach, but I want to be as encouraging to her as she is to me. "We're going to do more than hope. We're going to find some good men, not abusers or icebergs who only want to screw around and wreck our lives. They're out there, and we're going to find them."

"Preach!"

Feeling motivated, I return to my work, giving the floral statues a final inspection. "Hey, Court, hand me two more of those roses, and I'll be done."

She steps forward, grabbing two oversized pink flowers from the bucket of water. I stoop down to get them, ignoring the sway of the ladder. It's been doing that all day.

"Where is he now?" She asks as I straighten, leaning forward into the statue again so I can thread these last two pieces.

"Where is who?" Spencer's deep voice makes my heart jump to my throat, and my foot twists in the rung, causing the ladder to sway wildly.

"Oh, shit!" My hands go out, and panic grips my spine. "No... NO!"

I can't fall on the statues. They'll be ruined, and I don't have time to get more flowers. Hell, nobody will even have enough flowers to recreate them on such short notice.

These thoughts flash across my mind, but it's too late. The ladder is collapsing, and my body weight is headed straight into Belle and Adam.

"Oh my God!" Courtney screams.

"Joselyn!" Spencer shouts.

At the last second, I arch my back, doing my best to throw my body weight away from the statues. The ladder jerks like somebody grabs it. My forward momentum halts, but my balance is shot. I'm going down.

"NO!" I cry, bracing for impact, praying I don't slam my head against the floor.

With an *Oof!* I land on something hard. Spencer has me in his arms, and I grasp his shoulder. Only, we're still moving too fast. He lets out a loud groan as we go all the way down, crashing to the floor.

"Sly, oh my God!" Courtney is at my side, holding my hand, and I blink at the chandeliers overhead, trying to focus.

It all happened so fast.

"Dammit, Sin." Spencer grunts from under me. "Are you hurt?"

Courtney helps me roll to the side then onto my hands and knees, all while trying to catch my breath.

"I'm okay," I gasp.

Trembling breaks through my body, and a tear falls onto my cheek. I'm not really crying. It's all the adrenaline mixed with the relief I didn't just smash all our hard work… or my skull.

Spencer struggles onto his butt beside me, placing a hand gently on my lower back. "Look at me." Lifting my head, I meet worried hazel eyes.

He slides a thumb across my cheek, wiping the tears away. "Are you dizzy? Nauseated?"

"No…" I shake my head just before I collapse into his strong arms. They surround me quickly, muffling my voice against his chest. "You saved me. You saved everything."

Courtney sits beside us, stroking my hair. "You did some pretty impressive acrobatics getting away from it. It's more like you saved the flowers. He saved your head from splatting all over the floor."

I feel the muscles in Spencer's body flinch. "That does it," he grumbles. "No more sculptures without a safety net... and a football helmet and metal gloves."

Leaning back, I wipe my nose with the back of my hand. "Now I remember why I stopped doing these things."

"They're hazardous to your health." His voice is so grumpy, I start to laugh.

Tears fill my eyes again, and I can't stop laughing. I think I've lost it. "Thank you for saving my life."

"Sly?" Daisy's high voice echoes in the empty ballroom. "What the hell—Spencer? Are you okay?"

"Can you stand?" Spencer's voice is gentler than I've ever heard it.

He holds my hand and my elbow, helping me to stand carefully. Daisy is at my side wrapping her arm around my waist.

"What happened?"

"Oh, you know," I try to joke. "The usual Sly-near-death-experience on a bed of roses."

Her blue eyes are worried, and Spencer pats her back. "She's going to be okay."

"Whoa, what the hell? What did I miss this time?" Scout is with us, catching my other arm and helping me to a chair.

"I'm really fine." I try to push back on all the fussing. Now it's just overkill.

Spencer seems to have disappeared, and when I finally spot him, he's bracing one hand on a table and leaning to the side. His face is ashen, and his eyes are squinted in a grimace.

"Spencer, are you okay?" I angle through the crowd of my

friends, making my way to where my savior is clearly hurt. "Did I break something?"

His grimace is immediately replaced with a tight smile. "No, it's fine. I'm just catching my breath."

He isn't fooling anybody.

"Is it your ribs? Ribs can't really be fixed, but we can tape them." Scout steps forward, which only makes him withdraw more.

"It's not my ribs." Spencer holds up a hand. "It's an old injury. I tweaked my back playing racquetball with Miles. I probably irritated the muscle."

"If that's the case, Sly can help you. She got her degree in sports medicine, massage therapy. Give him the works, Sly." Scout motions between us, but I hesitate.

"I'm glad to check you out. We can do it here or at my mom's... Wherever you feel comfortable."

"I'm going to head up to my room and see if I can treat it with ice and heat. I've got a nice jacuzzi tub. If none of that works, I'll let you know. I'm glad you're okay." It's a dismissive retort, and he limps to the doors.

If I didn't know him better, I'd say he was running away. Only, not the great, cold and distant Spencer Carrollton. He's far too fierce for that... Right?

"That guy is such a dick." Scout shakes his head, but I punch him in the arm.

"That man just saved my life—and the centerpiece for the gala. Show some respect."

"Ow—don't hit me, witch."

I pretend to lunge at him, and he ducks like he'll tackle me. I lift my leg as if I'll kick him, but Daisy steps in the middle of our play fight.

"Okay, kids..." She puts her arm around my waist. "I'm glad you're okay. If Spencer's down for the count, I need you to help me greet our guests. You up for it?"

I glance over at Courtney, who holds up both hands. "I've got to find my lost boy. Do what you need to do."

Eight hours later, I'm standing outside the pristine white door of the executive suite, my breath a tight ball in my throat. Holding my fist up, I close my eyes as I rap firmly.

"Can't you read?" Spencer snaps angrily from inside. "Assuming you can't, I'll read it for you. It says, 'Do not disturb.'"

Slipping the tag off the doorknob, I use the extra key Daisy gave me to let myself in his room. It's elaborately elegant, much like his apartment in Columbia. Plush, white carpet covers the dark laminate floor, and a velvet armchair is beside a matching, dark wood table.

I walk further into the dim-lit space, past the bed to where Spencer is lying on his stomach on a divan facing the open balcony. A light breeze drifts in from the spectacular view of the ocean, and the shush of the waves drifts up to us.

He's not wearing a shirt, and his muscled torso is on full display. One hand is fisted under his cheek, and his eyes are closed. I take a moment to study his square jaw, his forehead slightly lined in what I assume is pain. A bucket of ice is on the floor beside him.

"It does not." I'm quiet and playfully firm. "It's much more polite. It says, '*Please* do not disturb.'"

His eyes pop open, and his body tenses as he lifts slightly. Just as fast he halts with a grimace of pain. "Joselyn," he groans. "What are you doing here?"

"You're hurt." I go to him, dropping to my knees beside the long couch. "Why didn't you say something? Why are you such a stubborn old mule?"

"I'm hardly old. I'm thirty-two." His dark brow furrows.

"It's a good thing." Reaching for his shoulder, I pull him forward onto his stomach again. "You're far more likely to heal faster at your age than if you were older."

"If I were younger, I wouldn't be lying here at all."

"Spilled milk. You saved my life and the entire gala, and now you're lying up here suffering for it, and you won't let anybody help you. It's ridiculous and prideful. I brought my bag, and I'm going to work out that injury. Right now."

He turns his head, resting his cheek on his hand, and squints up at me. "Is that so? Who died and made you queen? How did you get in this room anyway?"

"Daisy gave me your extra key. Now you're going to be still and let me help you."

He hesitates a moment, studying me, but I don't budge. My hands are on my hips, and my expression is as serious as my resolve—despite how delicious he looks in only his lounge pants.

His hazel eyes darken, and heat filters across my lower belly. I know that look, and I know where it leads, how good it feels.

Nope. I'm not even going there. His pig head told me how he felt, and I have no interest in violating his sacred rules—as if he's in any shape for it.

Still, I have to help him. When he never came back after the fall, I knew I had to come up here. I couldn't let him miss the gala or worse, be seriously hurt on account of saving my life. I had to do what I'm trained to do best.

"Just relax and stop fighting." My voice is gentler.

"What are you going to do?" His voice is gruff, even if it's muffled in the pillow.

Taking out a bottle of scented oil, I pour it on my hands and rub them together. "Lucky for you, I'm actually very good at treating sports injuries."

My lips press together, and my breath stills in my stomach as my hands hover above his body. He's an amazing specimen of a man. His broad shoulders are dimpled with muscles, and the line in his back is deep and luscious. Right at the base of his spine are two hollows just above what I remember is the most divine ass.

"I'm going to put my hands on your back." I shift into professional mode, speaking softly. "Now, I'm just going to work out the tension. I'll slowly apply more pressure. If it's too intense, let me know, and I'll ease up. Okay?"

He grunts his consent, and I'm ready. My fingers hum like the electricity is growing the closer I get to his skin. Closing my eyes, I exhale slowly and begin.

Usually, I don't talk to my clients when I'm massaging them. I simply do what needs to be done and let the music play, let them sleep or zone out, whatever they prefer. This time, I feel like I need to keep him apprised of what I'm doing... If only so he doesn't get the wrong idea and think I've forgotten his rules.

"I think the strain is located in your gluteus medius. That's the muscle that wraps around your left hip. Is it okay if I get closer there? I'll need to manipulate the top of your butt—"

"You have permission to touch my ass." Heat flushes my cheeks, and I almost laugh nervously.

Almost.

I maintain my professionalism and my dignity, luxuriating in sliding my hands over his strong muscles. Even if it's only to ease his pain, I can still enjoy it. He lets out a groan when I go deeper into the injured area, and I slide my hand higher to his mid-back.

"Tell me if it's too much."

He doesn't answer, and I chew my bottom lip as I move my hands lower again. I do my best not to think about what's hiding under his pubic bone. He has an impressive eggplant, and he knows how to use it. A flash of his mouth on my body heats my panties, and I slam that door.

So what if he made me come... four times. So will the next man I find. The better man.

"Are you doing okay?" I slide my hand along his narrow waist.

"That feels really good." He grinds out as I roll my fist along the muscle wrapping around his waist.

He's so damn gorgeous. Kneading my fingers along his torso, I distract my mind with thoughts of baseball and cold showers and Oliver's pet tree frog… Anything to keep from getting lost in the memories.

"God…" He gasps. "That's where it is…"

Pausing, I take my time, focusing on the specific area causing him pain. "Better?"

"I'm sure it'll be great once you stop."

I do laugh this time, but it's quiet, soothing. "I can't tell you how grateful I am to you for saving me."

"As if I would stand there and let you crash onto the floor. You could've been killed." He adds the last part quietly, just above a whisper.

"It was very heroic." I think about the split second when I was in his arms and our eyes met, just before we both went down. "Like something out of a movie."

"Not a Disney movie, I hope." He turns to the side and looks up at me.

A lock of hair falls over his left eyebrow, and my eyes trace down his straight nose, past the dimple in his chin to the light dusting of dark hair on his chest.

He's so handsome, like a prince.

"Maybe it was." Leaning to the side, I admire his face.

Just as quickly, his scowl returns. "Don't get any ideas, Joselyn. I did what I did because it was the right thing to do."

Embarrassment flashes in my neck, and I move away so he can't see the red flame in my cheeks. Why does he have to be such a bastard?

"Well, I'm here to try and even the scales." Swiping my forearms across the large muscles in his back, I notice a white scar stretching across the top of his right shoulder.

It's large and long, and I would guess it's from being struck with a whip or hit by a tree branch. I don't know how I didn't notice it before, although I was slightly buzzed and very overwhelmed with sensation the last time we were naked together.

"What happened here?" I place my palm on the top of it, and he flinches away.

"Childhood injury. Leave it alone."

Taking my hand away, I study the silver stripe. "Must've been pretty serious to leave a scar like that. Were you cut… or hit? Was it a car accident?"

"It's none of your concern."

"Actually, if you have a pre-existing injury, it can be helpful for me to know when I'm providing future treatment."

"I won't require future treatment. Thanks for the back rub."

He starts to move away, and I resist getting pissed by his dismissal. He's like a wild animal protecting a wound, and I want to put my hands on him again, slide them across this place where he's storing so much hurt. I want to ease him to safety.

My tongue slips out to touch my bottom lip, and I remember what he can be like when he stops being cold. It's addictive, and as angry as he makes me, I want to feel his warmth again.

Instead, I step back and take the towel, using it to wipe my arms before quickly packing my supplies in my messenger bag. "You might not feel so great tonight, but the healing should set in overnight. Maybe take some ibuprofen and drink plenty of water. By tomorrow, I think you'll feel well enough to attend the gala."

"I will attend the gala."

"Great, then I'll leave this with you, and here's this." I hold up the extra door card Daisy gave me and my business card, placing both on the side table. "You know how to reach me if you need anything."

I don't even look up before heading to the door. He's freezing me out again, but I did what I needed to do to feel better about what happened. I tried to help him, not sleep with him. He can kiss my ass if he doesn't want to be friends.

CHAPTER Twelve

Spencer

"YOU DON'T LOOK ANY THE WORSE FOR WEAR." MILES SLAPS ME ON the back as I enter the ballroom.

He's six inches shorter than I am, and his hand hits me right in my injury.

I stifle a noise of pain, forcing a smile. "It's not that serious—just a tweak. Besides, I couldn't miss your big event."

It's a lie. I'd miss this superfluous extravagance in a heartbeat, but knowing she's here, single, with all our richest clients in town from up and down the east coast, I dragged my ass off the divan, popped a pain pill, and put on a tux.

Of course, that's not the way I rationalize it. I'm here as a part of the team, to show our clients how much we value our relationships… and I'm scanning the room, searching for her soft, auburn hair.

The Grand Ballroom is transformed. The overhead chandeliers

are turned off, and instead, the room is lit by Ficus trees adorned with twinkle lights that also wrap around the perimeter. It gives the entire space a dreamlike, yellow glow.

A glass bowl holding a clutch of flesh-pink roses is on every table, and they look like brushed velvet. With the statues rising in the center, the entire room has a faint scent of roses. It's very elegant.

When I passed through the entrance, I nodded to Daisy at one of the tables with the list of names, checking off registrants and handing them magnetic name tags. Their friend Courtney was at the other table that held elegant, beige canvas SWAG bags with the same flesh-pink ribbons.

A live band is at the other end of the room playing standards, and a closer look reveals it's the same band from the Tuna Tiki. Only, they're not playing Marley and Buffett tonight—no "Red, Red Wine," as much as it's the running gag in this group. They're all spit-shined and putting on a good show for our neighbors to the north.

I wonder if Joselyn had anything to do with this, considering she has the catering connections. *Where is she?*

A server passes me with a tray of flutes holding pale pink champagne, and I lift one before stopping in front of the Disney characters Joselyn adapted to our needs. They're impeccable, like something you'd see on a Macy's Thanksgiving Day Parade float or in a botanical garden.

My brow tightens, and I have an unexpected flash of memory. I see her falling, her blue eyes wide with terror. My jaw clenches, and I swallow the sudden panic in my throat. I feel ill at the memory.

What is this? Fucking PTSD? I slug the champagne I'm holding and exchange it for another from a passing tray.

How could she think I wouldn't rush forward and save her? Lowering my chin, I rub my forehead, trying to massage away the image of her broken or worse on this hard wood-parquet floor. Fuck the injury in my back. I'd do it again in a heartbeat to protect her.

Then she showed up in my room last night in beige joggers and a tank top that showed off those gorgeous tits in the best possible way, like she was trying to taunt me.

Her pretty hair was gathered in a high ponytail on top of her head… ideal for wrapping around my fist when I fuck her from behind.

I thought I'd fallen asleep and was dreaming. I'd taken a THC edible to ease the pain and inflammation. It should have knocked me out, but she still got me hard. *Dammit.*

Her hands were like some divine remedy. It hurt like fuck, but this morning, I actually felt significantly better. Hell, last night when she wasn't torturing me by massaging my most painful muscles, her voice was like layers of warm cloth easing all the tension.

That probably was the drugs.

Clearing my throat, I try to dismiss the arousal she provokes simply by existing. I've had two glasses of champagne mixed with a pain pill. I need to eat something.

I stop at a set of long tables holding vast spreads of seafood and appetizers positioned in front of the giant floral statues. Perhaps Miles was right. Perhaps we can give these jaded New Englanders something they've never seen before.

"Spencer. Here you are." Rick Brimfield clasps my hand in a firm shake. "I've been looking for you."

"Rick." I return his shake firmly. "You made it."

Speaking of jaded New Englanders, Rick is our richest client out of Boston and a total asshole. Naturally, we're frenemies.

"Didn't see you at the welcome dinner last night. Let me guess, you found the only Marilyn in this tiny town and spent the night with her in your room." His smile is lecherous, but he does know my type.

"Actually, I tweaked my back playing racquetball with Miles. Had to call it early."

"Too bad." He looks around the room. "This is quite impressive, but I would expect nothing less. Only... What's a guy to do with this?"

He holds up the ultra-feminine beige SWAG bag with the flesh-pink velvet ribbon, and I shrug. "Give it to your wife. Where is Vanessa?"

He grimaces, looking into the bag. "Our divorce was finalized last week."

"Rick, I'm sorry. I had no idea."

"Yeah, fuck all that. You've had the right idea all along. There are far too many hot women in the world to tie myself down to screwing only one. I plan to make up for lost time, starting now. What do you say?"

My brow furrows, and strangely, I have no interest in his plan. In the past, I probably would have been fine with showing him around town, seeing what Oceanside has to offer. I take another passing flute of champagne.

Daisy swirls up beside us at that moment with her pituitary case husband who looks something out of *Hollywood Tonight*.

"Hey, Rick, I see you found Spencer." She rises on tiptoes to give him a hug. "He was looking for you last night, Spence. I think Rick wanted to pull an all-nighter."

"A missed opportunity," I deadpan, still feeling off my game. "You should have sent him out with your husband."

"Nah, thanks, but that's never been my style. I'm a one-woman guy." Scout looks down at his wife, and the adoration brimming in his eyes makes me angry.

I am not a one-woman guy. I need to fucking eat something. "If you'll excuse me."

I move away from them, returning to the food tables. I'm about to take what looks like a salmon croquette when I lift my eyes and there she is, entering the ballroom in a dress that makes me hesitate.

It's a floor-length white gown with a sparkling gold band wrapped around her narrow waist, crisscrossing her bodice, and curving over each of her full breasts, which are straining like pillows against strapless cups. My dick gets hard at the sight of her.

She's old-school sex kitten with her red hair swept back and falling in large curls around her shoulders.

Blue eyes land on me, and a hint of a smile teases her dark red lips. She crosses the floor, walking straight to me with all the confidence of a witch casting a spell.

"You made it." Her slim hand touches my shoulder, and she rises slightly to give me a kiss at my ear that sets my teeth on edge. "How's the back? Any better? I like this tux."

The way she's acting is worse than her anger. She's familiar and curious and wanting me to be well—or to help me get there. Blinking up, she touches my chin and smiles like I'm her hero.

I'm nobody's fucking hero. Not even my own.

"I told you I'd be here. I'm a man of my word."

"Yes." Her full lips part with a smile, and her eyes dance. "You're honest and not nice at all, and you never sleep with the same woman twice. I'm learning."

Is she teasing me? *Dammit*, the last time she did this, I kissed the shit out of her... and she was soft and pliant, and she tasted like honey. I want to take her mouth again, kiss her like I did before, like she belongs to me.

She doesn't belong to me.

That thought pisses me off even more.

Our chemistry is very real, but I won't let her have control over me.

"Why are you here alone? You should have brought a date." *Do I want that?*

"I knew I'd be seeing you." She's undeterred by my gruffness. "How did you sleep last night? Any pain?"

"I took an edible. I was asleep ten minutes after you left."

"Wait, are you saying you ate some weed?" She does that

adorable little pursed smile like she's scolding me. It shouldn't work on a woman her age, but it does.

So well.

"THC is a proven anti-inflammatory pain reliever, and there's no hangover." Unlike this alcohol of which I've had too much. I need to eat something.

"Why didn't you just smoke a joint?"

"It's a non-smoking room, Joselyn. Anyway, I don't like the smell of smoke, particularly pot smoke."

Her chin dips, and she exhales a laugh. "I'm not often surprised, but you've surprised me. I never expected you to be such a rebel."

"I've got seven years on you, Sin." Taking one of the salmon rolls off the table, I pop it into my mouth. "You can't possibly know all there is to know."

She slips her hand into the crook of my arm. "It's okay to be vulnerable. You've been hurt."

"I don't do vulnerable. If I appear to be on guard, it's because my partner has already seen fit to slap me in the back, and I don't know who might try to do it next. Fucking Miles. Probably trying to ensure he wins our next match."

"Oh no! He didn't!"

"He did."

"I'll get Daisy to tell him to stop hitting you in your injury. He seems to listen to her. And I'm available for follow-up treatments. I told you I'm rebuilding my client list."

We walk around the statues, and she takes a flute of champagne. The light glistens off the creamy skin of her shoulders. They're broad and elegant, and I'm struck by how perfectly proportioned her body is. I already knew this, but her dress accentuates it.

She's a work of art.

"You're very beautiful tonight. This white and gold combination suits you."

My voice is gentler, and she glances up at me from under her lashes. "Thank you. I know you don't give out compliments freely."

"Only an idiot gives out compliments freely. Or a person who wants something."

"And you want nothing from me. Don't worry. I remember."

She's so wrong.

I want to hold her again. I want to wrap my arms around her and sway side to side, tell her I can't stop thinking about her. It's because she fucking walked out on me last time. I wasn't ready to let her go, and yes, I know this goes against my principles. This sort of thinking leads to messy, messy trouble, and even my bullshit cold façade doesn't work when she's around... She *is* that fucking ember melting my walls.

"So you're saying you want to be friends?"

Her bottom lip slides between her teeth. It's a tantalizing quirk.

"I'm saying I want to treat you. I know we have a history, but I really do respect your boundaries. As your therapist, they would be my boundaries as well... and Lord knows I could use the work." She looks up at me, and this time she's not being coy.

"Why do you care so much, Joselyn?"

We're walking slowly towards the balcony, and I lift another flute off the waiter's tray. She does the same.

"Remember that old fable about the lion who was going to eat the mouse, but in the end let him go? Then later, when the lion had been captured by hunters, that same mouse showed up and chewed through the ropes and set the lion free?"

"Everyone knows that story. I don't know how it applies to this situation."

"No act of kindness, no matter how small, is ever wasted." She blinks those ocean eyes up at me. "I owe you one. Or several."

"I release you from your debt."

"You can't do that. The universe knows, and if I don't repay you, my karma will be all messed up."

Outside, the briny air is warm and breezy. It sends her pretty hair swirling, and the moonlight touches her in silver. The waves create a soothing backdrop, and I remember last night, the touch of her hands.

"Your position is giving me a massage is going to repay me?"

She turns and leans her back against the balcony rail. "Perhaps while I'm healing your muscles, you might let me heal whatever else is strained… or broken."

"I'm trying to decide if your suggestion is dirty or presumptive."

"I'm not being dirty at all. I'm being serious. Maybe I can show you it's safe to step outside that frozen castle."

"Why do I feel like this is more Disney?"

"It's only Disney if you're a tiny princess with magical powers. I don't think that's the case, is it?"

She's teasing again, her pretty, pretty eyes sparkling, and I polish off the rest of my champagne.

"No." It's time to go.

"Are you angry?"

I don't answer her. I simply leave the balcony, leave her there with her witchy ways trying to trap me. I haven't eaten enough, and I can't drink any more wine.

I've done my part to show up for Miles's gala. I haven't met with all my clients, but if I stay any longer, I'll do something foolish.

"Spencer?" I hear her voice behind me, and I'm caught in the center of the room by Miles.

"Here you are. I need you to lose the scowl and show a little love to Grafton. Heather is here, but she's pissed because of something Rick apparently said. I think he's been over-served, and now he's hitting on all the single women."

"Get Daisy to do it," I growl. "My back—"

"Oh, look, there he goes again." Miles nods his head in the direction behind me. "Although I'm pretty confident Daisy's cousin can kick his ass. She's a pistol."

Rage blazes in my stomach, and I turn around to see Rick with his hands on what my addled brain is insisting is mine.

I don't even try to fight it. I cross the room and take her by the wrist, pulling her to me.

"Oh, hey, I see you know Spencer..." Rick's voice goes from jolly to confused. "Wait a minute... What's going on?"

"Why don't we go and have some bread?" I hear Miles pinch-hitting behind me, but my patience is blown.

"What are you doing?" Joselyn tugs her wrist against my grip, but I only hold her tighter, pulling her into the foyer.

Her skin is so soft. "What are you doing, Joselyn?"

"What are you doing is more like it? How dare you manhandle me this way." Her eyes flash, and I can't escape her spell.

"What do you want from me?" I don't recognize my haggard voice.

Our eyes lock, and she's not afraid. She's rising to meet me. My roughness, my hands on her body doesn't intimidate her. I've never encountered a woman like her, so fiercely composed.

She puts both her hands on my neck and leans closer, almost brushing my lips with hers. "Thank you for liking my dress. I want you to call me when you're ready for your next treatment. Our professional relationship isn't over."

With that, she turns, and in a swirl of white silk, she walks away, leaving me alone in the foyer wanting more. I want to chase after her and pull her hard against my chest. I want to shake her and demand to know who she thinks she is speaking to me that way.

I want to fuck her so hard.

My face drops, and I growl as I scrub it with my hand. This isn't what I want. It's not who I am.

But the thought of another man touching her...

I don't know what it means or how far I'm willing to take it. I don't know if it will destroy me or if it could be the best thing to happen.

I've been a dick to her in my attempts to keep up the status quo—and to respect her need to keep it professional. I'm no longer her boss now, but I have to keep her from walking away.

She's at the door to the ballroom when I start to move. "Joselyn, wait." I reach out and catch her soft wrist in my hand, gentler this time.

She turns, lifting her chin, raising her gorgeous eyes to mine. "Have you decided to stop being an asshole to me now?"

"I'm going to try."

"Always so honest, Mr. Carrollton."

"The last time we were here, I made you an offer. Would you care to revisit it?" I wanted to fuck her all night. Will she remember?

"You need massage therapy, and I never sleep with my clients."

She remembers.

"I'm not your client. I haven't hired you, but if you want me to…" Pulling her to my chest, I wrap my arms around her waist and lower my face so I can inhale her scent of creamy magnolia.

"That sounds very much like blackmail."

"Only if you're interested in the work. You can always say no, and I'll let you go."

The last gasp of my resistance begs her to say no. This woman is nothing but trouble, and my dick is doing all the talking right now. It's a huge mistake, and fuck, I'm going to make it if she'll let me.

My entire existence hangs on her answer.

My throat is tight, and my teeth clench so hard, I'm sure they'll crack.

She lifts her chin, and her velvet red lips part ever so slightly. She takes a light breath, drawing out the torture like the succubus she is.

She looks around the room before tightening her fist in my coat. "Yes."

CHAPTER Thirteen

Joselyn

"GOD, I LOVE YOUR TITS." SPENCER LIFTS AND SQUEEZES MY BREASTS, tugging my nipples with his fingertips. My back is against his chest, and his cock is deep inside me. "So fucking gorgeous."

"Spencer," I gasp when his teeth pierce my shoulder.

It's like fuel to the fire. His thrusts grow feverish. My breasts bounce faster as he fucks me harder, and my pants turn to little sounds as the orgasm radiates through my pelvis.

"Give it to me," he growls. "Come."

My head falls back against his shoulder, and I succumb to the pleasure.

He ravages me.

He devours me.

It's incredible, and I come so hard, I cry out as I shoot to the stars.

We barely made it through the door of his suite before he slammed me against the wall. His mouth covered mine, and he gripped the top of my head in one hand, long fingers curling in my hair, pulling.

It was painfully erotic, as if all the fighting, all the holding back only made our reunion more powerful and desperate.

His other hand held my jaw as he tilted my face to the right angle so he could taste me. His lips pushed mine apart in a possessive kiss as his tongue swept inside, curling with mine, lighting the fire in my belly.

I pushed back, sucking his tongue, biting his lip. I was as hungry for him as he was for me. Our mouths broke apart with a groan, and he dropped to his knees.

His breath was harsh and fast as he pushed my skirt up, grasping my thong and ripping it off my legs.

"Oh," I gasped at the sting.

"I've dreamt of this." Pushing his face between my thighs, I collapsed against the wall with a low moan when his mouth covered my sex.

In one fast move, he lifted my thigh over his shoulder, and his tongue plunged into me before moving higher, up my belly to circle my navel.

"Oh, god," I gasped, threading my fingers in his soft hair.

His beard scuffed my sensitive skin as he groaned hungrily, making his way lower again. His teeth grazed my clit, and I almost screamed. I rose on my toes when his beard scuffed my inner thighs. It was so many sensations. I made noises I didn't recognize.

He pulled my most sensitive place with his lips, sucking and circling, devouring.

We were starving for each other. Rising fast, he turned my chest to the wall, quickly rolling on a condom before slamming into me with a groan.

"God, you feel so good." For a moment, he stilled, and we both panted in time.

My body radiated with orgasm. He pushed me onto my tiptoes, and I bucked my ass involuntarily against him.

"Fuck me…" I begged, unable to wait any longer. "Please… Fuck me."

"Sin…" He hissed at my ear, jerking the bodice of my dress down so my breasts would spill out into his hands. "My girls."

My eyes rolled back, and I exhaled a laugh at his obsession. Still, I wasn't complaining. His obsession translated into mind-blowing orgasms.

Now we're here. I've already flown to the stars once, and he's brought me back to the edge with him again. My eyes close, and we're grasping and clawing for that incredible release just within our grasp.

We're breaking all his rules, but my mind is too flooded with lust and need and orgasm to analyze it. I don't care if he takes it all back tomorrow. All I know is I need his cock driving into me right now, taking me to the far reaches of heaven again.

It's starting… I feel it rising…

Shimmering hot orgasm radiates the arches of my feet, snaking up my legs like a vine. My back jerks like I've touched a live wire, and with one more hit of his dick to my G-spot, I break, crying and clenching all around him.

"Fuck…" He groans, coughing as he comes. "It's so good."

He holds me tight to his body, one palm flat against my stomach, and I feel the power of his orgasm as he pulses inside me.

We both fall forward against the wall like we've just run a marathon. My face is turned to the side, and his chest is against my back, the little hairs tickling my skin. Salt is on my tongue from biting and tasting him, and we smell like leather and sage and flowers and sex.

His large hand cradles my breast, and a smile curls my lips. "You're like a little boy with his favorite toy."

"Fuck, yeah, it's my favorite toy." I feel his cheek rise at my shoulder. "Have you seen how hot your rack is? I'd have given my left nut to hold these babies one more time."

"Mm..." I exhale a satisfied noise. "I take it you're a boob guy."

His head lifts, and he kisses the side of my neck. "I've never really thought about it before. Until a witchy redhead waltzed into my life with a body to make any man weep and a brain sharp enough to make it all unfair."

Rolling against the wall, I turn to face him, lifting my arms onto his shoulders. "Who are you and what did you do with this asshole I know named Spencer?"

Smoky hazel eyes meet mine, and he's still grinning like a very bad boy. "You love assholes. It's why I had to get you away from Rick, the recently divorced douche."

"You didn't have to get me away from him."

I had no intention of going anywhere with anyone... Until I was sure Spencer was a lost cause.

He lifts his face and presses his mouth to my forehead, and a wash of emotion floods my insides. He's not angry right now. He's not pushing boundaries and throwing up walls. Damn him for melting my heart.

I'm sure it's all the champagne we've drunk, but I want to keep him this way. Where will he go in the morning? Will he remember his rules or will something have changed?

And as I think it, I know this is what he's talking about. The second night is supposed to make me think he's changed, and I've melted his heart. *Messy, messy trouble...*

It won't be me.

His lips trace down my temple to the side of my cheek. "Go to sleep. I want to fuck you again before dawn. I want to fuck you until I don't feel this way anymore."

My brow furrows. "How do you feel?"

His eyes are heavy, and my arm is around his waist as we stagger to the California king bed. Crawling beneath the sheets, he reaches out and wraps a strong arm around my waist, pulling me flush against his chest.

"I feel like the Beast." The sound of sleep is in his voice, and I thread my fingers with his.

Maybe I'm taking advantage of him, doing the things I want to do with him sober while he's slightly drunk. I don't care. I kiss his hand and pretend he's not an asshole. I pretend he's my boyfriend, and we fall asleep in our luxury suite with our bodies entwined like this every night, together, safe in each other's arms.

I exhale a sigh at this ridiculously rich, ridiculously arrogant man. He's cruel to taunt me with a peek inside his walls, but he's wrong if he thinks I'm like every other woman he's ever known.

I do have a brain to match his, and if he thinks he's got me, he's so wrong.

Lifting his hand, I press my lips to his knuckles wishing it wasn't this way. I wish it was easy, but when did easy ever lead anywhere good?

I slide my hand along that mysterious scar he guards so closely. His eyes are closed, and a dark lock has fallen over his brow. His lips are relaxed, and all the anger has momentarily subsided. He's gorgeous.

"You're safe with me, you know?" Exhaling a little sigh, I trace the hair off his eye. "No, you don't know."

I kiss him softly before closing my eyes and falling fast asleep.

"I've barely seen you all week." My mother has a pot of coffee ready when I push through her door at 5:30 a.m.

"What the heck are you doing up so early?" My heart is in my throat. "You scared the shit out of me."

"Language, Joselyn." She eyes me as if I didn't learn all my swear words from her. "Why are you doing the walk of shame? Didn't Daisy get you a room at the hotel?"

"I told her not to."

"So where have you been all night?"

"Sleeping with a random hot guy, of course. What do you think?"

She snorts a laugh over her coffee, and I love my mom. She's the witch who taught me to be the witch I am now.

Translation: She taught me that society brands women it can't control as witches. Or some other derogatory term. She also taught me to give that bullshit the big, fat middle finger.

"I love him, Ma." My eyes are on the table, and I want to cry. "God, I'm so stupid."

"Whoa, hang on right there." She lifts the mug and takes another, bigger gulp. "That's a lot of information to drop on somebody out of the blue at five in the morning."

"It's closer to six." Blinking fast, I pour myself a mug of java and sit across from her, giving it a dollop of cream.

"Either way, start at the beginning. Who is this guy?"

"He works with Daisy." Shaking my head, I roll my watery eyes. "God, he's such an asshole. He's gorgeous and rich and he has the perfect body, and he is the worst."

"And he's already making you cry?"

"I'm making myself cry." I huff a laugh, touching my eyes. "He's been nothing but straight with me. He has a rule. He never sleeps with the same woman twice. Want to know why?" Her eyebrow arches, and I know I don't even have to ask. "Because as soon as he sleeps with a woman twice, he says she thinks her, quote, 'magic pussy,' end quote, has changed him and he's going to leave behind his wicked ways out of love for her."

She sits back in her chair, eyebrows lifted. "He actually said the P-word?"

Pressing my lips together, I nod before taking another sip of really good coffee. My mom is killer at coffee. "Last night I slept with him for the second time." Her jaw drops, and I see the light of hope in her eyes. I put my mug down a little too hard and wave my finger back and forth. "No, no, no! That's the whole point. If I go there, then it's confirming what he said, right?"

Her eyes narrow, the light of hope fading, and she leans back in her chair. "Dang. This guy is some kind of special asshole. He's got it all fixed so even if he breaks his own rules, you can't do anything about it or you prove him right."

"Yee-up." I pop my lips on the *P*. "I want to strangle him... When I'm not dreaming of having his babies."

"Is he good in bed?"

My eyes press closed, and I nod my head. "I've slept with him twice, haven't I?"

Reaching across the table, she clasps my hand in hers. "Baby, I wish I could save you, but you got that gene straight from me. They're always irresistible. Your father was like that. He was a smart asshole, and the smart assholes are the worst."

"You never told me Dad was an asshole!" My chest tightens, and I'm not sure if I'm glad to hear this or horrified.

My father died when I was a little girl, so I only remember him doting on me. He was my first Disney prince, my first tragic hero.

"Your dad was a gorgeous, red-headed Scot, and I loved him from the moment he spoke to me in that accent. That man made me wet... then I discovered he was a notorious playboy, and I nearly took his head off. Then he changed his ways."

She says it all so fast, I don't have time to freak out over the status of my mother's underwear. Instead, I'm thinking about the last thing she said.

"What made him change his ways?"

"I showed him I'd walk away. He decided he'd rather hold onto me than continue his life as a tomcat."

"You were a badass." I sip my coffee.

"A witch."

"I'm not sure if I'm as badass as you… I seem to keep giving in to him."

"Don't do it."

Our eyes are locked when the screen door my mother insisted on having at the back of her luxurious Tudor mansion screeches and slams behind her best friend, Scout and J.R.'s grandmother, Alice.

"Lord have mercy, Regina. One of these days I'm just going to sit on that bottom step out there and holler until you come and get me." Ms. Alice is a fussy old lady, but I've known her all my life. She's also freakin hilarious.

"What's the matter, Alice?" My mom goes over to give her friend a hug. "Rheumatism?"

"Old age-ism. Sly, is that you? My goodness, you look just like a young Ann-Margret." She waddles over to give me a hug. "Elvis had a real thing for her. Almost didn't marry Priscilla because of it. Everybody hated her for it, but she came out on top. Elvis was a big cheater, and she's still kicking from what I understand. Mmm… Good coffee, Reggie."

"What brings you around so early?" Ma returns to her seat at the table after handing her fussy friend a mug of coffee.

"Couldn't sleep. I can't sleep past five-thirty anymore—because I'm old." She squints an eye at me. "Enjoy your youth while you can."

My lips press together, and I love these old ladies. I've sat and listened to them gossip and fuss since I was big enough to drink coffee milk and be quiet.

Giving her a squeeze, my hand slides across thick fabric under her blouse. "Whoa, what's under your shirt here? A back brace?"

"Oh!" Her whole face brightens and she rips up her blouse, exposing a flesh-colored bodysuit. "Got me some of those Skims. It's like a stretchy girdle made out of this slick material. That little Indian girl with the good birthing hips sells 'em. How do I look?"

She does a little turn, and I hold my nose to keep from snorting. "You look amazing. But… Do you mean Kim Kardashian?"

"That little girl who looks like Cher, except… fuller." She motions around her breasts and butt before taking a seat at the table. "If you ask me, Cher always looked like she needed to eat a whole pizza all by herself. I like that little girl's shape. Womanly."

"Why do you think she's…" I don't even try. "She's actually Armenian."

"Well, I don't care what tribe she's affiliated with. I believe in supporting women-owned businesses, minority-owned businesses—"

"I mean, she's not native—not that it matters."

"She's the same thing as Cher, right?"

"Right, they're Armenian."

Ms. Alice slaps the table, sitting straighter. "Are you telling me Cher's not… but she had that song where she dressed up like… and her hair…"

"If it helps, Armenians are still considered a minority group."

She takes a moment as her worldview shifts, and I stand, going to my mom. "My work here is done. I'm going to see if I can sleep another hour." Kissing her forehead, I go to Ms. Alice. "Sorry if I upset you."

"Don't be silly. I'm going to buy some more of these girdles and help that little girl out."

Chewing my lip, I can't hold back. "Kim Kardashian is a billionaire now. I think she's going to be okay."

"A billionaire! Mother of pearl!" She clutches her chest, and I press my lips together, fighting a laugh. "Maybe I need to start making stretchy girdles." I'm starting to go when she catches my hand. "Hey, Sly—have you seen that old book of ours? The Fireside Women's Society book? Daisy thought you might have it."

My heart jumps, and I hope she doesn't see the guilt on my

face. "Ahh… I don't know. It might have gotten mixed up in my stuff. I can check."

"Well, if you do, just bring it back next time you come. I don't want anything to happen to it. That book is a historical record. It's a powerful thing when women come together to help each other."

"I'll look for it." I'm retreating quickly when my mother calls after me.

"Joselyn?" I pause at the base of the stairs. "You deserve to be treated like a queen. If he can't see that, you're better off without him."

"Thanks, Ma." I give her a smile. "And thanks for helping with Ollie. I know I kind of sprung him on you this week."

"He's a little doll, and I love Chartreuse. What an amazing frog!"

"You're weird."

Climbing the steps to my bedroom in the early haze, I know I'm not going to sleep anymore. I'm too keyed up from everything that has happened. I'm considering taking a long bubble bath when my phone vibrates in my pocket.

Sliding it out, my heart squeezes at the sight of his name above a text glowing on the screen. ***Why aren't you in my fucking bed? What gave you the idea you could leave before I woke?***

He's pissed I'm gone, and I exhale a laugh, shaking my head as I tap out a reply. ***You were sleeping so well, I didn't want to wake you.***

Gray dots float, and I hesitate outside the bedroom Courtney shares with her son. I almost wish we could stay here, where it's safe. But then I'd be too far from my beast.

Spencer's text appears. ***You don't leave without telling me.***

My lips press into a sad smile, and I know what I have to do. He's not giving me a choice. ***Are you saying we're in a relationship?*** I hit send, knowing what his answer will be.

His reply is quick. ***No.***

Am I going to be your massage therapist?

Another quick reply. ***Yes.***

Then I won't be in your bed again. I don't sleep with clients.

Slipping my phone into my pocket, I decide I won't reply to any more texts until I get some perspective… and a soak in some lavender-scented water.

I'm kind of falling in love with him, but I won't give him all the power.

Like my mom said, men will do what they want until you make them decide. I know Spencer, and I know he appreciates things of value.

It all points to one clear path: I have to be something of value to him.

Let me rephrase that. I *am* something of value, but he has to see it. Or he'll lose me.

My throat aches, but I have to be strong. As great as the orgasms are, he's right. I'm a relationship girl. I do get attached, and he's not going to change that about me.

He'll figure out what's important to him, or maybe one day he'll realize what he lost.

CHAPTER Fourteen

Spencer

"WELL, IT WORKED." MILES BLASTS INTO MY OFFICE, STOKING MY already foul mood. "I just got the fall lists from our top three accounts—a month early—and Heather has granted us an exclusive first-look photoshoot of the top items from their summer auction. It'll be the cover of our June look book."

"Don't you knock?" I'm irritable, but Miles is undeterred.

"*Antiques Today* is Number 1! Take that, Link Sherlock." He does a little fist pump.

"We were never in danger of not being Number 1." *Not as long as I'm here.*

"Back still bothering you?" His eyebrow arches. "I saw Miss Winthrop is on your schedule for today."

His eyebrow arch pisses me off even more. "It's a back massage. Nothing more."

"Oh, come now. You left a trail of fire in your wake when you pulled her out of the gala. Rick actually apologized to me for hitting on your girlfriend."

"She's not my girlfriend."

"Sorry, sorry... I know, no girlfriends. Only *protégés*." He holds up both hands as he turns for the door. "I suppose travel is out until you're recovered? No worries. I'll work it out with Grafton."

He's gone and my jaw is tight. I flick a ball of paper after him, cringing at my lack of control. Joselyn is not my protégé. Calling her that makes it sound like I'm a lecherous old man, like my office has a casting couch. I've never slept with a woman who wasn't begging for it, and I don't groom them either.

As it stands with Joselyn, we've been home a week, and other than appointment-related messages, we haven't spoken. She doesn't sleep with clients. I don't do relationships. We're at an impasse.

Only, I'm pissed she's taking some moral high ground. I broke my rule for her. Now she's playing hard to get.

Fuck that, she yelped like a puppy riding my dick a week ago. She'll come around soon enough. The phone on my desk dings, and I flick the button.

My secretary announces, "Miss Winthrop is here for your appointment."

"Send her back." Standing, I round the desk as I shed my coat and loosen my tie.

Pouring a tumbler of ice water, I compose myself. If she wants to play games, she'll learn quickly I never lose.

The door opens, and when I see her, the ground shifts. Her hair is styled in a ponytail on her shoulder, sending red waves down her full breasts, which are straining against rust-colored scrubs. Her face is so fresh and glowing, but her blue eyes are all business.

It reminds me to get my shit together.

"Good morning, Mr. Carrollton." She rolls in a massage table and assembles it near the windows. "How's the pain today? Can you rate it on a scale of one to five?"

"First, you can call me Spencer. Let's not be obtuse. As for my pain, it only hurts when I move in certain directions, and then it ranges from one to five, depending on whether or not I'm lifting something."

Her full lips press into a thoughtful line, and she nods as she taps on her phone. "This is your second treatment. Based on how you feel this week, we can decide how many more are needed and the amount of time between them."

I've already decided if she insists on continuing this act, it'll be my last session with her, then I'll take her home and spank her bottom. That fantasy makes me happy.

I say none of this aloud.

Instead, I lift my tie over my head and unbutton my dress shirt, feigning indifference. "How's the client building going?"

She takes out a small speaker, a bottle of oil, and several towels. "Pretty slow. Would you prefer lavender oil or peppermint?"

"Considering it's the beginning of the day, peppermint."

She nods, placing what looks like a saucer of rocks on my desk and plugging it in. I watch as she pours a small vial over it and steam begins to rise, filling my office with the crisp scent.

Her eyes are averted as I take off my shirt, almost like she refuses to look at me. I'm about to comment on it until I turn back from placing the garment on the back of my chair, and I see her blink away fast, pink flooding her cheeks.

That one little tell, that one slip changes everything. Knowing she's drooling on the inside evaporates my frustration. It makes me want to toy with her.

She thinks she has the upper hand, but two can play this game.

"Should I remove my pants as well?"

My question seems to startle her, so naturally I unfasten my belt. *Let's do this, Sin.*

"No!" She quickly holds up a small towel. "I'll just tuck this in your waistband. It'll protect your pants, and the oil is washable."

"I'd rather not walk around with oil stains on my clothes all day."

"It won't happen. I'm very careful."

Hesitating, I decide not to push her too far on our first office visit. I've decided I do want her to return—this is fun. Going to the table, I lie on my stomach, closing my eyes as she carefully tucks the white terrycloth along my waist.

She switches off the lights, and the noise of whales and pan flutes surrounds us. It's very bothersome. The swishing sound of her scrubs alerts me to her approach, and I wait for her touch. It's sweet torture, my skin tightening in anticipation until she places her palm feather-light against my skin.

Relaxation filters through my bloodstream, and the tension leaves my brow as her pressure grows stronger. She's silent, letting the fake whales preclude any conversation. Fuck you, whales. It's the first time I've seen her since we've returned, and I want to hear her voice.

"When you treated me in my hotel suite, you talked me through the entire procedure."

"I didn't want you to get the wrong idea. Now that we've worked together, you can sleep if you want. It doesn't bother me."

It bothers me.

"What wrong idea would I get?" Yes, I'm pushing her to engage with me.

"That I was attempting to violate your rules by doing anything inappropriate." She's being sassy. "Now you know what I'm going to do, and I have my own rule about clients."

"So I've heard."

Again, the whales fill the void, and I allow it.

Her palms stroke my shoulder blades, sliding down my back to my waist. It makes me want to pull her close and kiss her long and hard, but I'll respect her rules. I'll wait until she's ready to break them, perhaps with a bit of encouragement.

I prop my cheek on my fist so I can see her profile. "It's quite a move from flowers to massage therapy. What prompted that jump?"

"It's not such a jump if you think about it in terms of service. I've always wanted to lift people's spirits, make them smile, or ease their suffering. Flowers led to aromatherapy and learning which scents eased anxiety and elevated the mood. That dovetailed into healing, which is how massage therapy works, and here I am."

As she speaks, she kneads her fingers into my strained muscle, and I hold my breath at the pain.

"You need to breathe through it." Her voice is soothing, calm.

I do as she says, and she gently moves away, dragging her forearms down the large muscles in my back. I feel her breath against my skin, and it's tantalizing. Her body heat surrounds me as she makes her way to the top of my back again, to my scar. Her palm covers it, holding steady, and I feel something like warmth transferring into my damaged skin.

It's a place I don't share with anyone, and her hand feels like it's opening the lid on a box I keep sealed for a reason. Anger rises in my throat, and my playful mood is gone.

I roll away abruptly. "Are we finished here?"

"Yes." Her tone is different, like she knows she trespassed. "I'm finished."

Heat burns in my stomach. I don't need pity.

"Thank you for your time." The ice wall is firmly restored. "I'll change in my bathroom."

"I'll see you in a week." She takes the towel from my slacks and uses it to wipe her arms.

Her expression is calm, and I wonder how we went from me having the upper hand to her acting like she knows some secret I haven't shared.

She knows nothing.

"Your payment will be in your Venmo account in the hour."

"Thank you." Her soft voice carries as I shut the door.

When I return, she's gone, but the scent of peppermint lingers. She also left a bottle of water on my desk with a note. It reads "stay hydrated" and has a little smiley face.

I swipe it off my desk ready to chuck it across the room when my phone buzzes. Glancing at the face, I see it's a text from her. ***Sorry if I pushed you today.***

My thumbs move quickly with my reply. ***I don't know what you mean.***

Several seconds pass, and she responds, ***It felt like things had changed in Oceanside. But you still don't want to share your scars with me.***

My answer is quick. ***I mixed a pain pill with alcohol in Oceanside.***

It's a dodge, but fuck it.

She doesn't immediately answer. Gray dots appear then disappear… appear, disappear. Finally, she replies, ***I don't sleep with intoxicated men.***

I huff a laugh at her throwing my words back at me. I was angry just now, but she always manages to make me laugh. I don't understand it. We're going somewhere I've never been, and even when I fight, I still go back to her.

I have to get on top of this.

Lowering my device onto my desk, I don't reply.

CHAPTER Fifteen

Joselyn

"TREE FROGS CAN LIVE FIVE TO NINE YEARS." OLLIE SITS ON THE opposite end of the couch from me holding his weird little pet with the oversized orange eyes.

He's got on a gray-camo Old Navy hoodie, and he looks like a little man with his blond hair parted to the side. He's such a cutie.

I'm using *Judge Judy* to distract me from obsessing over Spencer, and she's about to go off on some schmo giving her an obviously fake story. I love it when she does that.

Glancing at Ollie, my nose curls. "Why do her eyes have to be like that? It's creepy."

"She uses them to scare off predators. If she were in the forest, she'd blend with the leaves. If something gets too close, her eyes pop up." He does a little pop motion with his hand, and his brown eyes widen.

"She's a freak." I squirm, scooting farther away on the couch.

"Don't let her get on me, okay? If she got lost in my hair, I might have a heart attack."

"She won't hurt you." He flops away again, giving me a disappointed face. "People think frogs are poisonous, but they're not. They have toxins on their skin to protect them, but it won't kill you."

"Wait…" He has my full attention now. I pull my feet under me and move to a squatting position. "So you're saying that little lady is toxic?"

"If a dog ate her, it would get sick. But it wouldn't die."

"How sick?"

"Like throwing up and stuff, but it wouldn't die."

I cut my eyes to Courtney, who's studying her phone. "Did you know this?"

Her brow furrows, and she looks up at me. "What happened?"

"Chartreuse is poisonous?"

"Pfft, no she's not." Court rolls her eyes, shaking her dark, curly hair. "Ollie, stop scaring Aunt Sly."

"It's true, Mamma! She won't kill you, but she can protect herself!"

He seems so proud, I decide to go to the table and sit with Courtney rather than make him take his freaky friend to her cage. Judge Judy is midway through her lecture, but the expression on my friend's face pulls me away.

"Hey, is something wrong?" I put my hand on her forearm, and she gives me a weak smile.

"It's the usual." She glances to where her son is absorbed by his frog and lowers her voice. "He's back."

"Dammit," I whisper. "I'm sorry, Court. What can we do? Tell me. I'll help however I can."

"You focus on getting your business back on track. I'll worry about my personal life."

She tries to play it off, but I can tell she's worried.

It makes me worry, and I rub my hand up and down her forearm, thinking. "What happened? Anything new?"

"Oh, he's still going on about his son and wanting his son. I'm scared he's going to try something."

"Does Ollie know what to do if he shows up at school?"

"Yeah, and I've talked to his teachers. They're all aware of the situation."

Fine lines trace the corners of her eyes, and it aches in my chest. "You don't need this stress. I wish there was some way I could help you." Chewing my lip, I nervously try, "What if we moved to a different place? So he can't find you?"

"He's not going to run me out of another apartment. Anyway, he'd just find us again… He always does." Her voice simmers with quiet anger. "I need a gun."

Fear tightens my throat. She might be right, but I'm afraid bringing a gun into the mix could get the wrong person shot.

"Do you know how to use a gun?" We're speaking just above a whisper, leaning close.

"I'll learn."

My mind is racing, and I think about anything else we might do. She's talked to the school. She's talked to me. "What if we renewed the restraining order? You said the first one had expired… Maybe we could get a permanent one."

"What good is a piece of paper if he's determined to get what he wants?" She's so frustrated and angry, and while I can't relate, I can empathize.

"I won't leave you alone. If anything, you've got me here."

Her eyes tighten, and I wish I had something better to say. "Thanks." She squeezes my hand. "I'll figure it out. But enough of my shit. How did it go today with Spencer? Any progress?"

Shaking my head, I think about our session. He was so cocky in his office, acting like he was going to drop his pants to see me squirm. I'm glad he didn't, because I don't know what would've happened. I'm not sure how I'll respond if he decides to test my boundaries. I'm only human.

He didn't, though. He started talking, asking questions like he wanted to open up and get to know me. Then I put my hand on his scar, and he shut down so fast, it made my head spin.

I have no evidence, but my instinct tells me that white stripe across his shoulder is the key to why he's alone. Why one minute he's over the top possessive, then the next he slams invisible doors in my face.

"One minute he acts like all he wants from me is s-e-x." I glance towards Ollie, who is singing along with the theme to PAW Patrol and doesn't seem to be paying attention. "The next, he's asking questions like he wants something deeper. I feel like a yo-yo."

"You are not a yo-yo. You're an intelligent woman with a killer bod. You could get any man you wanted, and you deserve one who will treat you like a queen." She's defensive and awesome, even in the face of the fear I know she's feeling.

I hop out of my chair and go around to hug her tight. "So are you."

"No thanks." Her laugh is bitter, exhausted. "I'm off men."

"I understand," I sigh, dropping into my chair again. "But I do need the money, and hell, I kind of like the guy."

"You're screwed."

She's so blunt, I start to laugh, which makes her start to laugh. I'm sure it's the stress, but it is comforting to be together dealing with the shit.

"I'll make us some dinner. My problems really are minor compared to yours. I'm serious about getting that restraining order. Let's go tomorrow and just see what the cops say. Even if it's just a piece of paper, we can at least get it, right?"

Her smile is so hopeless. "Sure. We can do that tomorrow."

"What's your pain level today?" My hands slide down Spencer's warm skin, and I dig my fingers into his firm muscles as the soft notes of a muted piano waft around us.

Today, we're meeting after hours, which makes me nervous. On my way in, I passed Miles going home. He was friendly as always, but I didn't like the look he gave me, like he suspected something more than massage would happen during my visit.

"I still have some discomfort when I move in particular ways, but no more fives." Spencer's voice is muffled from being in the cushion. "You're very good at your job."

Leaning down, I spread my palms over his lower back, carefully making my way to his heavenly ass. My palms follow the lines of his muscles, and an image of his hard body pressed against mine, holding me down as he fucked me hard, flashes across my brain.

Clearing my throat, I banish the memory. "You're a quick healer. We can probably make next week our last appointment."

"Then I won't be your client anymore."

"I guess we won't see each other anymore." I'm not sure why I said it… Okay, I know. I want to know his thoughts on the matter.

He lifts up onto his elbows, and I step back. "I've heard some people get regular massages just for the hell of it."

Pressing my lips together, I nod. "They do. We could certainly continue along those lines. Usually it's a monthly type thing, but it could be biweekly."

"But then I'd still be your client." Hazel eyes narrow at me. "I'm not particularly happy with this arrangement."

"Lie down so I can finish. Please." My voice is quiet, and he hesitates a moment before doing as I ask.

I carefully step forward and resume working on his lower back, curling my fingers into the muscles along his hips, resting my thumbs in the large dimples at his waistband. *Luscious.*

"That feels good." His voice is husky, sexy, and heat filters through my lower belly.

I should not be aroused by his sounds.

I should distract my mind.

Too late.

"I don't know why you'd be tired of our arrangement. You said yourself you don't do relationships."

The oil is on my forearms, and I lean forward for my favorite part. Using my body weight for pressure, I slide my arms up the large muscles of his back, going all the way from his waist to the top of his shoulders.

It's a problematic move considering our past, because it's not just my arms, it's my body moving against his. My heat travels into him, and we're slippery and oily and close.

I can't stop my mind from remembering being naked with him, sliding all over him, riding his hard cock. As much as I fight against these feelings, my panties are drenched, and my face is flushed.

He's right. I getting tired of this arrangement, too.

Exhaling my frustration, I'm at the top of his right shoulder when I feel his warm hand on my inner thigh. I immediately freeze. My heart beats faster.

His palm moves higher, raising my temperature. It's flat against my leg, and when the side of his finger reaches the crotch of my pants, he slides it back and forth.

He's rubbing my pussy, teasing my crotch through my clothes, and I'm not moving away.

It's wrong and against my rules, and I'm so aroused from dragging my body against his, I could actually come.

"That's right..." His voice is a rumbling purr. "You're so beautiful."

My breath tightens in my lungs, still I don't move away.

I don't grab his wrist and make him stop. Instead, I rock my hips in time with his movements.

"You make me so hard." He growls. "I want to bend you over this table and fuck you until you can't walk. I want to slide my dick inside you and come all over your sweet ass."

"Spencer..." My insides clench, and I struggle against my rising orgasm. "What are you doing?"

"Tell me to stop, and I will." It's a rough order.

It's the voice of reason, giving me one last chance.

My promise to my mom, everything I know I have to do if I actually *do* want to be with him, be something of value, surges to the forefront of my brain.

"Stop." I take a step back, placing my hand on my stomach. My heart is beating so hard, I turn away, walking on wobbly legs to the door and switching on the overhead light to break the spell. "I'll just pack my things and go."

"Joselyn..." He's tender, but I don't look at him.

I don't know which version weakens me more, when he's being a total asshole or when he's being kind, lowering a bridge.

I'm not sticking around to figure it out. "You have my Venmo. I'll text you about your next treatment."

I wouldn't characterize it as running, but I don't stop until I've made it to the elevator. I don't look back.

CHAPTER Sixteen

Spencer

SHE RAN.

Again.

I couldn't resist anymore. She was so close to me, rubbing her body against mine. Her hair tickled my shoulders, her breath skirted across my skin. I'd done my best to be good. For three sessions, I'd followed her rules. I'd distracted us with conversation. I'd distracted myself with hating the whales.

Then she put on the sultry piano. The scent of lavender and patchouli was heavy in the air. She ran her fingers all over me, and I couldn't stop it.

I reached out and put my hand on her, and she ran.

I touched her in the way I know she loves. Why the fuck is it wrong to give her what she wants?

Growling as I slide my hand over the fading erection in my

pants, I know why it's wrong, *dammit*. I don't have to have it explained to me.

It's just...

It's Joselyn.

She's mine.

What?

What the fuck is that supposed to mean?

I saw this woman for the first time a year ago in Daisy's store. She hated me then because I'm sure Daisy told her I was an asshole, the Simon Cowell of the group, Mr. Freeze. She was there to comfort her cousin because of something that pituitary case had done.

I was there because Daisy had asked me for a favor.

I was the fucking good guy for once, and there was Joselyn, glaring at me like some sort of gorgeous, fiery banshee sent to suck my soul away and leave me trying to figure out what the fuck happened to my carefully ordered world.

Since she's reappeared in my life, I've been off my game. I don't know what I'm doing or why I can't maintain my unquestionable control.

It's intolerable.

She's casting her witchy spell over me, massaging my muscles, healing me... And god dammit, if another man touches her, I'll cut off his hands and shove them up his ass.

With a growl, I scrub my fingers over my eyes. I was right to let her go. This is not like me.

Snatching my phone off my desk, I hastily send a text to Miles.

You said something about travel? I'm up for it. The longer the better.

I'll get out of town for a week or so, fuck someone else, and I'll be back to normal. Nothing resets my compass like a trip to New England. I'll get on top of this, and we can reconvene when I've got my head straight.

Of course, that isn't how it goes.

Miles doesn't reply to my text until today, and it isn't what I wanted to hear. ***Too late, my friend. Heather is bringing the goods to us. She and Daisy have worked out a deal where they'll be on display in Daisy's store until the auction.***

Fuck.

I'm just reading his text when my phone lights up with another. It's her.

My friend Courtney has offered to take over your remaining sessions. She's very good. I highly recommend her as a replacement for me.

A growl rumbles in my throat, and I reply without even considering the consequences. ***I want to see you. Today. Meet me for drinks at Nightcaps, five-thirty.***

The phone falls silent. No gray dots to indicate she's thinking, nothing. I think perhaps she's going to treat me the way I did her and not reply.

She doesn't. ***I don't think it's a good idea.***

My jaw clenches. ***I'll see you there.***

No more running, no more bullshit. This ends now.

I have two martinis waiting when she walks through the door. Her red hair hangs in waves over both shoulders, and she's wearing a dress that looks like black overalls. Only, it ends at the top of her thighs, and she has a sheer top underneath.

She's stunning, and I stand to pull out a barstool for her. "I took the liberty of ordering drinks."

"I'm not planning to stay." Her voice is smokey sex, and her lips are full pink. I want to devour them. "Is this about working with Courtney?"

"I will not be working with Courtney. You are my massage therapist, and you will remain so for as long as I need you."

"You said you'd respect my boundaries, and you didn't."

"I apologize." I take a sip of my drink. "I suppose I find you irresistible, for whatever that's worth."

She doesn't drink her martini. Instead, her slim fingers toy with the base of the tumbler. "Why are you the way you are?"

"How am I?"

"Cold, distant—"

"I'm neither of those things as you well know. I'm realistic and in control of my emotions."

Her brow furrows and clear blue eyes blink up at me. "You can't be alone forever."

"Why not? I'm not uncomfortable being on my own. I don't understand why others have a problem with it."

"So you just go from woman to woman, no feelings attached? Doesn't that chip away at your soul?"

"My soul is quite well. Don't tell me you've become one of them—thinking you can change me."

"You said it's not possible." She's quiet as she studies the frosted glass.

So that's what's happening? My feisty redhead has become attached? Instead of being disgusted by her emotions, I feel gentle.

"I won't change." I slide my finger along the peach fuzz of her cheek, tucking a lock of hair behind her ear. "But it would be fun to let you try and change me."

I cup her jaw with my hand, and the vein in her neck pulses. Her breath quickens, and she won't meet my eyes. In this moment, she's the mouse, and I'm the lion.

Leaning closer, I slide my nose into her hair, speaking in her ear. "Do you want me to kiss you, Sin?"

Her voice is thick. "No."

"We could have a lot of fun if you'd relax your rules a bit. I did."

"I said no." She pulls away abruptly, and anger lights in my chest.

"Then I won't. I won't touch you again until you beg me for it. You're right, Joselyn, I do sleep with whatever woman I want, and I don't settle down because I'm honest, and like you, I don't cheat."

"And I don't beg." She stands, fire flashing in her eyes. "I also don't have a magic pussy. I only have me, and I am a relationship girl. That won't change, so we're wasting our time here. You can text me about your next appointment, and when we're together, you'd better keep your hands to yourself."

She turns on her heel and walks out the door, and something shifts in my chest.

No, I'm not melting. It isn't a sign of weakness, but *dammit*, she's magnificent.

CHAPTER Seventeen

Joselyn

"I'M SORRY, I SHOULDN'T BE CRYING ABOUT HIS SHIT." COURTNEY IS sitting on the living room floor with her back against the wall, tears streaming down her face, and my heart is beating so hard, I feel sick.

I drove back from the bar vibrating with energy after my conversation with Spencer. *Damn him. Damn my feelings for him*. I might have said too much just now, but I had to stand up for myself.

I'd been moving fast, chewing on the inside of my lip and thinking of all the things I could have said, when I unlocked the door to find the kitchen table overturned, a chair on its side against the wall, and my bestie sitting on the floor crying.

"Tell me everything that happened."

"Stupid Ozzy." She hiccups a breath, and a tremor shakes her whole body. "He's trying to scare me into coming back to him, like that'll ever happen."

"It looks like he was throwing things." I'm sitting beside her, rubbing her back. "What exactly did he say?"

"He said if I thought I could beat him, I was a fool. He said no friend of mine could stop him. He said no piece of paper could stop him..."

The blood drains from my face, and I notice red marks on her neck. "Did he do this?" I lightly touch her skin with my fingertips, and she drops her chin, fresh tears coating her cheeks.

"He grabbed me, but I pushed him away."

"That's it. We've got to call the cops." I push off the floor, taking out my phone and tapping 911. "They have to see this. They have to get it on the record and do something..."

"Wait, Sly... I don't want them coming here with Ollie in the house." She jumps up fast, gripping my arm. "I don't want to scare him with the lights and all the men and the guns. We can go to the station tomorrow. He won't come back tonight."

Our eyes meet, and I don't feel good about this. He said *no friend could stop him*, which sends ice through my veins. All my Spencer anger is pushed to the backseat of my mind.

"At least let me take a picture of your neck. It'll have faded by tomorrow." She agrees, holding back her hair. I take several different angles. "And you really think we're safe sleeping here tonight?"

Her eyes close, and she nods. "He did what he came here to do—he's trying to scare me. Anyway, where would we go? And Ollie's asleep..."

She exhales heavily, but I feel like we could find somewhere to go.

Going to the door, I quickly turn the metal switch. "We'll lock the deadbolt and check all the windows. I have pepper spray and a baseball bat. If we all sleep in the same room, we can keep each other safe if anything does happen."

She helps me pick up the spindly table off the floor, and I

arrange the chairs around it, then she tiptoes down the hall to Oliver's room and peeks in the door.

"I'm so glad he slept through it," she whispers upon return.

"I can't believe I missed it. It's like he knows our schedules or something." The thought scares me even more.

I've watched too many true crime shows to ignore what's happening here, but I hold it together for my friend. We'll get the police involved first thing in the morning.

Courtney looks at me with red-rimmed eyes, and I pull her to my side.

"Don't worry." I do my best to make my voice sound more confident than I feel. "We have strength in numbers, and we'll get this all sorted. I'll check apartment listings while we're at it. We're not exactly in the greatest part of town."

"It's all we can afford."

She has a point, and I hate I'm not bringing in more money yet.

This tiny apartment with its lack of security, creepy neighbors, and absentee landlord is the perfect setting for a horror film—or a serial killer attack.

"I'm still going to check. You never know what might be out there. Maybe we could sublet..." She shrugs, shaking her head, and I have another idea. Holding my finger in front of my lips, I motion to the table. "Sit down. I'll be right back."

Creeping to my room, I slide my suitcase from the closet, doing my best not to wake Oliver. Chartreuse watches me with her orange freak eyes in her terrarium, and I want to flip off her weird little self. Instead, I hurry back to the living room.

Opening the case on the floor, I take out a thick, ancient book. It's like something out of a Tim Burton film. It's a super-old scrapbook with pockets and plastic photo pages, and it has a fabric cover with "The Palm is Sacred" embroidered on a large panel in the center.

Grandma Alice wants it back, but I've held onto it since high school, reading it voraciously. It's filled with newspaper clippings and old black and white photos of women and groups of women.

They're suffragettes and early 20th Century protesters. Some pictures show them gathered on the beach or being hauled off to jail. In every one, they look so happy, so full of life. They were standing up for what they believed, trying to make a difference.

"What in the world?" Court's voice is hushed as she studies it with me.

"It's the ancient book of the Fireside Women's Society."

"Ohh-kay, and what in the world?" She looks up at me with wide eyes, and I hold up my finger.

"First, shots." I dash to the kitchen as she continues turning the pages.

Taking down the tequila and the salt shaker, I pull the refrigerator open and take out a lemon half.

"We don't have lime, but this will do, right?"

"What is this, Sly?" She looks up at me.

"I haven't been able to confirm it, but I think these ladies were witches."

She slides her finger over the stitched cover. "What's 'The palm is sacred'?"

"That was their motto. They were all about protecting Mother Earth and fighting for equality." I cut the lemon into two wedges and give her one. "Their primary focus was protecting Fireside and all its original families—of which I happen to be one." Passing her the wedge, I lift my chin. "Bottom's up!"

She starts to do the shot, but I grab her arm fast. "Wait! Not bottoms up! I meant to say, here's mud in your eye."

Court's nose wrinkles, and she tilts her head to the side. "What difference does that make?"

"I don't know." I hold up both my hands. "It's what I said last time we did this, and it worked. We have to repeat the process exactly like before. Now do the shot."

We throw back the liquor and squeal as quietly as possible, licking the salt off our hands and sucking the lemons. I cram my whole wedge against my teeth, trying to get all the juice out of it.

"Fierce like us," I whisper as soon as the shock has passed. "Now for the spell."

"Hold up..." Court scoots away from the table. "Stop right there. I didn't sign up for summoning demons or dead girls showing up in my bedroom or that kind of thing. I don't want that. Nope, nope, nope!"

She's out of her chair shaking her hands and her head.

"It's not like that!" I jump up, catching her shoulders and holding her eyes with mine. "Trust me. I did it with Daisy when Scout was gone. We brought him back! I'm telling you, it was crazy, and it totally works."

"Brought him back from where?" Her brow lowers, and she gives me a one hundred percent skeptical eye.

"Well, not from the dead," I laugh. "Back to town. He legit was back the next day."

"I don't like messing with the spirit world, Sly."

"Look." I turn the pages until I've found the protection spell. "This isn't about spirits. I mean, it *is* about spirits, but it's about good spirits wanting to help us. These women put this book together for situations just like this—to protect us through the ages. They don't want to hurt us."

"Dead old ladies."

"Just be cool." I slide my fingers carefully along the directions. "It says we need rosemary, sage, lavender, fresh basil, mint, and a handful of coarse salt. You grab the rosemary, sage, basil, and salt from the kitchen, I'll get the candles, lavender, and mint from my bag."

She's hesitant, but she does what I say. In less than ten minutes, we're sitting on the floor in front of the door. The lights are lowered, and five candles are on the corners of a makeshift pentagram.

"I don't like this…" Court whispers, scanning the room like she expects something to jump out at us.

As if kindred spirits are scarier than a real, live man threatening her.

I study the book. "Hold my hands, and I'll say the words. *Gods above and gods below, protect this home from wicked foe. Ancestors ancient and old, defend this home from hearts of cold. Spirits from beyond the misty silver, protect this home from those who pilfer.*"

We hold hands a few moments longer with our eyes closed, then we open them. Courtney's eyebrows are up, and she looks all around the room again.

"Is that it?" she whispers. "I didn't see anything."

"You don't need to." I stand, leaving the candles burning. "We protected this apartment from wicked foe and robbers… If anything, it'll help us sleep."

I don't mention that I hesitated over the cold-hearted part. *Could that mean Spencer?*

"The tequila will help me sleep. I'll get Oliver, and we can bundle up in my bed tonight. It's big enough."

She leaves me alone in the living room, and I look to the door, the candles, and the book. "Don't let me down Fireside ladies. The palm is sacred."

We don't go to the police station first thing.

Court has clients she can't reschedule, so while she's taking care of business, I spend the time going over my bills and the money I have, hoping I can find a better place for us to live.

Treating Spencer has been a nice Band-Aid, especially since he tips so well, and my payment for the gala was a nice little windfall, still, it'll be gone by the end of the month.

If I'm going to survive, I've got to pick up more clients. Scrubbing my hand across my forehead, I glance at the book still sitting on our table. "Come on, ancestors. Don't let me down."

Finally, after Court has her lunch, she agrees to drive to the station. I know she's nervous. She thinks they won't believe her. She thinks they'll take Oliver away. I try to distract her with my serious need to find more backs to rub.

"I can talk to the guys at Palmetto Rehab and see if they need an extra pair of hands." She's still in her navy Palmetto scrubs from her last appointment.

"You think they'd hire me? I've never worked in a clinic."

"I was straight out of school when they hired me. No promises, but I've been there a while."

"That would be fantastic, Court." My chest swells with optimism only to deflate as quickly when we pull into the parking lot of the precinct.

I'm just stepping out when my phone pings with a text. ***Is this Joselyn Winthrop who does massage? Are you still taking new clients?***

"Hey, you go on inside. I'll be right there."

She pauses to give me a panicked look. "Joselyn!"

Stepping forward, I pull her into a hug. "I'll be right inside, and you know these guys. We were just here last week getting the order. Talk to the desk clerk, and I'll be with you before anything else happens."

"You have the pictures."

"Right!" I text them to her. "Just let me set this up, and I'll be there."

She's not happy, but after crunching the numbers, I can't pass up an offer. I quickly reply. ***Yes. If you would, who is this?***

I wait as the gray dots float. ***Basil Santiago of Santiago and Associates.***

Sounds legit… ***Would you give me an idea of your needs and schedule?***

He answers fast, as if he knew I'd say yes. ***Strained my back. In a lot of pain. Can we do Fri at Member's Mark, 5:30 pm?***

Chewing my lip, I hesitate. Member's Mark is one of the downtown high-rises, and I did leave a card at the front desk there.

Still, at that time on a Friday, it'll likely be deserted. I typically don't see new clients after hours in their offices unless I know them or they've been referred to me by someone I know.

My stomach tingles, and I wish I had an alternative location. I don't, and these are desperate times. I can't go around leaving my card in office buildings and turning down follow-ups. When I first started out, Elliot worked in Member's Mark, and Santiago and Associates sounds like a legitimate organization.

I pull up Google and do a quick search. It's an international marketing firm, but they only list their services and contact numbers.

I'm not sure if that makes me feel better or not.

Fuck it. We need the money, and I'm sure it's fine. There's always a security guard on the first floor anyway.

I tap out my reply, ***Sure. Which office?***

Suite 22, third office on the left.

Making an appointment in my calendar, I shoot over a verification text then tuck my phone into my pocket before heading inside to support my friend.

CHAPTER Eighteen

Spencer

"A LEFT-HANDED FENDER STRATOCASTER!" HEATHER OLSEN HOLDS out the glossy white guitar, turning it side to side. "A vendor in Kansas had it, complete with case and papers."

"Kansas?" Daisy's eyes are bright as always, and as much as I tease her about her zeal, she does make our mundane work feel more like Christmas.

"Can you believe it?" Heather is equally enthusiastic. These two are a match made in antiques heaven, which is why they've been close since the time Daisy worked for us. "I was on a road trip with my husband, and I always make him stop at the flea markets."

"I brake for flea markets?" Daisy laughs. "I love it when that happens. Look at it, Spencer."

"Yes, it's a guitar." I lift the lightweight instrument, turning it in my hands. The lack of scars on the body tells me it was owned by someone who didn't play for long. "Dated 1962... Slab fingerboard. That's the year they changed it, yes?"

"Do you play?" Daisy's eyes are wide as she looks up at me.

"No, but the slab fingerboard makes it a very rare piece—and it's in mint condition."

"Are you ready?" Heather leans forward, nearly bursting with excitement.

"How much?" Daisy grabs her hands.

"Twenty grand!"

Daisy looks from Heather to me. "I don't know what that means. Is it good?"

"It's better than good." My eyebrow arches. "Nice work, Olsen. You'll easily get sixty for it at auction."

"I know!" She throws up her hands, bouncing on her toes.

Daisy makes a whistling noise and the women high-five like two cheerleaders at a home game. I leave them celebrating to inspect the next item, a three-foot bronze sculpture of a young woman, topless in a flowing skirt.

"This is a gorgeous piece." Turning it to the side, I see it's an Edward Onslow Ford sculpture. "Date?"

"1887."

Daisy joins me, gushing. "Just look at the movement in the skirt. So detailed, all the way down to the ruffles."

"It's distinctive of the artist." I muse, stepping around the table.

"I brought this one just for you, Spence. I knew you'd love it. Found it at an estate sale—the woman's grandmother had bought it in Germany in the forties."

"How could someone part with this?" Daisy shakes her head.

My eyebrow arches. "How much?"

"Ten." She waits, clasping her hands in front of her mouth as if she's anticipating my surprise.

I give. "You'll easily get twenty thousand at auction."

She claps, crying, "I know!" again.

Lifting my chin, I nod. "Grafton is very lucky to have you."

"What's this? A compliment from the great Spencer Carrollton? Am I dreaming?" Her dark eyes dance, and I shake my head.

These girls.

Sorry, these *women*.

Antiques dealers should not squeal like kids in a candy store, they should be composed, dignified... Still, I like working with smart people, and these two are rising stars.

Daisy traces her finger over the signature etched into the base of the sculpture. "She's so beautiful. I want her for myself."

Resting the tip of her pinky finger in the dancer's cupped hand, she tilts her head to the side, as if she's pirouetting with the statue in her mind.

Heather watches her with a grin. "She'll be in your shop until the auction. Maybe I can put a bug in someone's ear."

Our photographer steps around the items, taking pictures from every angle, and we continue on to a lighthouse clock under glass worth several thousand and a gorgeous Persian rug worth only a few.

Miles joins us to examine a pair of field binoculars Heather retrieved from a curbside trash bin. "Why didn't we hire Heather, again?" He quips, frowning at me.

"You can't hire her." Daisy puts her arms around Heather's waist. "If she leaves Grafton, she's moving to Oceanside to help me run my store."

He picks up a chunky ring with an oversized jade stone in the center and diamonds arranged in an art-deco-style along the black band. "Is this a Marsh? My God, Heather, where did you find it?"

"That is indeed a Marsh." Heather's expression is smug. "Can you believe it? They're so rare, and a jade—the rarest of them all. It's like a needle in a haystack."

"Let me see." Daisy takes the ring carefully. "Sly would love this."

My ears perk up at that bit of information, but I hold my expression neutral.

"It's missing one little baguette, but I have a fellow in New Hampshire I trust to repair it."

"Ten thousand?" Daisy squints at Miles, who breaks into a proud smile.

"Your jewelry skills have improved. I think that's right, yes?" He glances at Heather, who winks.

"I'm hoping to get at least fifteen if not twenty for it."

"I bet you will." My partner pats her on the back, and we continue going over the pieces she brought with her.

Another hour passes before Daisy says it's time for her to go. She kisses my cheek, and Miles walks her out. I linger back with Heather.

"This Marsh piece." Lifting the steel and jade ring, I study the polished stone. "What if I offered you twelve for it now?"

Her lips twist, and she squints one eye. "I had a feeling you might be interested when Daisy mentioned her cousin."

My brow relaxes, and icy calm fills my voice. "It's nothing like that."

"Now, now. Don't go all Mr. Freeze on me." She waves her hands at my face. "I'll sell it to you for ten, even though I could easily get fifteen for it."

"I'm not asking for any favors."

"Consider it a sacrifice to the gods for unfreezing your cold, cold heart."

I'm growing uncomfortable by the second. "Listen, Olsen—"

"No, you listen, Carrollton." She steps to me, but I see the glimmer in her eyes. "You've been this closed-off asshole for as long as I've known you. I don't get it. You're a good-looking man, and if Sly has somehow gotten through to you, I'm happy to keep the ball rolling."

"Females," I grouse. "You and Daisy deserve one another. I

hope you do retire from Grafton and go to work with her. From what I understand that town needs a fresh influx of interfering old biddies."

She laughs, but I tug on my tie, which for some inane reason feels too tight.

"I'll take your ten grand, and I'll send it to my guy for repairs. It'll take a few weeks, is that okay?"

"I'm changing my mind."

"No, you're not!" She skids over to grab my arm. "You're not going to kill my belief in happily ever after. I'm getting this baby fixed, and I'll tie it up in a pink bow. I expect you to name your first child after me."

I don't even respond to that. "Are you hungry? Let's get something to eat."

CHAPTER Nineteen

Joselyn

WE GOT SOME LUCK FILING OUR REPORT AT THE POLICE STATION. THE new desk clerk's first cousin had an abusive husband, and she seemed to take us under her wing as a personal cause.

She arranged for a patrol car to drive by the apartment complex every night between ten and eleven, and the deputy gave us his personal number.

"It's because you were with me." Courtney is packing for her Friday appointments.

"I think it's because the deputy has a thing for his dispatcher."

She steps over to kiss my head. "Whatever it takes. I'll follow up with my department chair about you joining Palmetto. He said if there's money in the budget, he'll find a place for you. Don't want him to forget."

"You are too good to me." I give her a tight squeeze, but she plays it off.

"If we're going to move to a better apartment, I need to get you earning some money."

"Speaking of, I've got that client tonight at five-thirty. Want me to grab a pizza on the way home? We can chill out and watch *Unsolved Mysteries* or something about frogs if that's too much...?"

"It's a date." She pulls her bag over her shoulder and looks past me. "Come on, Ollie! You're going to make me late!"

"Go on." I wave her away. "I'll drive him to school. You get to work."

"Sure?" Her nose wrinkles, and I wave my hand.

"Of course! I'll get him to school. You get to work and talk to your boss."

"He's not really my boss..." She's still talking as she heads out the door.

I dash to the bathroom to dust powder on my nose and pull my hair into a ponytail. I only have one appointment today, Court is doing her best to get me on at her place, but otherwise, it's time to start cold calling. I'll pay a visit to the different offices in town, and I need to look respectable. I add a little more blush so I don't look too pale, then I add some gloss on top of my lipstick.

We're in the van when Ollie squints at me from the second row. "You're wearing a lot of makeup."

"Too much blush?" I flip down the visor. God, the last thing I need is to look like a hooker.

"Your eyes are too dark, and why are your lips so shiny?" He puts a plastic cage on his lap and stares through the clear panel at Chartreuse.

"You can be kind of rude, you know?" I slide an eye over at

him while still rubbing at the purple eyeshadow I applied. Maybe I was a little heavy-handed. "Is something bothering you?"

His chin is tucked, and while I know he loves that creepy frog, he's acting more into her today than usual.

"Hey." I give him a nudge with my arm. "Talk to me. We're roomies, after all."

He doesn't look at me.

He studies the green amphibian a few seconds longer, like he's receiving messages from her eerie, oversized eyes. I put my hand on his shoulder, giving it a gentle rub.

"You can trust me, you know? I'm your aunt Sly. I might not look like the goddess of all wisdom, but I know a lot more than you'd expect—"

"Mom said all men are assholes. But… I'm a man. Does that make me an asshole too?"

My jaw drops, and I'm totally stumped. "Ollie… No…"

I want to pull the car over and give him a hug. How can this little guy possibly understand how his mother's feeling? We've worked so hard to keep all that ugliness from him, but is that even possible? I continue rubbing his shoulder, giving it a little squeeze.

"Sometimes people say things when they're upset, and they're really just exaggerating. Like that time you said you hated Chuck E. Cheese because it was closed when we wanted to go? It's like that. You don't hate Chuck E. Cheese, and your mom doesn't think all men are assholes. She'd never think that of you."

"It's because my dad's a bad man. He hurts my mom, and he wants to hurt me."

Swallowing the lump in my throat, I look out the window. Why haven't I discussed how to handle this with Courtney? I have no idea what she's told him about the situation or what I should say about it. Lord, here I go…

"Your dad is having some problems. We hope one day he

can get some help for those problems, but for now, it's better if you're not around him."

"He's still my dad. Jesse said he's going to grow up and be just like his dad." His voice trails off, and he studies the frog in his lap like he might cry.

Heat clouds my eyes, and I grip his shoulder. "Look at me, Oliver. You can choose what kind of man you'll be. Understand? Some people don't even have a dad..." Pressing my lips together, I try to think. "You could be like your mom. She's smart and strong and loving. What if you grow up to be like her?"

He blinks quickly, and I hope I'm saying the right thing.

Our eyes meet, and he seems relieved. He also seems determined.

His little jaw sets, and he nods. "I'll be a better man."

"He just canceled on you?" Courtney is at the table playing Uno with Ollie as I wrestle my massage table through the door.

"He said some work thing came up, and he'd have to reschedule." My chest is heavy, and I don't say out loud how much I needed that paycheck.

Now I'm really broke, and I promised Court I'd help put a deposit on a new place.

"Sorry I didn't get the pizza. We could still watch *Unsolved Mysteries* if you want? Or a nature show... I'll make mac and cheese!"

Oliver goes out with a Wild Draw 4 card, and Courtney hops up with a smile. "Nope—we're getting sushi!"

"Sushi!" Ollie jumps out of the chair and does a little sumo dance. "Sushi! Sushi! Sushi!"

"Are you sure?" My forehead crinkles. "I'm going to be short now that Mystery Client canceled."

"I have a coupon for Sakitumi—dinner's on me!"

"Grab the keys. I'll order while you drive."

We pile into my ancient Dodge mini-van and head for Sakitumi. "Best sushi in the Soda City," I cry, and Ollie cheers from the back seat.

We're heading down I-20, and my feet are propped on the passenger's side dash as I enter Court's credit card info. "Do you think I should get credit cards up front and threaten to charge a cancellation fee if they don't give 24 hours' notice?"

"Nope. I think you should come and work with me at Palmetto and not worry about it!"

My eyebrows shoot up. "I got the job?"

"You got an interview, but of course they're going to hire you. He'll take one look at your résumé and give you the job. It doesn't hurt that you're super friendly and likable."

"Tell me more..." I put my hand on my chest, fluttering my eyelids.

Courtney is turning the dial on the radio. "This old thing doesn't even have Bluetooth," she complains.

"Don't hate on Betsy. She gets me where I need to go with my massage chair intact."

"Good ole Betsy!" Oliver calls from the back. "This is Betsy, Chartreuse!"

"Ollie! You did not bring that frog!" I wail. "Do not—"

"I know, do not let her go in my van." He imitates my voice pretty well, I have to hand it to him.

His mother finally lands on a classic rock station playing Shania Twain, and we start belting out all the words to "That Don't Impress Me Much."

Ollie groans, pushing his head against the seat.

We head into The Vista, and I chew my lip, remembering the last time I was here with Spencer. All the feelings from our meeting at Nightcaps try to bubble up, but I push them right back down with a variation on Shania. "Okay, so you're a billionaire..."

Courtney pulls the minivan into one of the designated take-out spaces, and I turn the radio softer.

"You know, Ollie, you're a pretty cool kid to like sushi so much." I lift my head to meet his eyes in the mirror.

"California roll!" he cries.

"And edamame… and miso… and…" My eyes flicker across the street to the steak restaurant Rioz. "Mother of pearl!"

"What's that?" Ollie's nose curls. "Mother of pearl roll…"

Courtney frowns, squinting at the windshield. "What is it?"

The restaurant has a small, outdoor seating area, and big as day, sitting at a table is Spencer, right across from a woman with flowing dark brown hair. Her back is to me, but her legs are crossed. She's in a short dress, and it shows off her shapely calves.

"That flipping…"

I don't swear in front of Ollie, and Courtney cranes her neck, searching everywhere to see where I'm looking.

A pimply teenage guy taps on her window, and I snatch up my phone. ***Having a nice Friday?*** My eyes are glued to him, waiting to see if he'll pick up his phone, if he'll respond or ignore me…

I watch his eyes slide down. He nods to his date, smiling as he picks up his phone, then does a little wave and taps on the device.

Fury is blazing in my throat, and I'm already working on my reply. ***It's a beautiful night. Relaxing at my favorite place. You?***

I hope you step on a Lego. I hit send.

It doesn't take long for him to reply. ***Excuse me?***

My fingers are flying. ***I hope the worst day of your past is the best day of your future.***

I can barely read his reply for the anger burning in my eyes. ***Is that a curse?***

I hope everyone you shake hands with has moist hands.

Courtney cuts me a look as she pulls the minivan onto the street. "Are you okay? What's going on?"

I am *not* okay. I am not okay at all.

My fingers are flying. ***I hope you get an eyelash in your eye and you can never get it out. I hope every time you use hand sanitizer you have a paper cut. I hope every time the waiter walks by, it's with someone else's food.***

Where are you?

I throw my phone in my bag, and it's the stupidest thing ever, but I start to cry.

CHAPTER Twenty

Spencer

Where are you? I hit send on the quick text then stand, looking all around the outdoor dining area.

"What's happening?" The woman across from me grips the table.

At that second, I spot the ancient, frosted baby blue minivan pulling away from the sushi restaurant across the street. It's moving fast in a northerly direction, and I have no idea where she's going.

"I'm sorry, but I've got to go." Digging in my pants, I pull out my wallet and drop more than enough cash on the table before stepping over the wrought-iron fence surrounding the outdoor seating area at Rioz, my favorite steakhouse.

She's costing me yet another prime rib.

"Excuse me, sir! You can't do that." I hear the waiter calling from behind me, but I don't stop.

Looking left to right, I jaywalk as fast as possible across the street. An oncoming car honks loudly, and I flip the bird before dashing up to the takeout area of Sakitumi.

Catching the pimple-faced curbside waiter by the shoulder, I pull him to me. "I need to see the receipt for that last order—the blue minivan? I believe it's that one in your hand."

"I'm sorry, sir, I can't do that. Privacy laws, and all—"

"How much?" My wallet is still in my hand, and I start pulling out bills.

His eyes widen when I get to eighty. "The name is either Joselyn or Courtney..."

The kid hesitates, frowning at the flimsy scrap of paper. "Why do you want to know?"

I'm tempted to snatch it from him. Instead, I exhale slowly and force what I hope is a friendly smile. "I found her credit card, and I don't know how to get in touch with her."

The guy studies me, and I know he's not believing my lie. "Which one? Courtney or Joselyn?"

"Oh, for Christ's sake." I snatch the receipt out of his loosened grip, scanning it quickly.

"Hey!" He reaches for it, and I push it back at his chest along with the four twenties.

I've got what I need. "Sorry for your trouble."

I'm in my black Tesla speeding northeast towards Belmont when my phone vibrates again. Glancing at the face, I cringe. It's from Heather, and after the conversation we had earlier, I'm never going to live this down.

I pass a Piggly Wiggly and a liquor store before turning into a run-down apartment complex with a broken street light. Double-checking my phone, this is the address listed for Courtney's name.

A dented El Camino is in one of the spaces, and there it is, a few spots down, the old blue minivan. At least her vehicle fits in here.

The apartment building is only two floors, and it reminds me of an old beach motel rather than a place you'd live full-time. Glancing around as I tap my key fob, I notice a guy in a hoodie disappear around the corner.

I don't like this one bit.

Jogging up the steps, I make my way down to the correct number and knock forcefully. "It's me, Joselyn. Open the door."

Muffled voices come from the other side, and I hear what sounds like shushing noises. The door opens a crack, and it's her.

"What are you doing here? How did you get this address?" She has her chin up, but she won't meet my eyes.

"Get out here." I push the door open and catch her wrist, dragging her outside and pulling the door shut before I press her back against it.

"Oh! Stop this.... What are you doing?"

She's caged in my arms, and my heart's beating fast. I've wanted to have her body pressed against mine for a week. "Why are you following me?" My voice is thick, as desperate as I feel.

I look down at her, and we're both breathing fast. Her red lips remind me of a goldfish, puckered and full, and I want to smear that lipstick all over her face. Her hair is pulled back in another heavy ponytail with a few strands hanging around her cheeks. I want to wrap it in my fist.

"I'm not following you. I went with Courtney and Oliver to get sushi. You're interrupting our dinner." She struggles as if she's going to get away, but I hold her still.

"I'm interrupting your dinner." I exhale a laugh.

My thumbs are under her jaw, and I lift her face to mine. Her eyes are still averted, but I run my nose along her cheek as I speak, noting the uptick in her breathing, the slip of her tongue peeking out to wet her full bottom lip.

"Why all the texts, then? You said to keep my hands to myself. You said we were done."

Blue eyes flicker to mine, and I see the fire now. "So you went right out and found a new random hookup."

She's so sure of herself. I lift my chin, admiring her eyes. They say cold heat burns the hottest, and it's possible I could melt in her gaze. I wasn't lying when I said I might like it.

Leaning closer, I brush my lips over hers, light as a feather. She exhales a little noise, and my cock is awake. My whole body is awake. I want to be inside her. I want to lift her leg and take her right here against this door.

"Will you let me kiss you now?"

She blinks twice, and strain tightens her gaze. *Come on, Sin. Say yes...*

Her jaw clenches, and she bites out her reply. "No."

For the space of a breath, it's silent, no sound.

She said no.

Exhaling a chuckle, I step back, releasing her as the spell is broken. *God, this woman.*

"That was no random. I was having dinner with Heather. You remember Heather Olsen? You met her and her husband Jim at the gala. Grafton is giving us an exclusive on the prize selections from their summer auction. She'll be taking them to Daisy's store in the morning." Turning away, I rub my hand across the back of my neck. "We were hungry."

Joselyn hasn't moved from where I had her pinned against the door. Her chin is still lowered, and her eyes are still focused on the parking lot below.

Still, her breasts, those luscious breasts, rise and fall rapidly beneath her long-sleeved black tunic. She's as affected as I am.

"I guess I overreacted." It's a quiet admission. "I'm sorry."

Placing a hand on the metal balcony rail, I look up at the night sky. A smattering of stars is spread across black velvet, and it feels like something important is happening.

"You hoped the worst day of my past was the best day of my future." The creativity of it makes me smile.

"I read that somewhere."

"It's good." A police siren pierces the quiet, and I look over at her. "This is a terrible neighborhood. What are you doing here?"

"Trying to make ends meet. Something I'm sure you know nothing about."

"I've told you. You don't know about my past, Sin." I glance at the corner, where I saw hoodie guy go. "You have my number. Call me if anything goes wrong. Or you feel scared."

I can't imagine her being afraid, but this time when she looks at me, the fire has subsided. At least momentarily.

"Thank you." She steps away from the door, arms crossed. "I helped Court get a restraining order. Now we have a patrol car that drives by every night between ten and eleven."

She seems very proud, and I don't want to burst her bubble with how uncomfortable this makes me. "I'm available 24-7."

"I'll remember that."

My hands are in my pockets, and I start for the stairs. I hate leaving her here, this way, but it's what she wants. Just before descending, I pause. "I'll need to see you Monday at eleven." Sliding one hand up my waist, I squint. "Irritated my back chasing after you just now."

"I'll make an appointment and send you a confirmation."

"Goodnight, Joselyn."

I'm at my car when I hear the door slam and the lock click. Climbing inside, my phone buzzes with an incoming text. It has the letters *TY* and a little red heart in the Notes field.

Oh, Sin, if you think this is charity, you're dead wrong.

CHAPTER Twenty-One

Joselyn

MR. SANTIAGO REBOOKED FOR SUNDAY AFTERNOON.

He texted just as I was closing my eyes last night asking if I could see him today. Of course, I said yes, only mildly hesitant about appearing too available.

Hell, I need the work. Other than him, I've only got Spencer on the books for tomorrow morning.

I do have an interview at Court's place tomorrow afternoon, but I'm not sure how soon I'll get started or how much work it will be, or when I'll get paid...

"So, you see, I *am* desperate," I sigh to myself, scanning the office directory outside the elevators of the Member's Mark building.

A chubby security guard sits near the glass doors staring at his phone. He doesn't inspire a lot of confidence, but at least he's here, he has a gun, and he nodded when I said I was seeing Mr. Santiago.

The bell dings, and I step inside the glass tube heading to the top floor.

We spent the weekend scouring Zillow for apartment listings and doing our best to keep things upbeat and normal for Oliver. Our nightly police drive-by has continued, which makes us feel a little secure, and Spencer's offer has been burning a hole in my chest since Friday.

My heart is screaming I should have let him kiss me, but my head is a stubborn old nun saying I did the right thing. I won't be used and tossed in the trash... although, I am a bit embarrassed about overreacting to seeing him with Heather.

Way to show your cards, Sly.

The elevator dings again, and I step out into a dim hallway. With all the office doors closed, the reception area is illuminated only by the emergency exit lights. If it weren't five in the afternoon, it would be creepy.

I follow the directions to the third door on the left and tap lightly, "Mr. Santiago?"

The door slowly opens with a light creak, and lying before me on a table is an olive-skinned man without a shirt. He's face-down, so I only see his back, and he's not as defined as Spencer. Still, I can tell he works out.

The blinds covering the windows are closed, and the room is dim. He'd said in our text he had his own equipment, which is unusual but not unheard of. I didn't question it. The less I have to carry, the easier it is to get out of here if I feel uncomfortable.

"Miss Winthrop, I've been waiting for you." It's a mid-level voice with a touch of an accent I can't place, almost British.

A Bluetooth speaker is on the edge of the desk playing island music.

Shaking away my hesitation, I lower my bag into a chair. "Looks like you know as much about my job as I do."

"I've spent time with massage therapists." He doesn't look up, and it's starting to get weird.

"I'll just get started then." Taking out my oils, I place the warming plate beside the small speaker. "Would you prefer peppermint or lavender?"

"Neither, if you don't mind."

A quick nod, and I put the items back in my bag. "You said the pain is coming from a lower back strain?'

"Yes."

Rubbing my hands together, I start with light strokes on his shoulders slowly making my way down. "If the pressure is too intense, just let me know."

I'm quiet, working steadily, focusing on my hands. I assume he's fallen asleep when he speaks. "Tell me about yourself."

It's an odd question, but I don't mind answering. "Well, let's see... I grew up in a small town about two hours from here..."

"What brought you to the city?"

"College. I started at the university in horticulture, but then I switched over to Palmetto to study sports medicine. I really got into the massage therapy and wellness aspect of recovery."

"Horticulture to sports medicine is a big switch. Is it because you had friends in the field?"

I've answered this question before, and I start to relax as I talk about my goals. "I was drawn to the program because I've always been interested in the healing arts. Flowers bring joy and lift the spirit. Certain scents can elevate your mood. It's all related."

"So you made friends in college?" His question is forceful and a little confusing, jumping back to why I came here.

I return to my original assumption he's foreign—perhaps he's looking for a way to make friends? But he works in this busy office.

"Miss Winthrop?"

Clearing my throat, I move my hands into what he said was

the injured part of his back, deepening the pressure. He doesn't even flinch.

"Is this too much pressure?"

"Not at all."

My shoulders tense, and I step back, picking up my towel and wiping my arms. "You're not really injured are you?"

"You didn't answer my question." It's a smooth observation, a smile in his voice, almost like he's leading me with his words.

Picking up my bag, I take another step away from the table. "Why are you asking about my friends?"

"I'm wondering how you came to know my wife, Miss Winthrop. I'm wondering how you got the idea in your head you have any say in what she does with our son."

My heart leaps to my throat, and I bolt for the door, throwing my bag over my shoulder as I run.

Ozzy is off the table like a jaguar, nearly catching me. The whisper of his hand just missing my arm causes me to shriek, and I grab the doorknob, jerking it open. It's just enough delay for him to grab the back of my scrubs.

"No!" I scream, falling on my stomach in the hallway.

Clawing the floor, I manage to get my feet under me and pull myself up before he can land on top of me. Running as hard as I can to the door, I fling everything I pass in the way behind me—a chair, a potted tree, the computer screen off the receptionist's desk. It lands with a massive crash.

If I'm lucky, there's a security camera. Otherwise, whoever owns this office is going to be confused when they come into work tomorrow. Slamming the doors of the suite, I see his shadow rising up in the frosted glass, and I drag a long, metal planter in front of it.

He hits it with a slam, and I run hard to the elevator, pressing the button repeatedly, looking back over my shoulder, crying out as I pant for breath.

He's almost through the door, and I give up, scanning all over the place for the stairs. "Where are they?"

My eyes land on the sign for the restrooms. Deciding I don't have time to wait, I run full-speed into what turns out to be an enormous stone facility.

A powder area with sinks and a full-length mirror divides the front from the 12 stalls in the back. It's empty and dark, and I run to the middle stall, pushing open a door and quickly sliding the lock before crawling, military-style on my belly under the dividers to the very last one.

I lock that door as well and step carefully onto the toilet seat. I don't know if he saw me come in, and I clutch my hand over my mouth to muffle my breathing, straining my ears for any sound of footsteps.

Tears stream down my cheeks. I'm winded, and every snort, every heavy exhale feels magnified a thousand times in this stone enclosure.

"Joselyn…" Ozzy sing-songs my name like it's a horror film, and more tears coat my face. "I'm not trying to hurt you, Joselyn. I just want to talk."

He slaps the doors open, one by one, and I squeeze my eyes shut, praying to God and the saints, and the Fireside ladies to help me.

"Have you ever watched a house cat play with a mouse?" *Slam!* He pushes another door open, slowly moving down the row. "House cat's not hungry. He doesn't want to deal with all that fur and blood and guts…" *Slam!* Another door… "He plays with it until it stops fighting back. Then he gives it a warning…" *Slam!* He's one door away from… "Sometimes the warning is a little too rough, and the mouse dies. Either way, the mouse gets the message. Tell me, Joselyn, are you getting the message?"

Clink… He's at the door I locked, and my eyes squeeze shut. "Did you really think a flimsy little lock would keep me out?"

At the first *Boom!* of his boot striking particleboard, I step down from the toilet, sliding the lock slowly open.

Another *Boom!* and my lips squeeze shut against a scream. As soon as he breaks through that wrong door, I plan to run as hard as I can for the exit.

It's my only hope of escaping.

It's got to work.

My fingers grip the handle for his last kick when *Woosh!*

The toilet behind me automatically flushes.

I jerk the door open and our eyes meet. His glitter with satisfaction, but I swing my bag of massage oils, warming saucer, and rocks with all my might, aiming for his head as I run directly at him.

He's taken aback that I'm running at him, and the bag strikes his temple, throwing him to the ground. On the way down, he grabs my leg, and I go down, too, striking my cheek against the stall divider.

Light explodes behind my eyes, and I roll onto my back with a moan.

Ozzy pushes off the floor. "Look what you made me do."

The sound of his voice spikes adrenaline in my veins, and I shake off my disorientation. I'm on my feet again, snatching up my bag and running at top speed for the exit.

Sticky blood is on my cheek, but I don't stop running. I'm in the marble foyer, and I see the sign for the stairs.

Bursting through the doors, I run around and around, gasping for air, exhaling little cries of fear, flying as fast as I can down all twenty-two floors to the bottom. I slam the metal crash doors open and don't even pause for the security guard. I'm in the parking lot, in Betsy, screeching away towards the apartment.

We can't stay there tonight.

CHAPTER Twenty-Two

Spencer

Rocking back in my chair, I tap my finger against my desktop waiting for Joselyn to appear. It's Monday morning, and after our encounter Friday night, I didn't expect her to be late. She's very law-abiding these days.

On Friday, it took all my willpower to hold back from kissing her. Her reaction to seeing me having dinner with Heather was quite satisfying. What am I going to do with this woman—and Heather with the nonstop jokes.

Heather actually texted me, ***Some people are worth melting for***, which apparently is from a children's movie. I didn't reply.

At last, my door opens, and Joselyn breezes in, rolling her chair. "Sorry I'm late. Traffic this morning was crazy, and it took me a little longer to get out the door…"

She's wearing dark sunglasses and too much makeup, but she

can't hide the large purple bruise and cut held together with a butterfly bandage across her cheek.

"What the hell?" I'm out of my chair, crossing the room. "What happened to your face?"

"It's nothing. I'm fine." She waves her hand, but I lightly place my fingers on her chin, tilting her head to the side and doing my best not to hurt her.

"How did this happen?"

"I just... fell."

She turns away quickly, pressing her lips together. I notice a tremor in her voice, and my stomach knots all the way up to my throat. She's hiding something, and I have a sneaking suspicion I know what it is. All I can think of is hoodie guy disappearing around the corner outside her apartment complex on Friday.

I should never have left her there alone.

"What made you fall?" My voice is low, icy calm.

"Spencer..." It's a breathy retort, and she waves as if she'll brush aside my concern. "It's nothing for you to worry about. I've got it under control."

Catching her by the arms, I make her face me. "Did he do it? The husband?"

"It wasn't like that. It was my own stupid fault. I took an appointment with an unknown client. I should never have gone alone to an office building after hours for someone I don't know. It's just common sense."

With every word, the fury in my chest grows tighter. "What office building?"

"Member's Mark."

"Where is he now?"

"I don't know." She's quiet, subdued. "We went to the police station and filed a complaint. Since he didn't actually hit me, and I went there to meet him without being coerced, they're saying there's little they can do. I ran from him, and when he tried to catch me, I fell and hit my cheek on the bathroom stall."

"You were in the women's restroom… with him?"

She nods, and I can tell she's afraid.

Her fear has murder on my mind. "You're not going back to that apartment. You're not going out of my sight until this situation is resolved."

She laughs bitterly. "And how do you propose we resolve it?"

"It's very easy. You're going to pack your things and move into my house until we find you a better place to live."

Her jaw drops, but I hold up a finger. "No arguments. Tell Courtney and her son. I have plenty of room."

"Courtney will not go for this. Ollie has school, and she already said he'll find her wherever she goes."

My fist tightens, and darkness clouds my vision. I'd love for that bastard to try something at my home. I'd love to show him what a real man will do. Clearing my throat, I give a more civilized answer.

"Our office has security on call for when we're transporting expensive items. I'll tell them I need a man at my house around the clock until further notice. Better yet, I'll have him assigned to you until further notice. You'll be perfectly safe—as long as you don't do anything foolish like taking appointments from clients you don't know. Even then…"

"I needed the money, Spencer. And I'm not having a security guard following me around like I'm the damned Queen of England. I have an interview this afternoon with Palmetto Rehab. If they give me a job, they'll have security on-site, and then I won't need to take any more clients I don't know."

Her protests fall on deaf ears. I turn to my desk, punching up Allied Universal on my iPad and arranging for a guard to start today. "Did you report what happened to Member's Mark?"

"No."

"They need to know exactly what happened, when, and where."

"It was all so fast. I haven't really had a chance to process everything..." Her face lowers, and when she blinks, a crystal tear hits her cheek.

It's like a fist smashing in and grabbing my heart.

"Come here." I pull her to my chest, and she melts into me. "You're okay now. I've got you. We're going to find this guy and get him behind bars. In the meantime, you'll be safe with me."

"I can't do that, Spencer. I don't belong to you."

Sliding my hand up and down her back, I vaguely note the prick her words cause in my chest. "It's not about belonging. It's about your safety—and Courtney's. Men like that typically don't stop until they have what they want."

And I'll be damned if he hurts Joselyn again.

"I can't commit to something like that without talking to Court, and if she's not onboard, I can't leave her alone. I promised I'd stay with her, and we've been doing okay. We have a patrol car driving by every night—"

This stubborn, beautiful woman. At least she's letting me comfort her. I'd like to kiss her, take her home, and lock the door, throw away the key.

Enough.

I step away, going to the desk and picking up my office phone. "Call her now and ask her. I'll talk to her myself if necessary."

She watches me, looking from my face to the phone, but slowly she takes it and gingerly types the numbers into the keypad.

I take a seat in my desk chair, picking up a stress ball and squeezing it in my fist.

It's been a long time since I've been in a fight, but I can see myself smashing that guy's head against the concrete. Repeatedly.

"Court?" Her eyes blink away, and she turns her back. "Hey... I'm just at my appointment with Spencer. He's kind of angry. He wants us to live with him until Ozzy's off the streets." She exhales a laugh. "I know, that's what I said."

Leaning forward, I'm out of my chair, walking around to stand in front of her again.

When she looks up at me, I offer to take the phone, but she shakes her head no. "He says there's plenty of room, and they have this on-call security guard. I know it's silly…" Her eyes close, and I feel like she's not selling it until they open again, wider. "What? You think it's a good idea? Yeah, hang on."

Lowering the receiver from her ear, she holds it out. "She'd like to talk to you."

Taking the phone, I give her a knowing grin. "Hi, Court."

"Hey… um…" Courtney's voice is tense. "You'd be willing to let us stay at your house? What's the catch?"

I recognize the fear in her tone, the hopelessness. It touches a part of me I locked away a long time ago, and now, seeing this happening up close, I'm taken aback by the rage it unearths in me.

"No catch." I force the anger out of my voice in favor of calm reassurance. "I have two bedrooms on the first floor of my house no one is using. It's basically the same size as your apartment, so it should be sufficient for you, Oliver, and Joselyn. You won't even notice me upstairs."

"Ollie has to go to school. It's all the way back where we live."

"Would it be possible for him to homeschool the last month? I can call the principal if it helps."

"Why are you doing this?"

My jaw tightens. The whole truth of why is privileged information, but I can easily say, "I don't like seeing people I care about with black eyes. I don't like menacing cowards. Take the help I'm offering and don't over-think it."

Her reply is calm. "Okay. Thank you. I'm sorry—I don't have many people I can count on right now."

"You have Joselyn, and I hope you trust me to keep you safe."

"I think I do."

Her words move something in my chest. Maybe the fucking

ice is melting, but it's not for the reason Heather and Daisy like to tease me about. Or perhaps it is that... fueled by the past.

Replacing the receiver, I place my hand on Joselyn's. "Let's skip the massage today. I'll take you to the Member's Mark building to file a report, and I'll drive you to your interview. Allied said they'll have a man assigned to us by 6 pm. I can keep an eye on you until then."

Her lips tighten, and I see her struggling with an argument. I'm not going to hear it, so she might as well save her breath. She lets it go, and my reaction is bittersweet. That fucker must have really scared her, which has me seeing red.

No one threatens my girl.

The security guard at the Member's Mark high rise is an overweight incompetent with crumbs on his shirt. Joselyn's hand is in the crook of my arm, and I cut her a look.

"This is the guy you expected to save you if anything went wrong?"

She cuts me a look right back. "The appointment was on the top floor. I wasn't expecting him to save me. I was expecting him to be a deterrent."

"He's only a deterrent to a Twinkie." I step forward, placing my palm on the dark console in front of him, reading his nametag. "Hello, Doug, is it?"

"Hi!" He stands up fast, smiling broadly. "That's me. Doug. What can I do you for? Do you need assistance finding a floor?"

"How did a guy like him get a job in security?" I exhale under my breath. Joselyn pinches the inside of my upper arm, and I flinch away. "Stop." It's a level command.

"You are so sweet, Doug. I actually need to see Mr. Santiago. Is he in?"

Doug's light brow furrows, his fleshy face tilts to the side.

"Don't I know you? You were here this weekend… yesterday? That's a pretty bad shiner you got there. Are you okay?"

He's overzealous, childish, and I'm ready to call the proprietor when Joselyn cuts me off. "Yes, I was here yesterday, and I need to talk to Mr. Santiago if he's available."

"He should be." Doug looks down at the desk. "Oh… Oh, my bad, he's not. It says Basil Santiago is in New York until next week. I'm sorry. Say, weren't you here to see him yesterday?"

"Yeah." Joselyn's tone is placating, like she's about to let Snuffy off the hook.

"She was," I interject with a bit more force. "She had an appointment in Santiago's office. When did he leave for New York?"

Stay-Puff looks at his computer screen again. "It says he's addressing the United Nations…" He looks up at us with wide eyes. "He left on Friday. He stood you up?"

I'm about to rip into him, but Joselyn tugs my arm sharply again.

"Thanks, Doug. I actually found an intruder in Mr. Santiago's office, so I wanted to file a complaint."

"Oh!" His blue eyes go wide. "Oh no, Miss…"

"Winthrop. Her last name is Winthrop, and if you think—"

"Doug," Joselyn interrupts. "Listen to me. A man used Mr. Santiago's office to schedule a fake appointment with me yesterday. I need you to circulate a memo that the offices need to do a better job locking up on the weekends, and I'm going to send a letter to Mr. Green. The building needs better security."

Doug's eyes grow rounder with every word. "I'm sorry… They don't like it if we ask too many questions or hassle the visitors. They don't want us to seem unwelcoming—"

I'm ready to say more, but Joselyn grabs my coat. "Do better, Doug. I believe in you."

She drags me out the door, but I'm not ready to let this go. "You're going to let him off the hook?"

"He's right." She's walking fast to my car. "A building this size isn't going to question visitors. I had a name, an office number. It's normal to assume I had a legitimate appointment."

"Assume? You could've been killed."

"It's not a building with only one office like *Antiques Today*. I don't want to get Doug fired. It's not his fault."

Grabbing her by the shoulders, I turn her back to the car. "It's not your fault either."

She blinks rapidly, looking away over my shoulder. "I knew not to come here. My gut told me it was the wrong thing to do, but I ignored it. This is just as much my fault as it is Doug's."

My jaw grinds. "I disagree."

"Either way, I've got an interview in thirty minutes. Are you going to drive me there or argue?"

Reaching out, I grip the back of her neck, pulling her to my chest in a hug. I want to pull her mouth to mine. I want to pull her body to mine and hold her tight.

She trembles slightly, and her hand fists in the back of my coat. I hold her until her breathing calms, until she seems to have recovered control.

My hand relaxes and I massage her neck. I turn my face and inhale her hair. The idea of her being hurt or worse is unacceptable to me.

"You okay?" My voice is rough, and she nods. Stepping back, I meet her misty eyes. "Yes, I'm going to drive you to your interview. Now get in the car."

CHAPTER Twenty-Three

Joselyn

"THIS PLACE IS INCREDIBLE." COURT SOUNDS BETTER THAN SHE HAS in weeks. "Did you see that garden tub in the bathroom? I'm going to take the longest jacuzzi-bath *evah*! I might not come out. Girl, you've seriously got to hang onto this guy. He is a keeper."

I'm sitting on the foot of her bed as she doctors my eye with Neosporin and a fresh butterfly bandage. "He's not *my guy* to hang onto. I told you. He's been very up front from the beginning. He doesn't do relationships, and I do. We're at an impasse."

"But you said he's super-hot in bed, right?"

Pulling my bottom lip between my teeth, I blink away from her eyes. "It doesn't matter. I'm not repeating the same mistakes I made with Elliot. I gave up my independence and turned into someone I wasn't, and look how that ended. He was fucking his secretary, and I was getting screwed."

"This guy is definitely not Idiot Flick, and I don't know..." She grins down at me with her huge brown eyes. Her name should be Bambi with those gorgeous peepers. "Can't you sort of, have a little fun while it lasts?"

"Last time I slept with him, I sneaked out because I wanted to curl up in his arms and hold him forever. That is how I get screwed. He can love it and leave it, but I get attached. I want more."

She presses her lips together and makes a *whatever* face. "Say what you want, the way he freaked out over your shiner and moved us all in here in less than twenty-four hours tells me a lot. Mr. 'I don't do relationships' has it bad."

Standing, I exhale heavily. "I can't build my life around wishful thinking. I can only go off of the facts, and the facts are he's said plainly and repeatedly, *Don't get attached.*"

"I can't hear what he's saying. His actions are too loud."

Waving her away, I look down at the incoming text on my phone. It changes everything, and I jump to my feet. "I got it! Look, Court, look! Troy says I'm on the roster. I should start getting calls next week!"

She squeezes my waist. "I knew he'd give you the job. I'd kick his ass if he didn't."

The tension of the last two days drains from my body in a rush, and I want to sit down and cry with gratitude.

Oliver peeks into the room. "Mom?"

"Hey, come in here." She waves him over. "Aunt Sly got a job working with me. Isn't that cool? We're so excited."

His little mouth curls into something like a smile as he climbs onto her bed, but I can tell he's anxious. I think about our conversation in the car, and I'm worried about how he's processing all of this, from my black eye to our sudden move to his abruptly leaving school.

Sitting on the bed, I reach for his hand. "I don't start until next week. What if we go to the zoo tomorrow? I heard one of the koala bears had a baby!"

"They're not really bears." He looks down, tracing a fingernail along the leg of his jeans. "Koalas are marsupials... like kangaroos."

"Have I told you how smart you are lately?" I wrinkle my nose and muss his hair. "Maybe you can graduate high school early and be one of those child geniuses."

"Right." He gives me a tight smile. "I'm really not going back to school this year?"

"I'm sorry, hon." Courtney sits on the bed, putting her arm around his shoulders. "You only have a few weeks left, and we need to stay with Mr. Spencer right now. It's kind of the best thing. But you'll still pass your grade."

She gives him a hopeful smile, and his chin drops.

"Okay, Mom." He doesn't even question her, and it breaks my heart a little.

He'll do anything to make things easier for her, and I'm not sure he's ever told her the things he said to me in the car. I make a mental note to watch how we talk in front of him, and I've got to make time to tell her what he said in private.

She stands, waving us away. "Now you two vamoose. I'm going to take a nice, long bubble bath, and I don't want any interruptions!"

"Don't overflow the tub," I warn. "Once you turn those jets on, it's bubbles bonanza!"

"I know, I know." She's doing her best to make Ollie feel at home.

He lunges forward, giving her one more, big hug. "I love you, Mom," he whispers.

She kisses his cheek, and when I see the tears in her eyes, I hop forward to grab his hand. "Where the heck is Chartreuse, anyway? Does she like this big, nice house? Show me where you put her cage. I want to see her in it... I want to be sure it's secure..."

"Come on," he exhales heavily, taking my hand and dragging me out of the room. "Baby."

"I am not a baby!" I pretend to be offended, and when I glance back, Courtney mouths a *thank you* to me.

I give her a wink and follow Ollie down the hall to our shared room. We figured we might as well continue being roomies in this new place. Also, the second bedroom has two twin beds.

Spencer said the interior designer thought a children's wing would increase the resale value. Since I've seen his Master wing, I can believe he has little interest in what happens on these lower floors—other than the kitchen.

He was so insistent about us moving in here, yet at the same time, he's been very respectful about giving us our space. I won't let my romantic imagination run wild over this. It's over-protective, but he hasn't said anything to indicate his feelings about being in a relationship have changed.

"I hope you're getting settled okay." His voice at my back makes me jump, and I turn fast with a little yip. "Sorry, I didn't mean to startle you."

"No, I'm…" I exhale a little laugh. "I guess I'm still jumpy."

My confession makes the muscle in his jaw move attractively. Over-protectiveness is a good look on him.

He blinks it away, extending his hand to Ollie. "Oliver, it's nice to see you again. I hope you're comfortable in my house."

"It's a nice house." Ollie nods, looking around like a little man.

"Right." Spencer straightens. "I'd like to introduce you all to Tom. He's our security guard for the next few days. Tom, this is Oliver and Joselyn."

Tom steps up, and he's a tank of a man. I'm guessing he's six-six, with broad shoulders, a broad chest, and thick legs. The only thing soft about him is a swoosh of blond hair over his left eye. He doesn't speak, he only nods. He's like a cartoon superhero.

Spencer seems oblivious to Tom's appearance. "If you need

anything, if anything feels off, if you hear any strange noises. If you see a shadow you don't like." Spencer pats him on the shoulder. "Tom's your man. I'll text you his number—save it on your phone."

Ollie and I are still holding hands, and I'm pretty sure both our jaws are on the floor. Tom only gives us a curt nod. We nod back in unison, and Spencer dismisses the boulder assigned to watch us. "Thank you, Tom."

When he turns to me, everything shifts—even his tone is gentle. "Can I get you anything?"

"No, thanks." I don't know why I feel shy all of a sudden. "Dinner was fantastic. I think that's the best steak I've ever had."

We finally got an order from Rioz, and I completely understand now why he was so pissed I ruined two of his dinners from there—although, I think he forgave me for the first one.

Ollie gives my hand a pull. "We were just going to check on Chartreuse."

A small grin lifts Spencer's lips. "I've heard about this frog. Would you mind if I said hello as well?"

"I guess." Ollie shrugs, charging ahead of us towards the bedroom we share.

Spencer catches my arm. "You sure you're okay? You seem tense."

He has always been so observant of everything I do. Forcing a smile, I shake my head. "I'm okay… just getting over everything. I think Ollie's having a little adjustment period."

His brow furrows, and he looks in the direction the little boy went. "Does he know about what's happening? About his dad, your eye—?"

"I'm not sure how much he knows, but he knows enough."

Spencer seems genuinely concerned, and my heart melts a little more. Damn him. How can he be so wonderful and so infuriating at the same time?

"Perhaps we could take him to the zoo tomorrow. If you're

available, of course. I was thinking, he has that frog. He might enjoy seeing the amphibian exhibit, and it's been all over the news about one of the koalas having a cub."

Shaking my head, I smile. "You read my mind. I actually suggested it to him just now in Courtney's room."

"It's a date. We can leave after breakfast."

We start after Ollie, and I pause. "Just... if you were wondering, I got the job. I'm on the roster, so I'll have to work my way into the schedule. They said I should start getting calls next week."

"Congratulations. I'm not surprised. You're excellent at your work, although I do wonder what this means for me."

Pressing my lips together, I wonder what will happen if I say he has to find a new massage therapist.

I don't.

"I'm here for you as long as you need me."

His expression shifts ever so slightly. He's not the only one in this duet... dual? Tracking the other's every facial quirk.

"It's possible I won't require your professional services much longer."

"Just let me know."

"I will."

The temperature's rising in the hall, but like a good little cockblocker, Ollie tosses cold water all over it. "Are you guys coming or what?"

CHAPTER Twenty-Four

Spencer

"TURTLES CAN LIVE TO BE 150 YEARS OLD!" OLIVER SHOUTS, bouncing on his toes as he looks over the wooden fence surrounding the ancient tortoise exhibit.

"Heaven help them," I tease.

Joselyn leans into me and whispers. "You know he's happy when he's talking too loud and jumping around. It's his tell."

"I think it's every little boy's tell."

Before we left the house for the Riverbanks Zoo and Aquarium, I had Julien my personal chef, create an entirely new, little-boy-friendly menu for the duration. Apparently, when it comes to breakfast, it includes build-your-own pancakes, whipped cream, and chocolate milk.

I'd be concerned for the health of my little guest, but after last night, I think we're all focused on making him feel like this is a fun holiday and not a refugee situation.

Joselyn told me what he has said to her about his parent's situation. In my experience, children always know more than we think they do, and even more than they share.

His mother left for her job, smiling and behaving as if everything were fine, and watching him do his best to help her feel like he believed it, struck a chord inside me. It's a desire I remember well, albeit in my case, it was ultimately a failed one.

Joselyn is right there with the encouragement. "What do you want to see first? We've got all afternoon."

"Zebras!" He bounces on his toes, running back to catch her hand.

"Hang on, let me see if I can find them." She drags out the map, and I admire her devotion to helping them.

I sent Tom the Tank with Courtney this morning. He'll make sure she arrives and returns safely, and while she's working, he's on break. I've got these two covered.

"Looks like we need to go this way." Joselyn points towards the giraffe exhibit, and Ollie takes off running.

My throat tightens when he rounds a curve up ahead and we temporarily lose sight of him. "He needs to stay with us, Joselyn. Can you tell him without frightening him?"

"Oh my God, you're right." She takes off jogging at once, and I groan as I break into a run after her. My Italian leather slip-ons are not designed for sprinting.

As soon as I round the corner, my chest relaxes. Oliver is standing on a sculpted-stucco rock formation, gazing into a pen of black panthers.

"Look at them. They're fierce. Wakanda forever!" He pumps a fist in the air, and I have no idea what he's talking about.

Joselyn reads my expression. "Seriously? You don't know *Black Panther*?"

"In case you missed it, I don't have children."

"Still, it was groundbreaking. Revolutionary. An all-black Marvel movie? It kicked ass."

"Marvel... that's the comic book franchise? I prefer more sophisticated films." I lift my chin. "He's getting too far ahead again."

She points back at me as she takes off after him. "That's where you're wrong. The Marvel cinematic universe is deeply complex. People dismiss it because of all the explosions, but the movies ask real, philosophical questions. They comment on the state of the world..."

"Yes, I'm sure they're art house quality. Would you please?" I motion towards our escaping little ward, and she shakes her gorgeous head, taking off after him.

We're finally back together at the zebra exhibit, and I can't resist. "Black on white or white on black?"

Joselyn musses Oliver's hair. "What do you think, Ollie? Are they black stripes on white or white stripes on black?"

The little boy stands on the edge of the fence watching the small horses enraptured. "I think it's white on black."

"They have so much white, though." Joselyn's nose wrinkles, and I like seeing her relaxed and happy. "My vote is for black on white."

An ostrich walks slowly between two of the striped horses, lifting its powerful legs and replacing them slowly, turning its head jerkily.

Oliver is transfixed. "They're like robots."

We watch a little longer before turning away and entering the aquatic zone, and Joselyn claps her hands. "This is where the frogs are, Ollie!"

He jumps and starts to run, but she grabs him fast. "You can't leave us in here. I need you to stay where I can see you, okay?"

The little boy blinks a few times before nodding obediently, and to his credit, he's at our side the remainder of the trip—which tells me all I need to know about how much he knows about their situation.

"I thought you didn't like frogs." I arch an eyebrow, and she waves me away.

"It's for a good cause."

We see alligators, enormous green pythons, tree frogs, and of course, an adorable koala bear baby. It's a full afternoon of walking—or in Oliver's case, running, jumping, and climbing—and by the time we're driving back to my place, he's out cold on the backseat of my "cool space car," as he calls it. Something to do with the inventor sending bored billionaires into space.

Joselyn looks up at me from where she's sitting quietly in the passenger's seat. "Good work today. You couldn't have been sweeter to him, and I think it's so important for him to see a nice man outside of the teachers at his school."

Her words provoke a sad nostalgia, but I force a smile. "It was a fun day."

She squints an eye at me. "Why do I feel like you're not telling me something?"

It's uncanny how this woman can read my expressions. I'm accustomed to watching people, reading them for any change, any indication I need to take control of the situation. It's a reflex honed after years of survival, and I'm not used to it being turned on me.

"It's possible I have more in common with Oliver than you know."

"In what way?" Her brow furrows, and concern fills her pretty eyes.

My throat constricts, and a flight response seizes me. I've cracked the door on a past I locked away long ago, and I'm not planning to revisit it. I don't know what the hell made me do it, and knowing Joselyn, she won't let it go.

Thankfully, Oliver interrupts our conversation. "Can we get ice cream?"

"Of course." I lift my chin, meeting his eyes in the rearview mirror. "I can check in with Julian and see if he can whip something up for us after dinner."

"Does Mr. Julian make your food every day?" His little brow furrows like it's a wholly new concept.

"Not every day. He usually cooks dinner three days a week, and I cover the rest with leftovers or takeout."

"Don't you know how to cook for yourself?"

I see Joselyn covering her mouth, and I shake my head. "I hate to disappoint you, but my culinary skills are rather limited."

"What's cuuli..." Oliver trails off attempting to repeat me.

"*Culinary* means *of or for cooking.*"

"So you can cook some things?"

My lips quirk. He's smart. "Actually, I make a mean grilled cheese. I can also scramble eggs..."

Joselyn's face lights up with a smile. "I'd like to try some of your scrambled eggs and grilled cheese."

"I don't make them at the same time. Honestly, I can't remember the last time I cooked anything."

We're back at the house, and Courtney's car is in the garage. We left Joselyn's ridiculous bomb of a minivan back at the apartment complex to throw the ex off our trail. I can't imagine him looking for them here, although I'd welcome a confrontation with him.

"Mom's home." Ollie sits up straighter in his seat.

I turn off the engine and close the garage before letting him out—just in case. "Tell her about the koalas, and I'll be sure Julian has ice cream on the menu for dessert."

He jumps out of the car, and Joselyn gives me a warm smile. "Thank you for this. For all of it."

"You don't have to thank me. I had a free day, and I wasn't

going to let the two of you wander around the zoo alone. That seems careless."

Her lips press into a line like she's fighting a grin, and I'm not sure if she believes me. It doesn't matter. I need to know if the private investigator I hired turned up anything on Ozzy Clayton. I have no intention of letting that guy get away with what he did to her.

CHAPTER Twenty-Five

Joselyn

"TREE FROGS CAN'T SWIM." OLLIE IS SITTING ON THE COUCH ACROSS from Spencer with his little legs crossed. "They have to get water through their skin. They use mucus on their feet to help them climb."

Spencer looks like end-of-the-day-CEO slash sex-god in dress pants and a white shirt unbuttoned at the neck. His sleeves are rolled up exposing his lined forearms dusted with dark hair, but for all his overt, alpha masculinity, his nose curls at Ollie's fun fact. "Not sure I like the sound of that."

I pinch my nose so I don't laugh.

Chartreuse is perched on the lid of her box on the coffee table while Ollie finishes up his Häagen Daz "Caramel Cone" ice cream. Julien might not have made it himself, but he nuked it for fifteen seconds, making the ingredients all squishy and warm inside the frozen vanilla…

One bite, and I'm pretty sure my eyes rolled back in my head.

I know my toes curled.

Spencer is having a tumbler of what looks like scotch, and they're watching some nature show on Netflix with the sound off.

Ollie scrapes the last of his ice cream, nodding. "They can climb pretty much anything moist."

"Did somebody just say *moist*?" I make a face popping into the room in my *Unsolved Mysteries* pajamas. "You know *moist* is Number 2 in Buzzfeed's Top 12 grossest words."

Ollie sits up, scooping Chartreuse off her perch and moving away from me on the couch. "What's Number 1?"

"I'll tell you when you're older." I take his *moist* bowl off the mahogany table so it doesn't leave a ring. I'm betting the table is worth something outrageous like ten thousand dollars—like everything else in this mini-museum. "I'll take this to the kitchen."

"What are you wearing?" Spencer's tone is critical as he narrows his eyes at my black flannel pajamas with the bright yellow show logo all over them.

"Only my favorite PJs," I announce proudly, doing a little turn. "*Unsolved Mysteries...*"

"Why would anybody have PJs for that show?" Ollie groans falling back. "It's boring."

When I turn back, a smile curls Spencer's lips. "They're... not entirely unexpected."

"Are you two slob-shaming me?" I put a hand on my hip not caring one bit that I'm comfortable and completely covered in flannel. "I feel slob-shamed. I'm taking this bowl to the kitchen."

I leave the room with my nose in the air, and I hear Ollie behind me muttering. "Women. So much drama."

The beleaguered tone in his little voice almost makes me cackle. Instead I rinse the bowl in the oversized stainless-steel sink and place it in the dishwasher. On my way back, I slow down when I hear them talking.

"You seem to handle them pretty well." Spencer is being kind, and I smile. "The way you treat your mother shows the kind of man you are."

Ollie studies Chartreuse walking on his fingers. "You're nice to my mom and Aunt Sly. That means you're good, right?"

My nose wrinkles, and I wish I could see Spencer's expression. I can't, and I don't want to interrupt them. I'm stuck in the hallway, chewing my thumb as I listen.

"Are you worried about being good?" Spencer's question is easy, like he and Ollie are old friends.

"Sometimes." Ollie's voice is quiet. "Mom says I'm good."

"You seem like a good guy to me. I think you worry about your mom."

"She works really hard to take care of us. My dad doesn't help her."

"What do you think about that?"

Ollie tilts his little head to the side and looks straight at Spencer. "I think it sucks. My friends have good dads, and I don't. I think it means I shouldn't have kids."

To his credit, Spencer doesn't answer right away. It's quiet for the passage of several heartbeats, and I imagine him thinking about what our little friend said.

"I understand why you say that." Spencer's voice is grave, and my heart hurts.

"You do?"

"I do." He clears his throat, and I hear him shift in the leather chair. His voice grows calm, and I recognize now it's a defense mechanism. "I think we all have the potential to be good or bad, even your dad. From what I've seen of you with your mother, I think it's far more likely you'll be a good dad."

Ollie moves around, sitting back on the couch where I can see him better, and when he lifts his chin to the television, the tension has left his brow. My eyes warm, and I want to rush in and kiss Spencer's face.

I might even beg for it.

Instead, I clear my throat to announce my return. "Who's up for some *Unsolved Mysteries*?"

"No!" Ollie groans, turning to face me. "We're watching *Our Planet*. They're doing a show about tree frogs."

"You know everything about tree frogs." I take my place as far from him and his creepy pet as possible. "Let's watch something not gross."

"You know everything about *Unsolved Mysteries*."

"That's not even possible for anybody." I shake my head at him. "If it were, they'd have to change the name of the show."

Ollie exhales heavily like he's so disgusted. "Tree frogs don't hurt anybody."

"Unless you eat them!"

Courtney sticks her head out of her room. "Hey, Olls? Did you finish your homework? I told Mr. Peterson you'd keep up with your assignments."

"I finished them, Mom!" He calls, studying his frog stepping from his fingers with careful, shaky moves.

I don't know if she's growing on me, but Chartreuse *is* fascinating to watch.

"Okay, ten-minute warning. It's bedtime." Courtney lifts her chin. "Hey, thanks again for today, guys. I'm turning in. Early day tomorrow."

"Night, Court," I call, standing beside the sofa. "I guess we should turn in as well. I don't know about you two, but I'm beat."

I glance over to where Spencer seems lost in thought. He's so handsome, I wonder what would happen if I bent my rules, especially in view of how amazing he was just now with Oliver.

I'm about to say something along those lines when he stands.

A lock of dark hair has fallen over his eye, and he pushes it back, his heavy stainless watch gleaming in the dim light.

"I'll let you all get ready for bed. Today was a fun diversion. I hadn't been to the zoo in years." He pauses as he passes me, lifting the collar of my pajama top and giving me a ghost of a smile. "I'm glad you feel comfortable here."

I want to catch his hand and bring it to my lips. I want to find what he's hiding from me, from everyone, and shelter it. He gave me the tiniest peek in the car today. I want to tell him, *You are safe with me…*

Warmth aches in my chest for everything he's done, from this safe place to the ice cream to the reassuring chat with Ollie. I want to tell him so many things, but he doesn't allow it.

"Sleep well." His tone is final as he turns away, climbing the stairs to his tower.

I need to get this box out of my car. Elliot's text is in my face, and I growl as I tap out a reply.

I'm helping Courtney with her son. The last thing I want is to see Idiot Flick.

Send me the address of where you are, and I'll be there in ten minutes.

How can he know he'll be here in ten minutes? Either way, I text him Spencer's address. ***Tell me when you're here, and I'll come out to meet you.***

Gray dots float on the screen, and his asshole reply appears. ***I can meet you at the door like a civilized person.***

My jaw clenches and I can't even resist. ***You are not a civilized person.***

He doesn't reply, and I go to my room, stomping and huffing. I don't want to see his ass. I want him to drive off a cliff and his car to explode.

None of that happens, and ten minutes later, the doorbell rings. "I've got it!"

It's just Ollie, Tom the Tank, and me at the house today, and I take off to the front entrance. Tom materializes between me and it like some kind of phantom, and I hop back with a little yelp.

"How did you do that?" I put a hand on my chest, breathless.

His brow lowers, and he doesn't answer my question. "Are you expecting someone?"

"Yeah." I pat him on the shoulder. "Possibly my least favorite person on the planet, so if you feel the urge to beat the shit out of him, don't fight it on my account."

His brow lowers, and I realize this guy has no sense of humor. None.

I'm not sure I'm going to take back what I just said, though.

Pulling the heavy door open, I'm pissed when I see Elliot standing there in an Armani suit looking as polished as he always did. His light brown hair is carefully styled, and he looks around at the yard and driveway.

"What's Courtney doing here?" He turns back, his full lips twisted in a scowl. "Is this some kind of live-in masseuse type of situation?"

No, asshole, I made that mistake with you.

The fact he even uses that derogatory term says a lot, but I won't let him get to me. "We're staying with a friend. What's so urgent you had to give it to me right now?"

I'm impressed by how unaffected I sound... How unaffected I am by his cheating presence. He has effectively killed any love I might have had for him all those months ago.

"Nadine boxed up everything you left behind when you stormed out." He lifts a small box and holds it out to me.

Her name, the scenario he describes... I hate that it hurts, but I smile through it. "You didn't have to do this."

"Yeah, well, she said it was a good idea. No need for you to show up unexpectedly wanting to claim something that was yours."

His phrasing roils my stomach. Nadine can fuck right off if she thinks I would ever want this idiot back. I manage a little laugh at the absurdity of the suggestion. "That would never have happened."

"Still, here it is." He shoves the box towards me, and as my luck would have it, a black Tesla pulls into the driveway right behind his Mercedes.

My ex glances over, and when he sees Spencer stepping out of the luxury car, he turns to me with a sneer. "This isn't about Courtney. This is about you." Lifting his chin, he gives me a slimy wink. "Is this a new record?"

Heat burns in my face. "I don't know what you're talking about."

"We were together three weeks before you moved in—has it even been four weeks since we split up?"

"It's been longer." I shove my hair behind my ear. "Even if it hadn't, I knew him before I met you."

"I see you found a new sugar daddy to take care of you."

My body flashes hot then cold. "That is not what's happening. He's helping Courtney and Oliver—"

"And you just happen to be along for the ride." Elliot lifts his chin, grinning like a fucking Cheshire cat. "Or is he getting the ride?"

"You asshole." My fist tightens, my voice a heated whisper. "You're nothing but a lying cheater."

"And you're a gold-digging slut."

Spencer walks up to where we're standing, and as always, he reads my face quickly. He can tell at once something is wrong.

"Can I help you?" He takes a step forward, partially blocking me from the idiot.

"Nah, man." Elliot tosses his chin at me. "I was just saying goodbye. Enjoy her."

Elliot turns and saunters to his Mercedes. The door slams, the engine roars, and he squeals tires getting out of the driveway.

My eyes close in the wake of his departure, and I fight back a tear. How could I have been such a fool?

Strong hands brace my upper arms, and I blink up to see Spencer studying my face. "Who was that man?"

Shaking my head, I turn, carrying the box into the house. "Just somebody I used to know."

I pass Tom waiting with both fists clenched at his side. I'm sure he had a front-row seat to my humiliation.

Spencer gives him a nod, following me inside. "Is he a client?"

"He *was* a client." I put the box on the formal dining room table, wondering what in the world I left that Nadine was so worried I might go back to get.

Glad to know she's feeling secure.

Sarcasm.

"Hey." Spencer catches my arm, pulling me so I have to face him.

His dark brow is lowered. His hazel eyes are stormy and full of protective worry.

He looks like a man who cares, a man who would sit up at night, even if he was tired, to comfort a scared little boy and help him feel better. He looks like a man who would figure out a way to get ice cream on a moment's notice.

He looks like a man who knows how to be good…

Why isn't he?

"I don't want you seeing him anymore."

My teeth clench, and an old bitterness tightens my throat. "Are you saying I can't treat male clients?"

"I'm saying I don't like that guy. If he's a client, I don't want you treating him."

"Maybe you don't have the right to say that to me."

His eyes flash with anger, and he steps forward, jaw tight. "Maybe not, but I'm saying it."

"You know who else said I couldn't treat male clients? Fucking Elliot."

"I'm not saying you can't treat male clients. I'm saying you can't treat *that* male client. He's an asshole. He made you cry, and if I see him again, I'll punch his lights out."

We're both breathing fast, our bodies so close the heat radiates between us. I'm ready to collapse into his arms when a soft throat-clearing breaks the spell.

"If you're all done here." Tom the Tank stands at the doorway, seeming embarrassed and satisfied at the same time.

It's an odd combination.

"I'm done." Turning on my heel, I storm all the way to my room and shut the door.

When I open my eyes again, it's dark.

Grabbing the clock, I can't believe it's after nine. I came back here, curled up in my bed, and cried until I fell asleep—all over that idiot and his harpy girlfriend, which is so dumb.

So, so dumb.

The box he brought is sitting on the floor beside my bed, and I consider taking it outside and burning it. I don't want anything they've touched.

Ollie is snoring in his bed across the room, and I creep as quietly as possible out the door. I'm not starving, but I'm awake, and I didn't have dinner. Maybe I can find some of that ice cream Julien bought. It's one of the only two things that could make me feel better right now.

Creeping towards the kitchen, I stop short when I hear the clink of ice against crystal. Spencer is sitting in the same leather chair he was in last night when I watched him be so amazing with Oliver.

Again, he's in a dress shirt—light blue this time—with the

sleeves rolled up past his elbows. His hair is a delicious mess of dark waves dropping over his dark brow. Scruff covers his square jaw, and he seems perplexed. On the large screen attached to the wall is that nature show he and Ollie were watching, still on silent.

"Spencer?" My voice is quiet, and I walk closer to where he's sitting, seeming lost.

At the sound of my voice, he straightens. "I'm sorry. I thought you were asleep. Did I wake you?"

My lips press together, and I shake my head. "No. I'm on the quest for some more of that ice cream. Or something."

I shrug and exhale a laugh. He doesn't smile.

He studies me like I'm something he can't understand, like I'm something he's never seen before. With an exhale and a shake of his head, it's gone.

"I'm sure there's ice cream left in the freezer. I told Julien to get enough to last a week."

I take a step towards the kitchen, but then I stop. It's late, and we're both tired. He's had a glass of scotch… it seems like as good a time as any to ask.

"Yesterday you told me you understood Ollie. What did you mean?"

His expression is closed, and I feel certain he's not going to tell me. The room is quiet, and the tall, gold-faced grandfather clock beside the bookcase ticks loudly. My eyes flick to the television screen as a school of brilliantly colored fish swish past.

Nothing happens.

Still, I wait, hoping he'll tell me, preparing for him not to, wishing he would, wishing he would trust me enough to let me in those walls again.

My shoulders drop, and when I've decided it's a lost cause, he speaks. "My father was abusive." It's a quiet statement of fact, but my breath stills.

I don't know what to say, and he continues.

"He beat my mother so many times, I lost count." His expression is neutral as he tilts the crystal back and forth. "No matter how hard I begged her, she would never leave him, so I thought I could protect her myself. That's when he started beating me."

His eyes focus on the brilliant Persian rug on the floor, and he lifts the tumbler to take a small sip. He seems so far away.

"How old were you?"

"I was Ollie's age when they took me away from them."

I think about what he's told me, what I know about him, and I'm confused. "They took you away from your father? The antiques legend? I thought he left you all this money..."

"That would be my foster father, Drake Carrollton. My real father was a drunk abuser named Daniel Keane. My birth name was Spencer Keane. Drake had it legally changed."

Sadness tightens my chest, and I have no words.

He continues calmly, like he's reading from a history book. "For two years, I would have black eyes, unexplained bruises, cuts... The county finally stepped in when he hurt me so badly, I had to go to the ER."

Closing my eyes, I realize. "The scar on your back."

Hazel eyes flicker to mine, and they're so deep, I'm not sure what I'm seeing. I only know this is sacred ground we're treading. He's taking me into a hidden place.

"Drake Carrollton wasn't a good man either. He wasn't even a legend as much as he was a hoarder. He was a dusty old dragon who lived for finding and amassing treasure. He procured me because he was smart enough to know he needed an heir, and I suppose he saw some value in having a helper as he got older. No love was lost between us."

His eyes move to the shelves filled with what I'd always assumed were treasures he'd collected. I want to argue with him, to try and say he must be wrong. Instead, I listen, dropping to my knees beside him as he escorts me through this dusty, dark place in his past, this shadowy corner where the ghosts live.

"He taught me all about this stuff, taught me the worth of every piece. When he died, I was able to catalog his estate and turn it into even more money than he had when he was alive." Spencer places the glass on the end table. "He never traveled; he never lived his life. He stayed in his cave, clutching his gold like it would ever love him. All these precious things."

"Is that why they mean nothing to you?" My voice is so small.

"They're only things, Sin. Forgotten pieces of junk."

"Sometimes they're more. Sometimes they have meaning—heirlooms, wedding rings..."

He looks down at me and lifts his empty hand. "Sometimes."

With the tips of his fingers, he touches the edge of my hair along my cheek. I tilt my head to the side and give him a small smile. I want to comfort him if only he would let me.

"I didn't have anything else to do, so this became my life."

"You could have more if you wanted." Warmth fills my tone, warmth and longing. "You could have love, a family..."

His expression hardens. "My father was an abuser, which means I'll likely be one too. I don't know if that capability is in me. Perhaps it's not, but I'm not willing to find out."

"You're not an abuser. I've been with you; I've seen how you are with the people you care about. I've seen how you are with me, with Ollie."

"I have my share of dark thoughts. Possibly more than my share—"

"Of *thoughts*? Everyone has thoughts, Spencer. I have thoughts of wanting to kill Ozzy for threatening my friend, for menacing me, for ruining his little boy's life. Today I actually fantasized throwing that box in Elliot's stupid face."

His chin lifts, and he exhales a little *ah*. "That was Elliot. Good to know."

"My point is, thoughts aren't actions. You would never hurt me."

"Perhaps. I've never allowed myself to be in a situation I couldn't control."

The tone in his voice sends a tingle through my stomach, and I'm ready to fight for this man.

"You wouldn't. The beast never hurt Beauty. Hades worshipped Persephone—"

A grim smile curls his full lips. He pushes the dark hair off his brow and stands slowly. "It's a good analogy. I know the darkness in myself, what I can be, what I've wanted to do. I'm not capable of a normal life."

"How would you know if you never let yourself try?" Pushing off the floor, I stand beside him, holding his arm.

"I know." He pats my hand. "Goodnight, Joselyn."

My jaw drops as he crosses the room to the stairs, climbing slowly to his suite alone. I watch him disappear into the darkness, like he's done every night we've been here.

So respectful.

So distant.

So cold.

Only, I understand now, and he's dead wrong if he thinks I'm giving up on him, especially now that I know what I'm fighting against.

CHAPTER Twenty-Six

Spencer

Having them here is not how I thought it would be.

Of course, that's assuming I thought it through before I took one look at Joselyn's battered face and lost my shit.

It was an impulsive decision, and now her presence one floor down, one bedroom below mine, is a constant temptation. At the same time, Oliver is a constant reminder.

He's a tiny skeleton key slipping in and unlocking a lifetime's worth of memories. I've felt everything he's feeling. I'm well acquainted with all of his fears. I faced the dread he's struggling with, only he's in the very early stages of figuring out what it means, how his future will go.

I know where that lonely road leads. I know the questions he's asking himself. In my case, I never had anyone to show me what real love and sacrifice could look like. I went from a home where my mother chose a monster over me and herself.

Then I lived with a bitter old man, a different type of monster, who clutched his valuables to himself like they would keep him alive.

Oliver won't be like me. He has his mother and Joselyn to show him love and teach him a different way to live.

Stopping at the credenza, I brace my hands on the countertop and grip the wood. My shoulders are tense, and I drop my head, exhaling heavily. Not only did I revisit Daniel, I revisited Drake. My two dads, both with names starting with the letter *D* like some sick joke.

In those days, I had hope like Oliver. When the woman from the state introduced me to my foster dad, I thought I was going to be like one of those children in the C.S. Lewis stories.

Drake was an old professor type with a gray beard and disheveled gray hair. He pointed a long, crooked finger at me like I was a Limoges or a Qing dynasty vase.

He picked me out like he picked out all of his possessions, after much careful analysis and research. He ascertained I was intelligent and quiet. He taught me everything he knew, then he died.

He left me richer, and more broken than he ever was.

"You're not broken, you're only badly bruised." Her soft voice lights my entire body like the touch of a spark.

Joselyn is beside me, sliding her hand over mine, gripping my wrist as her body draws closer to mine.

"What are you doing here?" My voice is rough.

"I'm here for you." Slim fingers thread in the back of my hair, and my eyes slide closed.

"Joselyn…" It's half whisper, half groan. "I said I would respect your boundaries."

"You said you wouldn't kiss me again unless I begged you." She rises on her tiptoes, and her lips graze the shell of my ear. "Please, Mr. Carrollton, please kiss me."

Inhaling slowly, I turn to see her standing in front of me, so inviting. She's wearing a black tank top that barely covers those luscious tits I crave and her silly *Unsolved Mysteries* pajama bottoms. Her red hair is in a loose band over her shoulder.

She's the best thing I've ever seen.

I actually smile. "You followed me to my bedroom."

"I've been here before."

Placing my hands on her shoulders, I slide my palms up and down her creamy, soft skin. "You're bending your rules?"

"What rules?" She blinks, giving me a naughty little smile. "You're the one with all the rules. I'm just trying to keep up."

My walls are still down. I haven't had a chance to rebuild my defenses, and she's here, inside the gates, moving in front of me with so much heat and warmth and seduction.

I'm never vulnerable. I'm cold and distant, and she's standing on my mountain daring me to throw her off… or take her in.

"What are you doing to me?" I hear the change in my voice.

"I'm waiting for you to keep your promise." Her hands slide to my chest, and she lowers to her knees. As she drops, her palms follow, moving to my waist, to my legs, to the front of my pants.

Her face is at my cock, which has perked up and is ready to join the party. The last time she was in this position, she talked into it like a microphone.

And I laughed.

Again, a smile pulls at my lips. "What promise was that?"

"You said if I begged…" Her eyes return to my pants, and her nails trace the outline of my erection. It makes me groan.

"Get up here." Reaching down, I grip her upper arms again and pull her to me. "You want me to kiss you now?"

Our noses touch, and she's breathing fast. She nods quickly, blinking from my eyes to my lips and back again. Her breasts rise and fall, sheathed only in thin black cotton. Her nipples are tiny points piercing the fabric.

She exhales a reply. "Yes, please."

My lips cover hers at once, consuming her request. Releasing my grip on her arms, I slide my hands up to her neck, to her jaw, holding her face securely. Her mouth opens, and I sweep my tongue inside, tasting sweet caramel ice cream.

Pulling her lips with mine, I kiss her cheek, her nose. "You had some ice cream?"

My lips travel to her eyelids, which are closed.

"I had a bite..." Her voice is breathy. "Then I came for what I really wanted."

Leaning down, I kiss her again. This time, I drive my fingers into her hair, tilting her head so I can consume her more fully. Her head drops back, but her body presses forward against mine. She grips my wrists with her hands, exhaling a soft moan as she pulls me closer.

Only one way can I get closer.

Our tongues curl, and I nip at her upper lip with my teeth. She makes me hungry. She makes me feral. She makes me want to mark her body with my teeth, my hands.

Lifting my head, I meet her eyes, now navy with desire. "I want to fuck you, Sin. Can I?"

"Yes." She doesn't hesitate.

Catching the bottom of her tank top, I lift it over her head, allowing those luscious girls to spill out. I want to drop to my knees, but I lift her into my arms instead, carrying her to my bed, where she should always be.

I'm not analyzing that statement too closely right now.

"Come here." She reaches for me, and out of curiosity, I stop what I'm doing to comply. "You don't need this." She unbuttons my shirt starting at the top, following the progress of her fingers with her lips against my heated skin.

When she gets to the bottom, she slides her tongue over my

stomach, kissing a line around the waist of my pants and sending my dick to full mast.

"Jesus," I hiss, closing my eyes. I place my hands beside her ears, threading my fingers in her hair. "I want to be inside you when I come."

My thigh muscles twitch when she cups my cock with her palm over my pants. "Sorry, guy. You heard the boss."

A deep laugh rolls up from my belly, and I grip her under the arms, pulling her to her knees on the side of the bed, placing her face directly across from mine.

Her blue eyes sparkle with horny mischief, and I'm smiling. I'm actually fucking smiling after that trip through my macabre past.

My eyes are on her, and she's blinking up at me. "Don't overthink it."

"Too late." I'm not sure if my words are meant for her or for me.

I've thought about this so many times, and it's too late for turning back. My shirt is off, and I pull her to me. Her breasts flatten against my hard chest, and I feel her hands moving fast, working to unfasten my pants and push them down my hips.

Stepping back, I quickly finish the job, shoving them to the side, and going to the nightstand to grab a condom from the drawer. Ripping it open, I hesitate when I see her perched on the edge of the bed watching me, licking her lips.

"God, Sin, where did you come from?"

"A little farther south of you." I approach the bed, and she rises onto her knees.

While I grabbed the condom, she removed her pajama pants. Now she's leaning forward, back arched, lifting her gorgeous tits up to me. Her mouth is luscious and tempting, her red hair falls around her shoulders, and her creamy little ass is soft as a peach.

Normally, I wouldn't know where to begin. Tonight, I catch

her by the chin and kiss her slowly, growing firmer as my need flames hotter. I hold her waist, moving her onto her back on the bed, kissing her jaw, her neck, her shoulder as I make my way lower.

Leaning down, I run my nose along the crease of her thigh, teasing her bare pussy with my breath. She moans and slides her ankles together.

"First, my lady." Placing my hands on her thighs, I spread them apart, leaning down to drag my tongue slowly over her clit.

"Spencer," she gasps, her fingers shooting into the sides of my hair. "Oh, God…"

Her hips are quick to follow my tongue, and her fingers curl at my ears, growing more frantic as my tongue moves quicker.

"Oh, yes…" She hiccups, and I slide my palms along the insides of her thighs.

Her body spasms, and I can feel when the orgasm starts to rise. I feel her muscles flexing and trembling, I see her ass bucking. Her moans turn to little gasps, and I smile, moving my mouth away just before she climaxes.

"Oh, no…" She moans a complaint, but her fingers crawl along my sides, pulling me down to her body as I line up my dick and drive all the way into her clenching core.

For a moment, I can't move. It feels too good. It's like finding heaven. My forehead drops against her neck, and I inhale deeply, flowers mixed with sweat and sex. She truly is sinful.

"You feel so good."

Her ass bucks, and she whines, struggling to make me fuck her.

I don't make her wait.

I start to move, knowing I'm so close to the edge, I won't last long.

My eyes close, and I'm somewhere I've never been. I'm having sex with a woman, and I don't have her pinned to the wall, stomach first. I'm not pulling her hair, keeping her face turned away from mine so I don't see her.

Lifting my shoulders, I look down at her. A line pierces her brow, and her eyes are squinted. She's grinding hard, pulling my dick as much as I'm pushing. Her hands grip my ass, and her back arches.

Gorgeous tits rise to meet me, and I pull one into my mouth. I suck on her nipple, teasing the hardened peak with my teeth. She moans, moving faster. I wrap my arms around her back and move to my knees, drawing her onto my lap without ever losing contact.

Her arms are on my shoulders now, and she smiles down at me as her hair spills around us like fire, like the sparks from that blowtorch, like the chemistry we've always shared.

"Mm… I like this." She's riding me now, sliding forward on my cock.

A dimple is in her cheek, and I lean up to kiss it. The movement sends me deeper into her tight, clenching heat, and I can't hold back anymore.

"I'm coming, Sin." My chin drops and my hands grip her ass.

I'm moving her now, slamming her harder as the orgasm takes hold of my brain, as sensation rushes through my bloodstream, centering in my pelvis, driving into my cock, pulsing with so much force, I forget where I am.

"God, yes," I cough, dropping my head forward as my soul spills into hers.

This is more than scratching an itch or satisfying a primal urge. I don't remember anyone but her. It's only her. Has there ever been anyone else?

Her arms wrap around my shoulders, and I feel her clenching as she finishes. I hear her fluttered breaths, and I know she's with me in this place, melting with me.

Sliding to the side, I dispose of the condom before returning to pull her into my arms. I'm weary to my core from this night.

Our fingers thread, and I'm not ready to say all the things in my mind. I'm not ready to look at what I've done and decide what it means.

I only want to hold her and sleep.

A shaft of light streams in from the crack in my heavy, gray velvet curtains. I'm lying on my side in my massive bed, and last night comes back in a rush.

I turn, sliding my hand across the mattress, over cool sheets...

I'm reaching, searching. My throat tightens until...

My fingers encounter her soft skin.

Rolling over, I blink a few times at the woman beside me in this bed. Confusing warmth floods my chest, and a smile lifts my lips.

She's fucking adorable. Her hand is tucked under her cheek, and a wavy lock of dark red hair falls over her eye. She's asleep in my bed. She didn't sneak out again.

Her skin is flawlessly white. Lifting my hand, I trace my finger along the top of her shoulder, and it rises slightly at my touch. Her blue eyes blink open, and when they meet mine, she smiles.

I feel the smile still on my lips, and I push into a sitting position. "How did you sleep?"

She pushes into a sitting position as well, that fiery hair dropping around her shoulders. A curl loops under her nipple, and my cock is ready to go.

"Your bed is very comfortable." She props an elbow on the top of the pillows and traces her finger down my chin. "How do you shave in there?"

I capture her slim hand in mine, holding it to my lips for a kiss. "Very carefully."

She scoots closer, cupping my face in her hand and pressing her forehead to my cheek. I wrap my arm around her, turning us so I'm looking down into her face.

Her eyes hold mine, and I trace a finger along her brow, down her cheek. I've handled priceless heirlooms, one-of-a-kind artifacts, last pieces of million-dollar collections...

"Joselyn..." My voice is gentle, but I don't know what comes next.

These are uncharted waters, and I don't make deals I can't predict. How do I say what I've never said?

"Spencer..." Her voice lowers, and she's teasing, mocking my serious tone.

Our eyes meet, and she blinks impishly. Her full lips press together like she's suppressing a laugh. I drop my chin, exhaling a groan, and I'm ready to flip her over and spank her creamy, round ass.

Then bite it.

But first, I cover her lips with mine. My hand travels higher, cupping her breast. I'm gearing up for another round when a sharp voice rings through the house like a fucking police siren.

"Mom! Mom! Aunt Sly's missing!" Ollie's feet thud loudly up the hall then pause, almost like he remembers. "Mr. Spencer! Mr. Spencer..."

At the first pounding of his seven-year-old feet on the stairs, we're out of the bed, scrambling for clothes.

"Holy shit!" Joselyn's eyes are wide, and she has those flannel PJ pants on before I've even located my Jockeys.

A door flies open below, and Courtney stops his upward progress. "Ollie, stop! Don't go up there. Tell me what's happening!"

"Aunt Sly hasn't been in her bed. Get Mr. Spencer. Get Superhero Tom!"

"Calm down, and let's see what's happening."

They descend the stairs, and a fully clothed Joselyn skips across the room to plant a kiss on my mouth. "I'll take care of this."

I catch her before she skips away, pulling her to me. Her chin lifts, and light twinkles in her blue eyes. She's happier than I've seen her in a month, and dread pricks my chest.

Cupping her face with my hand, I slide my thumb over her full bottom lip. She's so beautiful. Leaning down, I kiss her. I inhale her soft hair, and I hold her forehead to my cheek. Her hands clutch my arms, and I have to let her go.

I hold a little longer, finding it difficult to take my hands away.

But I do.

My lips are warm from her kiss, and I turn to my armoire as she jogs down the stairs.

CHAPTER Twenty-Seven

Joselyn

"SO YOU FELL ASLEEP WITH MR. SPENCER?" COURTNEY MURMURS, nudging me in the ribs as we stand in front of the coffee machine in the kitchen.

Ollie is at the table sprinkling walnut pieces on top of the whipped cream he sprayed on top of the pure maple syrup he poured all over the massive chocolate chip pancakes Julien made for him.

Again.

"Ollie's going to have diabetes by the time we leave here." I nod towards the table, ignoring her elbow and her question.

"Stop changing the subject. What happened?"

I glance over my shoulder. Spencer always seems to materialize as soon as I start talking about him. Like the devil. "I'll tell you later."

Taking my cup, I walk slowly to where Ollie's sitting,

glancing up the dark hallway and wondering when he might make an appearance. My heart is hammering, but I have to act normal. No fawning or crowding.

His eyes were so stormy when he kissed me. We covered a lot of ground last night, and I don't want him to throw those walls back up.

"I'd better get going." Court sighs, joining us at the table. "What are you guys doing today?"

"I thought we might check out CMT. They're doing *The Wizard of Oz*, and it looks so cute."

"Cute?" Ollie's nose wrinkles. "I want to play Roblox."

"We're not sitting in the house all day while you play games after eating your body weight in chocolate chip pancakes and syrup." Also, I'm hoping I might sneak my hand into Spencer's during the show.

"CMT… That's the marionette theater?" Court drops her keys in her bag, and I nod. "Do you need any money or anything?"

"I think I've got it."

"Superhero" Tom enters as we're talking. He pauses at the coffee machine, but when he sees Courtney packing, he comes to where we're talking. "Are you leaving for work?"

"Yeah, but you really don't have to follow me. I shouldn't have any problems getting from my car into the building."

"I'm ready when you are."

My eyebrows rise, and I know this guy doesn't deviate from any rules. I guess Spencer would have his balls if he did.

"Ollie and I are planning to hit the CMT this morning, but maybe Spencer can go with us again? If he doesn't have to work, of course."

Tom frowns down at me. "Mr. Carrollton just left for the airport. Stay here until I get back, and I'll accompany you."

My heart drops with my jaw. "He… left for the airport?"

"He'll be in Boston until Sunday morning. I was just getting my instructions for while he's gone."

Courtney's dark eyes flash to mine. "He didn't tell you?"

"He must not have wanted to disturb us." Although, I was dressed and running downstairs before him.

Heat climbs the back of my neck, and I swallow the knot in my throat. Courtney is watching me, so I force a smile. I blink my eyes, doing my very best to seem unaffected, rather than confused and hurt he left town for two days without a word after last night.

God, I've got to find us a new place to live.

I step over and give her a quick hug. "Have a great day. I'm hitting the shower. When Tom gets back, we'll head to the park."

Skipping out of the room, I dash a stubborn tear off my cheek with the heel of my hand. I am not crying over him. I push into the bathroom and switch on the hot water, stripping out of my clothes and throwing them in a ball on the other side of the room.

Grabbing the shampoo, I step into the steaming heat. I want his seductive scent of sandalwood and leather off me. I want it out of my hair.

I'm rebuilding my own resolve.

We'll see who begs next time.

"I liked it when the lion jumped out, and all the other puppets started shaking," Ollie snorts, skipping along beside me and swinging my hand. "And the hot air balloon looked real. I think it was a real balloon!"

"Maybe..." I'm not telling him otherwise. "I liked Glinda."

"And the flying monkeys!"

I'm glad he's having another happy day. It's been years since I visited the CMT, back when it was in the Vista, closer to

Spencer's home. The new, larger space in the park means the productions are more elaborate.

We're walking through the park, along the red-brick canal path. Tom is never out of sight, but he gives us space. I almost want to call him to catch up and join us, but I don't. I let him do his job.

"Can we get a hot dog for lunch?" Ollie takes off running towards the vendor as I slide my phone out of my pocket to check for any missed calls or texts.

The face is blank, and my heart sinks a little more.

"Not doing this." I promised myself I wouldn't think about him again.

Shoving the device into my pocket, I hurry to catch up with my little friend waiting at the hot dog vendor.

One giant pretzel and a coney dog later, we're in the backseat of Tom's black town car headed back to our safe house. Staring out the window, I notice signs listing apartments for lease, and I wonder how long we're supposed to be in this holding pattern at Spencer's house.

Ollie has fallen asleep on the arm rest, and I slide forward to where the glass divider is lowered.

"Hey, Tom?" He lifts his chin to meet my eyes. "Did they give you an end date for this job?"

His brow furrows. "We're taking it on a week-by-week basis."

"A week!" My voice goes high, and I shake my head.

He's got another thing coming if he thinks I'm staying past Sunday.

"Is something wrong, Miss Winthrop?"

"You can call me Joselyn… or Sly. That's what everybody else calls me." Shaking my head, I scoot back in the seat. "I have to talk to Courtney. We need to find our own place."

He doesn't answer. We're at the house, and I pick at a loose thread on my jeans, thinking about how Spencer swooped in and took charge, installing us here like helpless children.

I was shaken and scared, and I let him.

I'm more angry than scared now.

After dinner, when I present it to Courtney, she does not cooperate. "He's helping us stay safe until we can find a better apartment." She says it like it's the most normal thing.

"But for how long? We can't stay here forever, Court." I'm walking around the room, feeling hurt and mad and angry. "He's not even related to us. He's not your boyfriend or mine..."

Her lips press into a frown. "You're upset about him leaving. I get it. But you haven't started working yet, and we can't go back to the old place. This is the longest I've gone without hearing from Ozzy, and I confess, I'm scared. I know he's problematic, but I like Spencer. I like the extra security."

For the first time, I see the tension in her eyes, and I feel bad for pressing the matter.

"Maybe we could stay at a hotel for a few days. I think some of those places rent rooms by the month."

"None we could afford." Ollie's splashing and making noises from the jacuzzi tub, and she stands. "I'd better check on him before he makes a big mess. I have a few appointments in the morning, but we can hop online and see what's out there if it makes you feel better. For now, I think we should stay put."

"I'll start looking in the morning. Maybe it'll help us narrow down our choices."

She smiles, hugging my shoulders. "I'm glad to look."

Tightness is in my stomach, and I head to my shared room with Ollie. Who says I can't start the search right now? Pulling out my otherwise useless phone, I open the app and start swiping.

My phone buzzing with a text startles me awake. I fell asleep last night searching for apartments, and I discovered Courtney was right. I need to get working.

Lifting my phone, I hold my breath… Is it him?

It's not Spencer. My chest sinks, but it quickly rises when I see it's my first appointment at Palmetto.

They send me a cool little client dossier. Mrs. Wolfe is a geriatric patient recovering from a hip replacement. Her upper body and shoulders are tense from the physical therapy…

So nice not to have to collect all this information myself. I can plan my course of treatment and be ready when I see her Monday.

Momentary disappointment forgotten… sort of…

I choose to focus on the positive angle of preparing for a new client. Mrs. Wolfe sounds like a nice old lady and not a maniac who'll chase me into a women's restroom then down twenty-two flights of stairs. The memory gives me a shiver.

Hopping out of bed, I quickly put on leggings and a sweatshirt. Stopping at the mirror, I sweep my hair into a ponytail. The bruise on my cheek is a faint yellow now, and the cut is healed. Courtney stopped bandaging it shortly after we came here.

Perhaps that's why he could leave without a second thought. With the visible reminder of what happened gone, he forgot why he was so concerned in the first place.

"Nope," I say out loud to my reflection. "Still not going there."

"Going where?" Ollie's voice is a whine from across the room. "Aunt Sly, my stomach hurts."

I go quickly to put my hand on his forehead. "You don't have a fever. Do you feel nauseated? Crampy?"

He rolls to his side with his little brow tight. "I want my mom."

"Your mom had to work this morning, babe." Dropping to

my knees, I try to smooth his bangs off his face, but he turns his face to the pillow. "She'll be back after lunch. Want me to see if I can find you something?"

"I'm not hungry."

Chewing my lip, I want to say it's because he ate all the junk food in the world yesterday, starting with breakfast, but I don't. If he really is sick, I'll be eating those words later and feeling like an asshole.

"Just stay in bed, and I'll try to find something to help. Do you like ginger tea?" He makes a groaning sound, and I guess he'd be an extra special seven-year-old if he did. "I know, let me find some Sprite."

I manage to track down a sleeve of saltines and a warm Coke. Scooching in the bed beside him, I put the nature show he likes on the big television in our room.

His head is in my lap and my phone is beside me as we watch hour after hour of wildebeests running across the African prairie or neon schools of fish swirling in the ocean or his favorite tree frogs hiding in green leaves or climbing limbs.

I'm getting bored when I hear his little-boy snore and realize he's asleep. Sliding my hand under his torso, I ease out of the bed and quietly into the hall. Checking my phone, it's almost one. Courtney should be here soon.

The house is dark and empty, and I guess Tom went to escort her from work.

Walking through the elegant home, I stop at a built-in bookshelf. A round switch is beside it, and I twist it to turn on the recessed lights. A soft yellow glow illuminates a collection of antique trinkets.

A large and shiny brass clock sits under a glass dome. A round spinner in the back seems to serve as the battery, and on the side is a plate reading Simon Willard.

The shelf above holds a glowing purple vase with hobnails

all down the sides. The lip curves dramatically and it's strangely beautiful. On the bottom shelf is a leather notebook, and when I open it, I see it's actually a ledger. Beside it is a lapis blue cloisonne pen. It's like a Mont Blanc, but with brass filigree and pale pink and green flowers etched in the sides.

I know from Daisy's work this stuff is valuable. Considering what Spencer told me, it's probably worth several thousand dollars or more.

Leaning my head to the side, I pick up the pen and turn it in my fingers. I wonder if he's ever even written with it or if it even works. Taking a step away, I walk along the hall to the stairs leading up to the master suite.

Climbing slowly, I pass the small sitting area to the left with its balcony facing the river. The enormous, navy king-sized bed is perfectly made. No sign I was ever even here.

I go to the bedside table that holds a blue and white porcelain lamp covered in Chinese lettering. I slide my finger along the top of the polished mahogany when I realize...

He doesn't have a single picture.

Lifting my chin, I look all around the bedroom, to the dresser, the nightstand on the other side of the bed, not even on the credenza in the sitting room.

All these old things and not a single framed photo.

Spencer said his foster dad was like one of those old dragons, and I imagine a thick, reptilian man curled up on a pile of gold coins, protecting them with all his might as his life slips away, as he never knew the little boy in his care.

Dropping into the oversized leather chair, I pull up my knees, resting my cheek on them. "You don't have to be this way," I whisper.

Sadness presses inside my chest, and I take out my phone. I'm breaking my promise... But I was doing a shitty job keeping it anyway.

My fingers tap quickly, and I hit send. Then I switch off the sound, lean my head to the side, and close my eyes.

My head pops up, and I can tell it's late. "Courtney?"

The house is quiet, and it seems we're still alone.

I quickly check my phone, but I don't have a text. Jogging quickly down the stairs, I hurry to our room. Ollie is still asleep in his bed, and I don't wake him.

Fear is tight in my throat as I jog to the living area then into the kitchen. No one is here, I don't see a note, I don't see anything. Pulling out my phone again, it's after four. Courtney should have been here two hours ago.

At least I know Tom is with her. I can't imagine Ozzy or anybody being strong enough to overpower Tom. Still, I don't like it. If she'd decided to go shopping or something, she'd have told me.

It feels wrong.

Tapping quickly, I send a text to her. ***Everything okay?***

I think about what she told me last night. It's been a long time since she heard from Ozzy—too long. She was worried about us disappearing without a trace, and we both know he won't let her go without a fight.

We might be here, Ollie might be homeschooling, but Ozzy still has Courtney's phone number. He still knows where she works.

"Oh, God," I whisper. "Please keep my friend safe."

Returning to the bedroom, I contemplate waking Ollie to see if he'll at least drink something. His little head is tucked in the pillow, and he's sweaty. I lean down and place my lips lightly against his forehead. He still isn't feverish, and I take his cup and plate.

I put Ollie's things in the sink and wash them quickly. I don't feel worried about us here. Spencer has state-of-the-art security, and we're surrounded by metal gates. Still, I can't relax. I won't feel better until Courtney checks in with me.

Walking to the living room, I sit in the window seat, looking out at the perfectly groomed yard. Leaning my head on my hand, I push back against the fear. Tom is with her. Nobody could get past him. I just can't take much more of this radio silence.

I'm about to stand and start pacing all over again, when Tom's black town car swerves into the driveway fast.

The massive gates close slowly behind him, but he's already out, racing around the back of the car. The door is open, and he dives in, pulling out Courtney. She's leaning heavily on him, and I'm on my feet, racing to the front door.

"What happened?" The words are out of my mouth, and I see a swarm of cars pulling up outside the gate. "What's going on?"

I don't have time to finish my sentence before Tom is past me, putting Courtney on her feet and slamming the door. "Take her to her room. Nobody goes anywhere until further notice."

My jaw drops, but Courtney's head against my shoulder snaps me out of it. I realize she's been crying, and only one person makes her cry.

"Are you okay?" I search her face for any sign of injury. "What did he do?"

She shakes her head, and her eyes are heavy, miserable. "Courtney, tell me what happened."

Both her hands cover her face, and her shoulders hunch. A shiver moves through her body, and I give her a hug. "It's okay," I soothe, rubbing my hands up and down her back. "Just breathe."

We walk slowly to her bedroom, and I guide her to the bed where she sits on the foot. Then I step over to close the door. She's breathing more normally, and she clears her throat, blinking several times before lifting her chin to meet my worried eyes.

"Sly... Would you be willing to take Ollie? If something happened to me." I'm ready to argue, but she grips my forearm. "Would you?"

I blink back and forth between her dark eyes, placing my hand on top of hers. "What happened?"

Her lips tighten. "Ozzy won't bother us anymore."

My chest squeezes, and I'm not sure I can inhale.

I know the answer, but I have to be sure. "Why not?"

It's quiet.

She's quiet.

The tears coating her cheeks now are like a release, and when she speaks, it's calm resolution. "I shot him. He's dead."

"Oh, God." It's a soft whisper, and I'm so afraid.

I'm afraid of her being taken to jail. I'm afraid of Ollie being taken away, even though I promised to take care of him. Can she give him to me? Is that allowed? I don't know what happens now, and I don't have anyone to ask.

Actually, I do. This time when I send the text, it's for my friend.

CHAPTER Twenty-Eight

Spencer

"Well, that sure is a nice suit." The mean old bastard sits across a glass partition from me, and I search his hazel eyes, exactly like mine, for anything I might recognize.

I find nothing.

"Yes." My answer is short, clipped. "It is."

His shaggy, dark brows lower. His hair is long and cut in an old mullet style, and his gray beard grows into a point. He reminds me of one of those guys who used to fly drug planes between Houston and South America.

Only he's in an orange jumpsuit.

"I guess that means you're a rich man." He slides a pack of Parliament cigarettes out of his pocket. "So what do you want from me?"

He actually snarls, but I don't flinch. I've never loved this biological contributor to my creation, and I'm not afraid of him now.

"Last time I saw you, the police were taking me to the hospital."

He rocks back in the chair. "What? You want an apology?"

I almost laugh at the suggestion. "My forgiveness is not available. No, I'm here out of morbid curiosity."

He holds out a hand. "What do you want to know?"

My eyes flicker to the beige Formica counter then to him again. "Were you the same with every woman or was it just with my mother?"

The vulnerability inherent in my question makes me cringe. I hate that I fucking need to know the answer. The only gift this animal gave me was a deep and abiding mistrust of myself.

"I met your mother when I was twenty years old." He lights up, but the glass keeps it on his side. "They let me out of the army after I helped liberate Kuwait, and I went home to find this pretty little lady with a big heart. She wanted to help me. She loved me to the end."

"An end you helped her find. She died as a result of the injuries you caused."

His eyes narrow, and my body instinctively reacts to the flash of anger in them. That flash was a prelude to one of us being slapped across the room.

My throat heats, and I'd love to shove these barriers out of the way and let him try it.

"I guess you boss people around now. Is that right, boy?" He lunges forward, speaking in a low hiss. "You don't boss me."

I lean back in my chair, relaxing into my cool grin. "Be thankful for that glass. Striking me now would be your last mistake. Now answer my question."

Our eyes clash and hold. We're locked in a silent battle for a moment, two... three...

Until he sits back with a chuckle. "Looks like you got a bit of the old man in you after all. Is that what's got you worried? Afraid you'll turn out like me? Don't want to give up your fancy suit, your cushy lifestyle? Don't get cocky, boy. Half of you is me."

I turn his words over in my mind, thinking about what they mean.

Perhaps there was a time when this man wasn't a feral beast. Perhaps if that part of him had been stronger, I might feel a kinship. As it is, my insides are empty as a ghost town, and I have nothing for him but contempt.

Standing, I slide my palm down the front of my blazer. "I don't see anything I recognize here."

I tap on the door, and a guard appears to open it. Stepping into the hall, I pause when he calls after me. "You're no better than me."

"Actually, I am. I just needed to see it."

I'm speeding down the Interstate from Providence, turning east and following the highway farther out to the coast.

After I settled my adopted father's estate, I swore I'd never return to this strip of land on Aquidneck Island.

When I was a kid, Drake avoided all activities on the island. He didn't go to parties or host dinners. His castle-like manor was as silent as a tomb.

It wasn't on Bellevue Avenue, where the Gilded Age mansions of the Vanderbilts and the Astors were located. He preferred a remote location farther south, where we were completely isolated.

Every year, when the America's Cup would come to town, I'd stand on the roof as the people gathered to watch the sailors race around the coast.

He would be in his study admiring his latest find, and I would gaze down, longing for the world happening around us.

I was a lonely church mouse, wandering his cavernous cathedral, caring for my father when he'd had too much to drink or simply fallen asleep in his chair clutching his gold, then reading myself to sleep.

The day after his lawyer read the will, leaving all of it to me, I got to work. I sold the mansion and almost everything in it. I had a few treasured items he'd allowed me to play with as a child. The rest was gone, and I had enough money to buy the island.

Turning the car into the cemetery, I follow the path slowly past the historic monuments. A life-sized statue of an angel covered in a green patina sits between two headstones, and I know I'm on the right track.

Drake had no family, but I found a deed to a plot in this esteemed burial site as I was going through his things. I took his urn and had a marble headstone fashioned for it.

He didn't leave an epitaph, so I installed a black granite obelisk with his name and dates engraved on it. When I see it, I park the rental car and step out, walking slowly to the quiet stretch of bright green grass.

The landscape is perfectly manicured, and seagulls cry in the distance. I stop at the place where I planted his remains and read the marker, *How terrible it is to love something death cannot touch.*

It seemed like an appropriate epitaph. In life, he clung to things he could never take with him, and ultimately, he died the way he lived.

Alone.

Like me.

Standing in front of the black stone, I think about what drove me here. Up until this point, I told myself I wasn't like this man. I did engage in human contact. I had carefully selected friends, I held a job, and when the need arose, I would have a woman in my bed.

When I kissed Joselyn's lips and gazed into her eyes that morning, I had a startling realization—I wanted to be the man she believed me to be.

With that realization, the loneliness of my childhood, the self-preservation instinct that kept me safe from the crushing pain of my mother's rejection, my father's dysfunction, and Drake's narcissism, yawned wide like a black hole. I didn't know how to be that man.

In my arrogance, I convinced myself I could accomplish anything, but lying in that bed, I realized my carefully constructed rules were a façade covering the truth. I don't know how to touch, to care like a normal human.

"Why couldn't you have given me that?" My voice is quiet, and I don't really expect an answer.

I don't expect closure here in this quiet field.

I remember a little boy standing at the entrance of a massive, mahogany-lined office so hopeful. I remember Drake looking up at me with derision, asking if I wanted to play. I remember being ashamed to say yes, like wanting his attention was a weakness.

Now my stomach burns with anger. It wasn't wrong to need someone. I had lost everything.

If only I'd had a sibling or even one extended family member. I had nothing but that shriveled reptile of a human whose heart had dried up long ago.

Our interactions were reserved for formal walks through his mansion, while he pointed out his possessions and made special note of their value. He wanted to be sure his massive collection lived on after him.

Then he died, and I was free.

Only, the joke was on me.

I'm not free.

"You taught me to be cold like you, and I was a star pupil."

Reading the epitaph again, I realize I wrote the words for me, for when I came here again as I knew I would one day.

The real lesson I learned from this man is love must be shared with something that *can* be lost.

Giving it to possessions only diminishes its value. Love becomes priceless when you have to earn the right to keep it.

True love takes risk. It takes vulnerability.

Only then have you found something irreplaceable.

"He does such a good job on repairs." Heather stands on the other side of her mahogany desk, moving the heavy ring back and forth on the black velvet mat. "You can't even tell a stone was replaced."

"It's an unusual piece. I can't say I would've picked it out myself." Lifting the ring, I inspect the baguettes lining the sides for any sign of looseness.

"True. It's not the most romantic ring I've ever seen." Heather slides it on her slim finger. "It has a fierce quality, though."

"Fierce." My mind drifts to the last time I saw Joselyn. "It's a good description."

"Just so you know, my middle name is Lynn, which can be a boy or a girl's name."

A smile fidgets at the corner of my mouth, and I shake my head. "You can hold the baby names. I'm not proposing with this."

"You're not!" Her jaw drops, and she's so disappointed. "Then why are you here? I told you I'd bring it to you."

"I had some business to settle in Providence. It was just as easy for me to collect it from you."

"What business? Are you stepping out on me, Spence?"

I hate that diminutive. "It's not hard to say the *R*."

"Stop changing the subject. What were you doing in Providence?"

"Wrapping up some family business. I would expect by now you'd know we deal with Grafton before anyone."

A smile breaks across her face. "Being careful is what keeps me on top."

"Yes, I know." I hold out my hand, but she shakes her head in disgust.

"I'm not giving it to you like this. I have a box and tissue. I'll wrap it up and make it look nice. Maybe then… if you're lucky, she'll accept it."

If I'm lucky. She has no idea.

I'm about to make a comment when my phone buzzes in my pocket. She texted me last night, but she didn't want an answer.

Now when I see her words, my shoulders tighten. "Sorry, Heather. I've got to go."

Sliding the ring into my pocket, I make a quick call to the airport and arrange the private jet. The rest I'll handle on the flight home.

CHAPTER Twenty-Nine

Joselyn

"He asked if I would meet him for coffee." Courtney's voice is so small in this enormous conference room.

She sits across a wooden table from a team of lawyers led by an older woman in a St. John suit.

The day after the incident, we took Ollie to stay with my mom in Fireside. Tom suggested it to get him away from the news and the reporters. Then Courtney and I moved to a penthouse suite in a downtown Westin, supposedly in case there was a backlash. Courtney and I were both confused, since as far as she knows, Ozzy has no family in the States.

She was taken before a judge for arraignment, and now we're meeting with Spencer's team of lawyers in preparation for her preliminary hearing.

All these things are happening at his direction, but I haven't seen or heard from him.

I've become an expert at pretending I don't care.

The female lawyer glances at a yellow legal pad. "You agreed to meet your ex-husband for coffee knowing he had a history of violence?"

"It was in a coffee shop. Tom was always with me. I didn't think—"

"Exactly, Mrs. Clayton. You didn't think, which is precisely why you won't speak in your defense. They'll rip you to shreds."

Courtney's chin drops, and I want to scoot forward in my chair and hold her hand, give her my reassurance. It's just the two of us here at this meeting.

"He said he wanted to talk about Oliver." Her voice is a bit louder, a touch angrier, and I'm surprised by her sudden show of strength. "I thought I could get him to leave us alone."

"And how did that go?" The woman's eyes never leave her notebook. She's impatient, and I want to throw something at her.

My friend's shoulders droop, and she exhales. "He told me I was moving home with him. He said I couldn't hide forever."

One of the younger male lawyers sits forward. "Tell me, Mrs. Clayton—"

"If you don't mind," Courtney interrupts him, "I don't go by that name anymore. I use my maiden name now. It's Shaw. You can call me Miss Shaw."

"Sorry." The guy makes a note. "Miss Shaw, can you tell me how the gun was introduced into the situation?"

"I didn't mean to take it out. I was leaving, going to my car, and he followed me." Courtney talks fast, like she's embarrassed. "He grabbed my arm, and my bag fell. It hit the ground and he saw it. That's when he lunged for it, but I beat him to it."

"So he saw the gun in your bag and tried to take it from you?" The guy repeats.

"Yes. I didn't want him to get it because it's registered to me. I didn't trust him."

"So you never at any time intended to kill your ex-husband?" The older woman is back in the lead.

Courtney's eyes go to her lap again, and she doesn't answer right away. I want to jump in at this point and show them the pictures I took of her neck. I want to show them the pictures she took of my eye after Ozzy chased me into the women's restroom, but they have all the evidence.

"We're your lawyers, Miss Shaw. Whatever you tell us is protected by attorney-client privilege."

She still hesitates, and this time I do scoot forward to hold her hand. She glances at me, giving me a weak smile.

"The last time Ozzy came to my apartment and threatened to kill me, I bought the gun. So I guess you could say I bought it specifically for him. I just never knew when I'd use it."

Her answer seems to satisfy them.

"How was your first appointment at Palmetto?" Courtney sits on the end of the bed polishing her toenails. She's strangely calm, considering what she's facing.

"It was really great, actually. Mrs. Wolfe is a sweet old lady, and it was cool having someone taking care of all the paperwork for me."

"I really appreciate you taking over my clients this week."

"Yeah, well, we need the money." I exhale, dropping to the bed beside her. "I would say you're too upset, but I don't think that's true. What's going on?"

She shrugs, moving to her other foot. "I talked to Ollie. He's so happy being in Fireside. Jesse is out of school already, so they've been playing together."

"You haven't given up, have you?"

"No, I'm feeling good. Spencer texted me to be strong, and Ollie said he went to see him yesterday—"

"He did?" A pang of hurt cramps in my chest.

She must hear it in my voice, because she frowns up at me. "He still hasn't called you?"

"It's okay. I'm sure he has a lot going on." Such a lie, but whatever. "What did you say? He texted you to be strong? What does that mean?"

"I don't know exactly. He just said he was working on new information for the defense."

"And he visited Ollie?"

"Ollie said he dropped by yesterday. They fed Chartreuse, then they walked to Daisy's house. Ollie was fussing because he had to play with Melody."

My head is just spinning, and I don't know whether I'm angry or touched. "That's... really sweet."

"Yeah, he told him not to worry about me, that he was taking care of us." She blinks up at me with worried eyes. "I want to be pissed at him for ghosting you, but he's so damn good to my son."

Chewing my lip, I shake my head. "Don't be mad at him for me. I broke my own rules sleeping with him again. I should be mad at myself." Scooting closer, I put my arm around my friend. "If he helps get you out of this, I'll be willing to forgive him for disappearing."

I just won't be getting in his bed again.

"In this preliminary hearing of the people versus Courtney Shaw, the honorable Beverly Wright presiding, all rise." The bailiff stands at the front of the empty courtroom, and the few of us in attendance stand.

It's only me in the front row of the seats behind the railing separating the spectators from the small table where Courtney sits with her team of four well-dressed lawyers.

Across the aisle from us, two disheveled attorneys in messy suits, hastily sort through papers. They seem disorganized and disinterested.

I'm having a hard time understanding why anyone would care that the world has one less abuser today.

I guess that's why I don't work in law enforcement.

The judge calls for the prosecution to present their case. A woman from the messy lawyer table with tightly curled hair and a pinched expression steps forward. She briefly outlines the case for the judge.

"Miss Shaw left her husband without notice, taking their young son away in the middle of the night." The woman acts like she knows anything about the situation. "When he tried to meet with her about sharing custody of the child, she pulled a gun on him. He attempted to wrestle it away from her, and she shot him."

I'm ready to jump to my feet and yell that's not even close to the whole story when the judge turns the floor over to Courtney's attorney.

"Your honor, we can establish a pattern of abusive behavior on the part of Mr. Clayton. Miss Shaw filed numerous restraining orders, which he violated." The woman steps over to a small projector and flips a switch. "These photographs were taken just one month ago when Clayton showed up at the defendant's apartment and attempted to strangle her."

"What are you asking, counsel?" The judge lowers her gaze on Courtney's lawyer, and the woman holds out her hands.

"This is a clear case of self-defense. The prosecution has no one bringing charges against Miss Shaw. The victim was a criminal with no one to vouch for him. Miss Shaw acted in self-defense. We're requesting all charges be dropped."

The male lawyer across the aisle jumps to his feet. "Your honor, that's outrageous. We still have laws in this country. A man cannot be shot in cold blood and nothing done about it. We're requesting a trial for first-degree murder. No bail, as Miss Shaw is clearly a flight risk."

Courtney's hand flies to her mouth, and her face turns ghastly pale. She reaches out, and I want to hug her.

Instead, her lawyer rises slowly, calmly. "Your honor, there is no reason to hold Miss Shaw without bail. She has a job, clients, a son. If she were a flight risk, she would already have run. She clearly believes in the system and justice. We're asking you to simply review the facts of this case and decide what is clear to see."

The prosecutor begins to speak, but the judge holds up her hand. "I'll take a five-minute recess to review the defendant's case."

With the bang of a gavel, she stands and leaves the courtroom. We all collapse in our seats. I take a deep breath and sit forward, reaching for Courtney's arm.

"She's going to see the truth. I know she is."

Worry lines my friend's eyes. "I hope so. I hope it's enough."

Holding my smile steady, I say a prayer under my breath. My phone is set to silent because Daisy and my mom are blowing it up with texts wanting to know what's happening.

We wait what feels like an eternity for the judge to return from reviewing Courtney's case. I wish I had included pictures of my cheek after Ozzy chased me into the ladies room, but if the police are anything to go on, it wouldn't matter. I saw him of my own free will. He didn't touch me. I fell.

It's the same thing they're saying about Courtney. If she were so afraid of him, why would she willingly go with him to a coffee shop?

It's like none of these people have jobs or children.

My heart jumps when the bailiff returns to the front of the courtroom. "All rise."

We stand like it's church, and Judge Wright gathers her black robe as she takes her seat inside the small booth. My breath is stuck in my lungs as I wait for her to tell us her decision.

"It is the opinion of this court Mrs. Clayton acted in haste when she met with her husband last week, armed with a loaded weapon.

I'm not convinced she had reason to believe he would harm her that day or she would not have gone to meet him."

My throat is tight, and I feel the bile rising in my stomach. How can she say this? Didn't she even see the restraining orders? The pictures I took? He was completely unpredictable.

The black-robed woman continues, her tone actually sounding bored. "I do think Mrs. Clayton was in a difficult situation, but she didn't pursue the proper remedies to help herself. She didn't file for divorce; she didn't seek sole custody—"

"Your honor, if you please." Courtney's lawyer is on her feet. "Miss Shaw did file for legal separation on August 27—"

"If she was able to do that, she was able to finish the process." The judge snaps. "She didn't leave Columbia or even behave in a manner that would suggest she feared for her life. She continued going to work, sending her son to the same school, living in the same apartment."

"Your honor, she was attempting to maintain a normal life. She had to work in order to pay her bills. Miss Shaw is not independently wealthy. She's a poor, single mother with no family nearby, no support system."

"Regardless, a man lost his life violently in my city." The judge doesn't even hesitate. "Based on the information before me here today, I see no reason to dismiss the charges of first-degree murder, and I hereby set a trial date for—"

The wooden doors at the back of the courtroom fly open, and a male voice I know well echoes through the near-empty room. "Your honor, my apologies, if you would please wait. I have new information that will impact your decision."

Spencer strides up the aisle dressed as always in an expensive suit, but he's disheveled, his hair's a gorgeous mess, and he's not wearing a tie… And I hate how fast my heart beats at the sight of him. I hate that I'm so stupidly happy to see him.

"I object!" The prosecutor is on her feet. "Your honor, we have no idea what this new information might be or who this person even is."

The judge frowns at Spencer, and he motions to Courtney's lawyer to join him. "If you would just take a moment, your honor. I came straight from the Dentsville Magistrate with a notarized confession."

All of the lawyers congregate around the judge's desk, and Spencer slides several sheets of paper from a brown manila envelope.

"I'll call a ten-minute recess while we examine this new information. Bailiff, please provide copies to the prosecution and her defense team."

She stands and leaves the courtroom with the envelope in her hands, and the guard passes out the copies to the lawyers. Spencer walks to the defense table, speaking urgently to the lead attorney. From where I'm sitting, I only catch bits of what he's saying.

"...hired a private detective the day she came to my house. He's been following Clayton for weeks..." His brow is lowered, and he's so focused.

He's so damn gorgeous.

Courtney stands, and he takes her hand, giving her a smile. "Don't worry. That piece of paper should wrap this up pretty quickly."

My friend grasps his hand, and her eyes are so hopeful. I'm standing behind the rail watching with gratitude and pain aching in my chest.

Hazel eyes flicker to mine, and his brow relaxes. "Joselyn—"

His voice is like warm butter, but the bailiff interrupts. "All rise."

We turn at once to see the judge again taking her seat, a grim expression on her face. My scalp tightens, and I'm not sure how much more of this I can take.

"I spoke to the judge in Dentsville, and it appears these documents are in order. Mr. Carrollton's private investigator uncovered a conspiracy to kidnap Miss Shaw and take her to a second location where this man had agreed to bury her body. He confessed under oath in exchange for a commuted sentence."

"Oh!" It's a sharp gasp from my friend, and I lower my head to my hands.

"Oh, God." The words slip from my lips, and a sharp bang comes from the podium in front.

"Order in my courtroom." The judge snaps. "In view of this new evidence, I dismiss the charge of first-degree murder against Miss Shaw. She has confessed to shooting her husband, but as this document establishes imminent danger, I will commute that charge and expunge this from her record."

The gavel bangs, and the bailiff tells us all to stand again, which we do. I feel outside my body, like I'm not sure what just happened.

It's all over.

Just like that.

The lawyers shake hands, and tears stream down Courtney's cheeks as Spencer pulls her into a hug. I step side to side trying to figure out how to get around the silly wooden railing between us when she turns and catches me in a big hug.

"He did it." Her body trembles in my arms. "He saved us, just like he said he would."

A knot is in my throat, and I blink back tears as I meet his eyes over her shoulder.

His head is bowed slightly and his jaw is tight. He's not smiling—he watches us with detached satisfaction. It's so like him to do something this monumental and then to resist being proud or even to show emotion.

One of the lawyers taps his shoulder, and they shake hands.

Courtney lifts her head and speaks to the woman leading the team. "Can I go now? I really want to see my son."

"You are free to leave, Miss Shaw. It was a pleasure working with you."

"Thank you." Courtney nods. "Thank you, Spencer. So much."

I'm holding her hand, and we start for the double doors at the back of the room. They're just closing behind us when a strong hand grasps my upper arm.

"Joselyn, do you have a minute?" Spencer's hand slides down my arm, and Courtney's dark eyes meet mine.

I don't know what she sees, but she pulls out her phone. "I'll just call Ollie and tell him we're on our way."

My heart is lodged in my throat, and I'm not sure I can have a proper conversation with him right now. At least not the one I need to have with him after this week.

Still, it seems I have no choice. He guides me to the side hall, away from the crowd of attorneys leaving the courtroom.

"Your text said you wanted to talk when I got back in town." He gazes into my eyes with so much intensity. "I didn't know if you meant now or if you wanted to wait until you came back from Fireside."

My lips part, and I almost can't believe him. "You could have texted me then."

"Should I have?"

He literally seems confused, and I close my eyes as my heart screams, *Yes, you should have. We're in a relationship, dammit!*

But my brain reminds me he never said we were…

"Only you can answer that question, Spencer. I have to go. Courtney wants to see her son, and it's a two-hour drive."

"Maybe we can have a drink when you get back. Best martinis in town?" He gives me a sexy little half-smile, and I can't hold back.

My voice is sharp, and fire burns in my chest. "When you told me about your childhood, I was sad. I understood your walls, because you were taught not to love. Maybe you don't even think you deserve love, but you're wrong.

"I love you. I want to give you what they never did. I want to be there for you, to make you laugh and bring you in from the cold.

I want to show you a different life, one where you have someone to count on, someone who's always there for you no matter what.

"But I can't, and I can't keep hoping for something you told me wasn't possible. I wish I could've been the woman to make you want more, because I do want more. So this is goodbye. I hope you have the life you want, and I wish you well."

Turning on my heel, I leave him standing there, watching me go, and in my mind, the last petal falls.

CHAPTER Thirty

Spencer

"I checked all the rooms, and I reset the alarm codes." Tom strides into the living room with a black duffel in his hand. "It'll prompt you to enter a new code when I leave. Then it'll just be you."

"Thank you, Tom." My voice is quiet. I'm sitting in my favorite wingback chair.

It's thick brown leather with heavy brass studs along the edges. I found it in Boston at an estate sale where the seller claimed it once belonged to John Quincy Adams.

It was my prized possession.

Gazing at the hand-knotted Persian rug covering the floor, regret tightens my chest. I'm just like him. Alone, in an empty house with only my things.

Why does this bother me? I never minded being alone before.

"Sir?" Tom waits, and I glance up at him.

"Yes?"

"I just wanted to say, it was a great thing you did today. I've always thought of myself as something of a silent hero, keeping people safe, but you were the real Tony Stark swooping in there like you did and shutting down that judge."

My brow relaxes, and I exhale with a smile. "I was only the messenger."

"You were more than that. You hired the private eye, you chased down the evidence, and I don't know, but I'm sure you had to grease a few palms to get a notarized confession that fast."

Leaning back in the chair, I hold up my hands. "No laws were broken in the liberation of Miss Shaw."

He surprises me with a grin. "Either way, I just wanted to say it before I left."

He's said more just now than in the whole time he's been with us. "Thanks, Tom."

"Also… it's none of my business, but I think Miss Winthrop is a great gal. You two seem like a good match."

Her words are still ringing in my ears, her goodbye smarting in my chest. I haven't been able to shake a sense of dread since she left me standing in the gallery of the court.

Looking up at my suddenly gregarious security guard, I figure he's as good as anyone to run this past. "Tom, you've been in this business a while, yes?"

"Yes sir, seven years."

"Tell me, have you ever done something you thought would make everyone happy then ultimately felt like you screwed up everything?"

His brow furrows, and he actually thinks a minute. "I'm not sure in what way you mean, but I did rescue a kitten once. I took care of it, fed it for two weeks, took it to the vet… Only to find out later it belonged to a little girl around the way who'd been crying for two weeks over her lost pet."

Hesitating, I guess that is a type of good-deed backfire. "I thought Joselyn would be happy about what I did. Instead, I feel like I lost her."

"Well, you did take off without a word. She wasn't happy about that."

I blink up at him, realizing he was with them every day. "Did she say something?"

"She didn't have to." He points two fingers at his eyes then turns them on me. "She has the fire that shoots out of her eyes."

The gesture makes me chuckle sardonically. "I should have called her."

"You never did?" He makes a face like I just stepped in dog shit.

"No, I was… taking care of old business. Exorcising old demons."

He inhales loudly and sits on the couch across from me, with a gesture. "Do you mind?"

"Of course not. Have a seat." He might as well.

"You're a smart guy, and clearly you have a lot of money. I'm guessing you know how to make deals and handle people."

"Usually…" I'm pretty sure I haven't done the right thing since a witchy redhead fell on me… however long ago it was.

It feels like a short time ago, yet it also feels like my whole life.

"Women like to know you're thinking about them. They want to feel important to you, like they matter. You fucked that up, if you don't mind me saying so, but maybe, if she really cares about you as much as it looks like she does… A grand gesture would be a good place to start."

"Grand gesture." I think about all the things we've discussed…

I'm not the beast or a prince or Mr. Freeze, despite what everyone likes to say.

He stands and walks to where I'm sitting lost in thought. "What you did for Miss Shaw was pretty grand." He pats me on the shoulder. "Maybe you could do some groveling. Women also like being reminded when they're right, because trust me, they usually are."

CHAPTER Thirty-One

Joselyn

"He didn't even try to stop you?" My mom leans on her kitchen table clutching her coffee mug of whiskey.

Courtney and I stopped off at the Westin to collect our things and check out before driving to Fireside. She decided to wait on telling Ollie about his dad until after meeting with her therapist. Again, something Spencer arranged.

It's like he thought of everything but me.

Courtney cried silently most of the drive, and I held her hand. I can't imagine how she's feeling, although she claims to be relieved. Still, when she and Ollie were finally together, they hugged like it had been months.

We had a good old-fashioned dinner of fried pork chops, mashed potatoes and gravy, and corn and black bean maque choux, which happens to be my mom's specialty. Then my friend said she was exhausted, which was completely understandable. The two of them went upstairs for baths and bed, and I hung back to fill in all the details—or as many as I know.

"He just stood there and let me walk out the door." I exhale heavily into my coffee mug of whiskey. It has Dolly Parton on the front and the phrase "Cup of Ambition."

She rocks back in her chair, setting her mug, which reads "Maybe Coffee," on the table. "I just can't get over that. When he came by yesterday, he seemed so different. Whatever he said or did, he is not the same man I met at Daisy's wedding."

"He's always sweet around Oliver." I frown, taking another small sip. "That's what's so infuriating about him. He's incredible with Ollie. He swoops in like a superhero to rescue Courtney... and yet he lacks these basic human skills of just saying goodbye or returning my text when we're apart."

My mom looks down, and I feel like I know what she's about to say, and I close my eyes. She reads my face and stands instead, walking around to hug my shoulders.

"I think you should all stay here a few days. Can you do that? It's almost the weekend. Courtney's eyes are so tired, and I've got plenty of room."

Shrugging, I stand as well. "I don't see why not. I saw my only client for the week, and Court rescheduled most of her appointments just in case."

"Good." Ma pats my arms before pulling me into a brief hug. "Go upstairs, take a nice long bath, get a good night's sleep... And turn off your phone."

My eyebrow arches. I know what she's suggesting, and I do exactly as she says.

"You found it!" Ms. Alice clasps her hands as I carry the big Fireside Ladies Club book downstairs. "Oh, let me see it. I don't' want anything to happen to this book."

She helps me carry it to the table, and Ma joins her bestie as they flip through the pages. "I haven't seen this in years."

Daisy elbows me in the ribs, obviously pretending to be surprised. "Oh, look. You found it."

I pinch the skin inside her arm and she squeals. "Don't get me in trouble."

She slaps my hand, and Courtney wanders in with a mug of coffee to blow my cover completely. "Hey, isn't that the book we used to cast that protection spell?"

Ms. Alice squints one eye and looks up at me. "Protection spell?"

Courtney leans in closer, looking at the book. "It didn't work. He still gave you a black eye."

"What?" Ma steps back inspecting my face with a horrified expression. "Who gave you a black eye? When?"

"I'm fine, Ma, it was nothing." I glare at Courtney to shut up. "Anyway, the spell did work. We're all here, aren't we?"

Ms. Alice waves us away. "These women didn't need spells. They had each other. It's a powerful thing when women support one another, and we're here to support you."

"Thank you." Courtney squeezes my mom's bestie. "You all have helped me so much through this. I can't tell you how much I appreciate it, and Ollie..." Her voice cracks, and my mom puts her arms around her as well.

"Is a wonderful boy and so smart! Why the things he can tell you about frogs is amazing."

I shudder, putting my arms around the three of them. "Just keep her away from me."

Courtney laughs, dabbing her eyes. "Don't forget Spencer. He was amazing."

Daisy scoots into the group. "What about Spencer?"

"He was really great." Courtney shakes her head, taking the

fresh cup of coffee from my mom. "He saved me from a long trial and maybe even jail."

"What? How did he do all of that?" Daisy looks from her to me, and we quickly fill her in on his last-minute save in the courtroom.

My cousin cuts me a grin. "I thought he was just looking for an excuse to spend more time with you."

Heat rises in my stomach, but it's silly heat.

Silly, wasted heat.

"Spending more time with me was not on his agenda." I shake my head, but Daisy's hand goes to her mouth as her eyes widen.

"I wouldn't say that." Spencer's deep voice makes me almost spill my coffee. "Good morning, ladies. I hope I'm not interrupting."

I turn around quickly to see him standing inside the door, stunning as always in a tan blazer over a black shirt. His hair is messy like he hasn't slept, and he looks like he stepped out of a magazine.

"Sweet baby Jesus, my lady bits." Ms. Alice fans herself, and Ma hurries around grabbing a fresh mug of coffee.

"Spencer, I had no idea you were coming. Would you like some coffee? Alice made scones."

"You can have all my scones," Ms. Alice holds out the platter.

His eyes are leveled on mine when he answers my mom, and that silly wasted heat floods my face. "Thank you, Regina, I was hoping to speak to Joselyn if she's available."

"What's on your mind, Spence?" Daisy pipes up from her spot at the table, but he doesn't look away from me.

I know because I haven't looked away from him.

"I hoped you might take a walk with me?" He steps closer, lowering his voice.

Swallowing the knot in my throat, I shrug. "I don't mind walking."

I do not take his hand.

Lifting my chin, I brush past him towards the front door, and Ms. Alice calls after me, "Don't walk so fast!"

I roll my eyes, shaking my head as I push through the door. My insides are hot and zippy, but I'm not letting him get the best of me. I'm not going back to the way things were before.

He does a little jog to catch up with me, and for a minute we walk in silence.

I follow the sidewalk outside Ma's new house, which is several blocks from the house where I grew up. Eventually, we meet up with the path leading to the small wooden bridge.

"I'm not sure where we're going." Spencer finally breaks the silence. "I'd wanted to go somewhere private so we could talk."

When we get to the bridge, I stop in the middle. I'm not taking him all the way down the path into the alcove where the palmettos grow in thick clusters. My stomach is tight, and as much as I want to take him to that place, I'm not.

"We can talk here." I turn to face him, leaning my hip against the railing. My arms are crossed so I don't do anything foolish like reach out and touch him.

He puts a hand on the railing beside me, positioning his body so it's in front of me. The wind blows his hair forward attractively around his temples, and his clean scent of leather and sandalwood touches my nose.

I blink away to keep from being distracted. "What do you want, Spencer?"

"Last night I had so many things to say, but now..." He looks out over the water, and I watch the line of muscle move in his jaw. "I'm not very good at this."

Shifting my stance, I wait. I said all I had to say to him in the courtroom, and now the ball is in his court.

He blinks back to me, and his eyes are tight. "I'm sorry I left that way. I didn't do it to hurt you."

His words squeeze my chest, but it's not enough. "You did hurt me."

"I realize that now. I was thinking about the past, my past, and the things I had to handle, doors I had to close before..." As he speaks, his gaze falls to the water again. "I wasn't thinking about you or how it must have seemed."

He hesitates, sliding a hand to his hip, moving his jacket back, like he's a model or something. My heart thumps in my chest, but I won't help him with this.

Clearing his throat, he straightens. "You want something I've never done. I can't promise I'll be any good at it. I can't promise I won't fuck it up." Hazel eyes lock on mine. "I can promise I'll try."

I blink, and a tear hits my cheek. His brow furrows, and he steps forward quickly to wipe it with his thumb. "I don't want to make you cry."

"Too late," I hiccup, covering my mouth with my hand. My chest is twisting with heat and love, and I'm trying to be firm and push back on all the emotions he's stirring inside me. "You're a very frustrating man."

"I know. I never cared before." His voice is hoarse, and he slides a hand in his pocket. "I went to Rhode Island because I thought if I saw my dad, if I visited Drake's grave, I might understand why."

"Did you?"

"Not until I came back and saw you again. Sitting alone in that empty house last night, with only my things... I hated him. When he died, I sold everything he had so I'd never be like him, only I turned into something worse. He only hurt me. I hurt you."

When his eyes meet mine, they're more open than I've ever seen him. He almost seems lost, like he's in a place he doesn't understand. "I want to change for you, Sin. I want to be the man you deserve. Is it too late?"

Shaking my head, I rush into his arms. My face is pressed into his chest, and he holds me close. I hear him inhale deeply at the side of my head, and my heart swells so fast it hurts.

"It's not too late." My voice is a muffled whimper.

His arms loosen, and he slides his hands up my arms, holding my shoulders before cupping my cheeks and covering my mouth with his. Fresh tears fall, and I grip his sleeves as our lips part, as his tongue sweeps in and curls with mine.

Heat floods my lower body. It's a possessive kiss, demanding as always. He's claiming me, but I'm claiming him right back. I pull him to me, wanting everything he's giving me.

Lifting his chin, his face is relaxed. He's brighter as he exhales a chuckle. "What are you doing to me?"

Reaching up, I slide my hand across his cheek. "I'm going to make you so happy."

Looking down into my face, his pretty eyes are so full of emotion. "You already have. You have no idea."

Our lips collide once more, pulling and chasing, tasting and nipping. My body is on fire, and I want to rip his clothes off. Too bad, we're in the middle of Fireside, where everybody knows everybody.

His lips move to the bridge of my nose. He kisses my forehead, then lifts my chin again, studying my face with so much love. "While I was in New Hampshire, I got you something."

"Is it a surprise?"

"I have it here." He slides a hand in his pocket and takes out a ring.

The band is black with diamonds arranged down the sides in an art deco style, and in the center is a polished jade stone. "It's so strange and gorgeous."

"Daisy said you'd like it." He almost seems worried.

"It's the coolest thing I've ever seen. Jade stones are magical. They represent luck and happiness." I take it at once and put it on the middle finger of my right hand tilting it side to side.

"It's a promise." He covers my hands with his. "It's my promise to deserve you."

Blinking up at him, I smile. "I love it."

He lifts my hand to his lips, and his brow furrows. He blinks a few times, and fear tightens my throat until he meets my gaze. "I love you."

"Spencer..." My voice breaks.

Wrapping my arms around his neck, I close my eyes as he lifts me off my feet. We hold each other as it all surrounds us, from the first time he caught me when I fell to the day he saved me when I needed him most.

So many times his actions said the words that are now promises. He's my beast, my frozen savior who rescued me, but who I also rescued from a lifetime of loneliness.

He's the man of my dreams, the fierce, wounded prince saved by love.

He's the kind of trouble I never want to be without.

CHAPTER Thirty-Two

Spencer

Nine months later

"I'LL GIVE YOU TWO THOUSAND DOLLARS FOR IT." I'M SITTING IN THE kitchen of my future mother-in-law's home attempting to convince the most reluctant buyer I've ever met.

"Two thousand!" Alice spits the words in disgust, like I've just kicked her dog. "You might be the best-looking man I've ever seen, but I'm not parting with the Fireside Ladies."

"Come on, Alice. I'll treat it with the utmost care." I also happen to know Joselyn loves this book.

"This book is going in the Fireside Public Library for future generations to learn what the founding mothers did for the beach, for women's rights, and for each other."

Moving from my chair to sit beside her on the couch, I play dirty. "You know as well as I do kids these days would rather play video games than read books." Slipping my arm around her shoulders, I lean into her ear. "How's thirty-five hundred?"

She does a little shiver before standing and rebuking me. "Get behind me, Satan, I'm doing this for future generations!"

Leaning back, I cross my arms with a grin. "Would it make a difference if I told you I want to give it to Joselyn for a wedding gift?"

Her blue eyes fly wide and she throws up both hands. "You popped the question?"

"No, and if you spill the beans, I won't give you five dollars for it." I stand, speaking firmly, and she's so short, her gray helmet of hair only comes to the center of my chest.

"Oh, how I wish you were my grandson. He likes to pick me up, you know." She waggles her eyebrows, but I'm still doing my best to be stern.

"Don't tell Regina."

"I won't tell her!" She crosses her heart. "Fireside Ladies promise."

"Are you going to sell that book to me or not?"

"Of course not," she shakes her head, waving me away. My jaw tightens, and I'm about to steal the damn thing when she cuts me off. "I'm giving it to you as a wedding gift. Sly's a founder's daughter. She has as much right to this as I do."

Lifting the heavy book, she puts it in my hands, and it's better than the best deal I've ever closed.

Except for getting Joselyn to take a chance on me.

"You're a tough nut, Alice."

"You're still wet behind the ears." She winks, driving her pointy elbow into my ribs. "I've wrangled with the best of them, son."

It's no wonder Joselyn stole my heart. She's the same as this crazy town, the best kind of antique, the quirky kind that only gets better with age.

"I think you love this place so much because they all know you here." Joselyn leans forward across from me at Rioz, and the slinky black dress she's wearing dips low on her cleavage.

My eyes follow the line of thin, black silk with spaghetti straps over the soft curve of her full breast, and I want to forget dinner, take her home, and unwrap her like a present.

It's been nine months since that day in Fireside, and I've never been surer of anything in my life.

Once we found Courtney and Oliver a safe, affordable place to live, I moved Joselyn back into my house. No surprise, Tom started dropping by to visit her friend pretty regularly, claiming he wanted to be sure they were safe. Now they're a couple, and Oliver is happy every time I see him—he bounces on his toes and talks too loudly. I'm a fast learner.

My biggest lesson, however, was I can't live without this woman, and I've got plans for tonight.

"Up until I met you, I was a good customer here. It's only been in the last year I've gotten... less reliable."

We're sitting at the outdoor patio. It was a warm day, but with the sun down and the stars out, it's lovely. Our waiter Pat is cued up to hold dessert until I give him the signal.

Her red lips curl in a naughty grin, and she winks. "I can't help it if you're not always hungry for food."

My cock twitches, and I have to focus my mind on the business at hand. "How was your steak?"

"Perfect as always."

"Ready for dessert?"

"Mm..." She tilts her head to the side, placing her napkin on the table. "I've been feeling fluffy lately. Maybe I'll skip dessert tonight."

"Women are supposed to be fluffy. You're having dessert." She has to have dessert.

That makes her laugh, and she shakes her head. "You won't say that when I can't fit through the front door."

I'm about to say I'll buy a bigger house when her expression changes. She slides down in the seat making a face like she smelled something rotten.

"What's wrong?" I sit straighter, looking around the outdoor area, until my eyes land on a man I've only seen once before.

Still, I made a mental note when it happened.

He has the nerve to walk right up to our table with a busty brunette on his arm. "Well, hello, Sly. Funny seeing you here."

My girl sits up straight at once, flashing a bold grin. "How's it going, Elliot? Nadine?"

The woman on his arm wrinkles her nose when she tries to smile. "Joselyn."

I do a quick take from her to Joselyn to the guy, and I quickly read the situation. He's being an ass, Joselyn is cringing, and this Nadine chick is threatened.

"Sorry," I stand, extending a hand. "I don't believe we've met. Spencer Carrollton."

The idiot looks down at my hand like I've offered him a dead fish. "So you're the new guy." It's not a question. "You should know she makes a habit of moving in with a new rich guy after only a few weeks."

My extended hand turns into a fist, which I quickly lower to my side. "You're Elliot, is it? I've heard you make a habit of banging your secretaries and being an all-around douchebag."

Nadine's jaw drops, but the idiot has the balls to get offended. "People don't talk to me that way."

"Is that so?" I look down on this little man. "From what I understand, no one should talk to you, but if they do, they should only use small words."

Joselyn's fingers fan over her full lips to hide her smile, and the bimbo jerks the idiot's arm.

"You're not going to let him talk to you that way?" She does a little sniff, and Elliot's face turns pink.

"You take that back!" He sounds like a child on the playground.

I might feel sorry for him if he hadn't insulted my girl. "You preyed on Joselyn, convinced her you cared about her, and then cheated on her. If anyone deserves an apology, it's her."

"I'll never—" I quickly step forward, catching him by the front of his shirt.

"You've got two seconds to apologize or you'll wish you had." My voice is low, but the threat is real. I'd like nothing better than to throw him on the ground and put my foot on his neck.

"How dare you!" He sputters, the red growing hotter in his face. "I'll have you know my father—"

"One second." My jaw is clenched, and I'm actually growing excited. "Three, two…"

"I'm sorry!" He yells, far louder than I expected.

It's very satisfying.

"To whom are you apologizing and why?" It's more of an order than a question, and I steer him around so he's facing my date.

"Joselyn!" He's still shouting, and our fellow patrons stop eating.

Two of the waiters rush out then stop when they see what's happening.

I give him a sharp jerk. "Continue."

"I'm sorry, Joselyn, for saying bad things about you." He's breathing fast like the sniveling loser he is.

"Will you ever do it again?"

"I'll never do it again."

Leaning forward, I look down into his face. "Good. Now get out and never come here again. This is our restaurant, and I don't want you spoiling our dinner."

I let him go with a shove, and he bounces off an empty table behind him before staggering to the exit. Looking around, I straighten my jacket, meeting a mixture of curiosity and approval.

"I apologize for the disruption. Just removing some old trash."

A light murmur and some laughter, and I look down at Joselyn, whose eyes are shining up at me. "Now I'm really ready to go home."

Pat stands at the door, and I do a little shrug. He waves me away with alternating thumbs up and fast air clapping.

"Come on."

We barely make it through the door when Joselyn pins me to the wall with a kiss. "Have I told you how happy you make me?"

I'm right there, meeting her lips, grabbing her face, and turning her back to the wall so I can kiss her deeper. My hands slide up the slippery silk of the dress, lifting her breasts and teasing her nipples through the thin fabric.

"Then I'm doing my job." I trace a line with my lips along her jaw to her ear, inhaling deeply soft white flowers and the warmth of her body. "I love this dress."

Sliding my hands down her hips, I cup her ass, but she holds my wrists, kissing my neck before dropping to her knees. Fuck, yes.

Her hands are on my pants, sliding up and down as she gives me a naughty look, curling her fingers so her nails tease my thighs before rising higher to unfasten my pants.

"Joselyn…" I reach out to brace my hand on the wall, and she has my fly down.

My cock springs free, and she wraps her fingers around it. "Hello, Jock!"

I can't help a laugh. "Stop talking to my cock."

"Just ignore him." She leans forward to kiss the tip before flicking out her tongue and tracing it all around the edge. "Does that feel good?"

"Yes," I groan, and she looks up at me with big blue eyes before pulling me all the way into her mouth on a long suck.

My eyes roll shut as she does it again.

Her mouth pops off, and she looks up at me. "You were very good tonight."

Sliding my fingers along her cheek, I'm still amazed by how much I feel for her. "I'll always take care of you."

She grins, returning to my dick, tracing her tongue around it before pulling it between her red lips, smearing lipstick on my shaft, licking and sucking as her head bobs faster.

"Sin..." I groan deeply.

Both her hands slide up my legs, scratching her nails lightly over my ass. My eyes squeeze shut, and I do my best not to thrust forward and drive my cock down her throat.

She's sucking and pumping me with her fist, making little hungry noises as she does it. She's on her knees, feasting like I'm a fucking ice cream cone, and when I look down and see her breasts bouncing, I can't take it anymore.

"You're too good," I gasp. "Come up here."

Reaching down, I catch her under the arms and pull her up, turning her stomach to the wall and ripping the silk over her ass. Fuck, I love this ass.

I rip the thong off her just before I slam into her and hold. My heart is beating so hard, I can't breathe, and she whines, bucking against my pelvis, sending me deeper into her clenching core.

My teeth are tight, and I grind out, "I'm going to come."

"Me too," she moans, twerking against me.

Fumbling with the front of her dress, I find the top of her thighs and slip my fingers between them, massaging her clit fast as I thrust harder, faster. Her palms flatten against the wall, and she pushes against me, fucking me backwards as I do my best to wait for her.

It's no use. I'm too far gone as the ripples of orgasm climb my legs. My knees buckle, and I push up and hold, closing my eyes as I pulse into her so hard.

My arms tighten around her waist, and I hold on so I don't fall as the planet shifts beneath my feet. Her hand fumbles over her shoulder into my hair, and I turn my face to kiss her neck.

"You are the most amazing woman."

Her cheek rises, and I turn her to face me, looking down into her lazy blue eyes. "You're my hero."

For a moment, I take in her beauty. Her hair falls around her shoulders in messy, just-fucked waves, and her black silk dress is off one shoulder. Reaching down, I slide it up her arm. She leans closer, pressing her lips to my neck.

My eyes close, and I want to carry her upstairs and repeat what we just did in my bed many times.

Instead, I place my hands on her shoulders. "I had other plans before we left the restaurant tonight."

She leans against the wall, smiling at me. "Other than making that fucking Idiot apologize for living and making me love you even more as if that were even possible?"

"That was pretty good, but it wasn't on my original agenda."

"It was better than pretty good."

"What I wanted to do was this." Lowering to my knee, I pat the pocket of my jacket, locating the small item our waiter was going to bring out with the tiramisu.

Her eyes widen, and she places her right hand over her heart—the same hand that holds my promise ring, which she never takes off.

This item is more delicate. It's an 18-karat, white gold diamond engagement ring with a three-karat oval diamond in the center and two baguettes on each side. In the band, I had the words "My queen" engraved.

"In the last nine months, I hope I've proven myself to you. I intend to go on making you happy, fighting for you, protecting you. Will you marry me?"

She drops to her knees as I slide the ring on her left hand, nodding as she puts her arms around my neck. "Yes, of course, I will. I love you."

My eyes close, and I hold her tightly to my body, feeling the warmth of her, the beating of her heart, the fire in her soul. This woman, who brought so much trouble into my life…

She broke me free from my prison. She melted the ice around my heart. She taught me to love—she taught me I could love.

I'll never let her go.

Lifting my head, I smooth my hands down the sides of her fiery red hair, gazing deep into her sparkling blue eyes. I kiss the freckles on her nose, so thankful she fell into my arms, my witchy angel, my queen.

"I love you."

Epilogue

Joselyn

"WHY AREN'T YOU WEARING YOUR HELMET?" SPENCER STALKS across the parquet floors of the Oceanside Hotel's Grand Ballroom with a football helmet in his hand.

"I thought that was a joke." I'm at the top of a ladder threading the final flowers into a larger than life-sized sculpture of Belle and Prince Adam.

It's a slight variation from the one I made for the ball in that Belle's hair is redder, and they're embracing closely rather than just dancing. It's my one contribution to the reception for our wedding, coming in only two days.

Gazing down at him, holding that ridiculous helmet he got from Daisy, I wonder if I could love him more if he weren't so over-protective.

Short answer: No.

"It's most definitely not a joke. I won't have you walking down the aisle in a neck brace."

I place the final coral rose in the side of Belle's hair then I sit back on the ladder, smiling at my creation. "It's perfect. Just like you."

"Come down from that ladder at once. I don't want to injure my back before our honeymoon."

My nose wrinkles at my fussy fiancé, so sexy in an Armani suit. His dark hair is messy around his temples like he's been walking on the beach, and his hazel eyes are broody. That muscle in his perfectly square jaw moves like it does when he's annoyed with me.

He still takes my breath away.

It's been a year since he proposed, and I want to say a lot has changed. The truth is, we've simply gotten to know each other better, and as a result, we've grown deeper in love. Not everybody can say that.

We've also established a rule—neither of us can leave without a kiss goodbye.

On Saturday, we'll be man and wife, and we're back to the beach with the whole gang turning out to celebrate with us.

The noise of running footsteps precedes a little girl in a pink dress with a fluffy tulle skirt flying across the glossy dance floor. Her blonde hair bounces in curls around her chubby cheeks, and two little boys in matching black suits are hot on her heels.

"Go far, Ironman!" Melody yells just before passing a football to Spencer.

He drops the helmet and catches it with a grunt a half-second before it nails him in the groin, and Daisy's daughter flies past him, steps ahead of Jesse and Ollie.

"Pass it to me!" Melody screams, now on the other side of the room. "Don't just hold it!"

"We got you. It's our ball now." Ollie holds Spencer's arm, trying to get the ball from him.

"Throw it to me, Ironman!" Melody's hands are over her head, and with every jump, her skirt rises and falls like a cloud.

Spencer's brow lowers. "Who taught her to call me that?"

Ollie makes a guilty face, and Jesse only laughs. "Don't hold up the game."

"Football." Spencer grouses, and my lips press together to hold back a laugh as he tosses it underhanded just short of my little cousin.

It bangs the ground on a corner and flies wildly in the opposite direction, and Melody jams her hands on her hips stomping after it. "He might be a superhero, but he can't play football."

Jesse and Oliver take off after it, and she breaks into a run just beating them, scooping the ball into her arms, looking so much like her daddy, and heading across the dance floor in the direction they came.

Spencer looks up at me and holds out his hand. "Will you come down now?"

Exhaling a happy sigh, I step down the ladder, dropping lightly into his arms. My arms go around his neck, and his go around my waist.

"You've been a naughty girl, Miss Winthrop." His tone makes my insides clench. "You need a spanking."

Leaning closer, I kiss his perfectly straight nose. "Maybe I did it on purpose so you would."

His eyes flare, and I start to laugh when my cousin slams through the double doors. "Sly, have you seen Melody? She's going to ruin that dress… Oh!"

We look over to my cousin, who isn't paying attention to us. Her eyes are lifted to the floral statues I just finished.

"Just look at them." She whips out her phone and takes a picture while I'm still in Spencer's arms.

He lowers me to my feet, hugging my back to his chest. "My bride is a genius."

He kisses the side of my neck, and Daisy watches him, smiling. "It's so nice to see you so happy, Spence. It's like a vote of confidence in humanity."

"Your cousin is a kook," he whispers in my ear, sending chills down my shoulder.

"Melody ran through here with the boys and a football less than a minute ago. They're probably out at the beach."

"Your mom said the lady from Karen Willis is here for your final dress fitting. I'll get the kids, but you'd better get back there."

Tilting my head to the side, I exhale a sigh. "I guess my spanking has to wait."

He slides a hand down to my ass, giving it a squeeze. "I'll take care of you."

Warmth floods my chest, and I place my palms on his jaw before kissing his lips. "You always do."

Tears are in my mom's eyes, and she attaches the small veil to the top of my braid. "Your father would be so proud of you."

"Ma!" I cry, looking up at the ceiling and touching the tears away as soon as they form in the corners of my eyes. "You're going to ruin my makeup."

"Nothing will ruin this makeup. It's ultra-waterproof performance wear." Daisy steps up to smooth my hair down my back. "You're going to need a triple wash to get it off."

"At least it won't smear on my dress. I hate when that happens."

"Spencer's going to pop a boner when he sees you."

"That's the goal." I wink, smoothing my hands down the thick white satin of my mini slip-dress.

The front has a deep V-neck that shows off my cleavage, and the back is also plunging, held together by a delicate string tied in a bow. Daisy helps me into the white blazer I'll wear over it.

"When you two disappear, I'll know not to go looking for you."

The door to the dressing room suite opens, and Courtney sticks her head inside. "How's it coming? You should see the guys out there. It's like one of those cover-model calendars."

"They do make an impressive lineup." Daisy fastens a necklace with a round blue sapphire charm resembling the night sky with three diamond stars on me. "This is your something borrowed and blue. Scout found it at a museum auction last month."

"Are the three stars the three of you?" I lift the unique pendant and study the circular pattern.

"Maybe..." Her voice trails off suspiciously, and my eyes widen.

"Are you?" Spinning around, I grip her wrists as she tries to act cool, which she totally sucks at doing. "Are you pregnant?"

"It's your special day! We can talk about my stuff later."

"Daisy!"

"The natives are restless, ladies." Ms. Alice barges into the dressing room. "Let's get this show on the road before Melody finds her football."

I give my cousin a tight hug, holding her hands before leaning back. "We're going to have the biggest party when I get back."

Ma clutches my upper arms. "I'm out first. Love you, darling. You're absolutely beautiful."

JR escorts my mother to her seat, and Tom leads Courtney next. I'm so happy to have him be a part of our lives now that they're dating.

Scout appears to escort Daisy, and from where I'm peeking behind the door, I catch his sparkling smile. He pulls her close and kisses her cheek, smoothing a hand over her stomach before starting for the front.

I'm so excited and happy for them, and looking around, I realize it's my turn. Sliding my hands down my skirt and adjusting my veil, I pick up the bouquet I arranged to match the sculptures. It's coral roses and oversized white peonies with thin white feathers cascading down the front.

Walking myself down the aisle was my idea. I read it was a dramatic statement of independence and doing what I want…

Now, I'm wishing I had agreed to let Miles escort me. Even if he's shorter, it would be nice to have an arm to grip. I'm a squinky bundle of nerves.

The wedding march begins, and I clear my throat. I square my shoulders and head out to the crowd waiting beachside.

Everyone stands when I appear, and my heart beats faster. I fix my gaze on Spencer and focus on putting one foot in front of the other. When he sees me, desire smolders in his eyes. It squeezes my stomach, and I wish I could kick off these shoes and run the rest of the way into his arms.

As if sensing my anxiety, he leaves the front, meeting me halfway down the aisle and taking my hands. "I've never seen anything more beautiful than you right now."

I blink fast to keep the tears away and clutch his arm, pulling my body securely against his. "Thanks for rescuing me."

I lean in close, and he wraps an arm around my waist. "I will always rescue you."

We're at the front, and the minister begins with the traditional service.

He leads us through the vows, and when he asks us to present the rings, Melody skips up in her tulle dress with Spencer's hammered titanium and ironwood band tied to a pillow. Heather found it at a vintage store in Boston and gave me a deal, something about our first child being named after her.

Ollie has my ring in his pocket, a simple platinum band that connects with the beautiful diamond engagement ring he gave me a year ago. It's breathtaking and ridiculously expensive… but it's nothing compared to the steel jade ring I always wear on my right hand. Spencer's promise ring.

"I now pronounce you man and wife. You may kiss the bride."

Looking up into his eyes, my heart is so full, it hurts. This bossy, arrogant, wounded, wonderful man is exactly what I've always wanted.

He cups my cheeks in his large hands, and before giving me my wedding kiss, he looks all the way to my soul.

Light shines in his smoky gaze, and I know he's thinking the same thing as me. We're back where we started, where he first caught me when I fell. I had no idea he would save me twice.

"Thank you for saving me," he whispers, sliding his nose along mine before covering my mouth with his.

It's a proper kiss, but it lights my body from the tips of my toes through my stomach all the way to my scalp. I clutch the front of his blazer, knowing I'll never let him go, and the noise of applause reminds me we have to stop kissing and be with our guests a little while.

He lifts his head, looking into my eyes once more. I reach up to place my palm against his smiling cheek.

"I love you," I whisper, imprinting this moment in my mind.

It's the best we've ever shared. This kiss is our promise to love and protect each other forever. It's a promise in front of the people who know us best, and it's a promise I know we'll keep.

This man is the best kind of trouble.

He's the kind that belongs to me.

The End.

Thank you for reading Spencer & Joselyn's romance. I hope your heart is as full and your cheeks as achy as mine are right now!

What to read Now?

TWIST OF FATE *is Scout and Daisy's second-chance, friends-to-lovers romance. It's funny and sexy and full of heart.*

Start with the short prequel story, ***"You Walked In,"*** *then binge the rest in* **TWIST OF FATE***...*

Or go straight to **TWIST OF FATE *Today!***

Also available on Audio*, narrated by Sebastian York and Samantha Brentmoor.*

Keep turning for a special Sneak Peek!

Already read it?

Meet Daisy and the whole Oceanside gang in **WHEN WE KISS** *a super fun and sexy, "enemies to lovers" romantic comedy—***FREE** *in Kindle Unlimited!*

Keep turning for a special sneak peek...

Never Miss a Sale or New Release!

Sign up for my newsletter (http://smarturl.it/TLMnews) so you don't miss it—and get a ***FREE 3-story book bundle...***
and/or
*Get a New Release Alert by messaging TIALOUISE to 64600 now!**
**Text service is U.S. only.*

Twist of Fate
By Tia Louise

A friends-to-lovers, second-chance, stand-alone romance by USA Today *bestselling author Tia Louise.*

To be "just friends" with a guy, you've got to follow The Rules:
Don't touch him unnecessarily.
Don't share your intimate dreams with him (even if he asks).
Don't kiss him, and *definitely* don't sleep with him.

Scout Dunne and I have been "just friends" since childhood.
He's everything you could want—sexy, charming, confident—
every girl's wet dream.
Until we broke The Rules.

We broke them in the ocean, in my aunt's bathroom, in my bed…
It was the hottest week of my life.
I'm one of the few people who knows the first-round NFL draft pick wants more than a life of sports.
Because we're friends, right?
Not anymore.

Now he's gone, and I'm trying to get my career back on track.
Mamma said a guy would never put your dreams ahead of his.
But *the twist of fate?*
It's something you never see coming.

(TWIST OF FATE is a STAND-ALONE friends-to-lovers, accidental pregnancy romance. No cheating. No cliffhanger.)

Prologue

Scout

PEOPLE USED TO SAY I COULD SWEET-TALK THE DEVIL INTO GOING TO church.

My mom, who was a librarian and English teacher and one of the smartest people I ever knew, said I was a *misunderstood character*.

She said people looked at me and saw a handsome young man—her words—with blond hair and blue eyes who slept with a football instead of a pillow and didn't make very good grades and assumed I traded on that to get ahead.

That's where they were wrong, she said. Mom said talking to people and listening to what they said made me just as smart as any valedictorian. She said my brother John, who we all call J.R. is more serious because he's older.

I loved my mom, but I'm not sure she's right either. I just learned pretty quickly growing up in Fireside, South Carolina, one of the smallest towns this side of Charleston, I'd get a lot further with being nice to people than being shitty.

For example, when I was in fourth grade, Ms. Myrna was going to flunk me because I couldn't analyze *Stargirl* to her liking. I just didn't understand it. The girl was weird, and I get it, Leo was a nerd with no friends, but what was I supposed to be learning from this story?

What was way clearer to me was Ms. Myrna's husband had thrown out his back working construction at the new development down on the coast, at Oceanside Beach. He was laid up in the bed for weeks, and I could tell by the tightness around my teacher's eyes, it was wearing on her.

So maybe I couldn't write an *A* paper, but I sure could mow her grass and cut that old vine off her back fence and hold the door for her when she carried too many books from the teacher's closet.

Ultimately, she said if I could at least recite the plot of the story, she'd give me credit for reading the book.

What did that teach me? Getting in there is better than keeping people at arm's length like my brother. It's not manipulation. It's simple facts.

Facts I never shared with my mom.

She was also the kindest person I knew. Laying in that sick bed, she would trace her fingers along my forehead as I knelt at her bedside, and I never wanted her to leave us.

The night she died, the man from church said heaven must've needed another angel. He said she was too good for this earth—something even I knew. He said it was fate.

Losing my mom was a truckload of bullshit. I've never felt anger so intense, burning so hard in my chest it radiated up the back of my neck. It made me want to break things. It made me almost forget...

My life was like an etch a sketch Fate scooped up and shook hard. I hated that feeling. It sucked. I never wanted to feel it again.

J.R. and I were left with my dad to figure out what the hell to do with ourselves, so we did what we knew—football. Dad threw himself into work, only noticing us when we were in the backyard drilling, and when J.R. and I became superstars.

Then I was cast in a few school plays, and I discovered I could be somebody else. I learned all that anger and pain disappeared on the stage. People liked watching me, and when I made them laugh or gasp or cry, I felt like I'd done something huge.

I've only ever told one person that story, a girl in glasses I discovered at a junkyard. She didn't misunderstand. She wanted to know more.

FEAR WAS MY EARLIEST MEMORY.

I can still see my mom looking out the kitchen window at the horizon, her body rigid and her mind far away. Even then, she was planning her escape, and it scared me.

I'd go to her and tug on her shirt, but she wouldn't pick me up. She'd exhale a noise of resignation and go back to hand-washing the dishes. Sometimes she'd break one.

Sometimes, when she was sitting in her chair, tearing the pages in one of dad's old books, she'd tell me to forget about trying to be pretty.

"Smart is the only thing that matters," she'd say. "No matter how pretty you are, it's our fate to be alone."

I didn't know what she meant. I thought she was pretty. I can still see her hair shimmering like turned maple in the sunshine, rare and beautiful, and I was here.

She left us in late May. I don't know what finally made her do it.

I was a junior in high school, listening to boy bands and

wishing my stick-straight blonde hair would have the slightest bend. I had a crush on the cute boy in my Algebra 2 class, but he turned out to be a real dickhead.

"Don't ever expect a man to put your dreams ahead of his." Fear knotted my throat as I watched her slamming her clothes into the open suitcase. "Men are selfish, self-centered… You have to look out for yourself. Men won't make you happy."

What about me? The question pressed against the insides of my temples. *Daisy* means happy. She'd told me a thousand times. *The daisy is the happiest flower.* I could make her happy.

I followed her to the door, unable to make my voice work, and she paused one last time. "I'll send for you as soon as I'm settled."

But she never did.

She wasn't the person I thought, either. She threw us away like old trash. Then one day, standing in a junkyard, someone magical found me….

Start with the short prequel story, "You Walked In," *then binge the rest in TWIST OF FATE…*

Or go straight to ***TWIST OF FATE Today!***

Also available on Audio, *narrated by Sebastian York and Samantha Brentmoor.*

When We Kiss

Exclusive Sneak Peek

"Kiss me…

You're too law-abiding for me.

What makes you say that?

That uniform. Those handcuffs.

Maybe I should put you in handcuffs.

Maybe I'd like to see you try…"

Tabby Green:

Preacher's niece.

Website designer.

Bad Girl.

Chad Tucker:

Retired military.

Deputy sheriff.

Hero.

He's a hot cop with a square jaw, a sexy grin, and a tight end. I'm a bad girl, a "Jezebel"—just ask all the old biddies in town. We're oil and vinegar. We don't mix. *But when we kiss…*

She's got flashing green eyes, red-velvet lips, and luscious curves in all the right places. She's a bad girl all right, and after what I've lost, I'm not looking for trouble. *But when we kiss…* Oil and vinegar DO mix, And when they do, *it's electric.*

A full-length, STAND-ALONE, opposites-attract romance about heroes, bad girls, and what happens when you stop fighting and surrender to love.

CHAPTER 1

Tabby

August, last year...

THE AIR IS ELECTRIC WHEN YOU'RE BEING BAD.

Little currents zip through your veins like lightning bugs grazing the tips of tall grass, and your stomach is tight. You're right on the edge, holding your breath...

Or maybe it's just me.

"Climb through." Blade squints up at me, the devil in his blue eyes.

He's holding the corner of a chain-length fence, and it makes a metallic screech as he lifts it higher.

Eleven thirty, and the night air is hot and humid—a warm washcloth on my bare skin. I duck through the opening, putting my hands up to protect my hair, my ears.

The space is just big enough for me to fit, hidden behind the tool shed. A rustling and a *BANG!* lets me know we're both through the breach. My naughty escort stands grinning in the moonlight. His hair is dark, his skin pale, and shadows deepen his eyes, nose, and mouth. He's like one of those scary-sexy vampires.

Or maybe I'm a little high.

"Let's do this!" He lets out a whoop and jerks off his black leather jacket.

His white tee is next, revealing a coiled serpent tattooed on his upper back. Jeans off, I catch a glimpse of his tight ass as he runs straight to the pool and breaks the glassy surface with a loud splash.

I shimmy out of my calf-length jeans and unbutton my short-sleeved shirt. I'm buzzing from the pot we just smoked at my small house, the old parsonage in town near the church, before we got the idea to break into the Plucky Duck Motel pool.

The Plucky Duck is off the Interstate, too far from the beach to be a tourist attraction. It's a million years old and completely deserted.

"Nobody ever stays here." I walk slowly down the steps into the shallow end.

The water is warm as it rises up my calves, to my knees, to my panties, to my waist. Blade is under the diving board watching me, his mouth submerged like a shark or a crocodile. His eyebrows rise as the water reaches my waist.

Through a blue haze of pot smoke, he demanded we do something I've never done before. I said there isn't much in Oceanside I haven't done. Until I thought of this old place.

Skinny dipping with Mayor Rhodes's tattooed bad-boy nephew is the perfectly spontaneous, irresponsible way to kick the last memories of Travis Walker from my heart.

Acid burns in my stomach. Tattooed Travis blew into town three months ago on a Harley, kissed me, and said I was the prettiest girl he'd ever seen. We screwed around for six weeks, until I caught him sneaking out of Daisy Sales's bedroom window.

He didn't even deny sleeping with her. He said Oceanside was getting "too restrictive," then he hopped on that Harley, lit up a cigarette, and drove away.

Asshole.

Serves me right for letting my guard down.

Pushing off the bottom, I keep my head above water as I glide to where Blade waits at the deep end. It's darker under the diving board.

"How long you planning to stay in Oceanside?" I don't really care. Blade's a fling I'm going into with my eyes wide open.

"Not sure." He reaches for my waist, his palms hot against my bare skin. "Ma said Uncle John needs to straighten me out."

He grins, and a dimple pierces his cheek. That bit of information makes me laugh, and I rest my elbows on his shoulders.

"I've been told something like that before." I give the field where we came in a longing glance. I wish we had more pot or at least a six-pack.

"Who's trying to straighten you out?" he asks, running his fingers up and down my sides.

My eyes return to his, and I do a little shrug. "My uncle's Pastor Green."

"No shit!"

The way he says it with a laugh makes him seem young, like a kid. I don't like the way it makes me feel, especially with the iron rod of his erection pressing against my stomach.

Twisting my lips, I reach up to hold the sides of the diving board, moving out of his arms. "I lived under his roof, his rules, until I was old enough to get out."

"I hear that." Blade reaches up to hold the diving board, mirroring my behavior.

We're facing each other, and I admire the lines of his lean muscles. Another snake is tattooed around his upper arm, but it looks amateurish, almost like he did it himself.

"So you're staying?" My red velvet lips purse, and he winks.

"That's what they tell me."

His muscles flex as he walks his hands forward, bringing our bodies closer together.

"Future's a lot brighter now that you're here."

I don't know if I'm sobering up or if his enthusiasm is killing the mood.

Blade had waltzed into the bakery where I work earlier this afternoon looking for trouble. The memory of Cheater Travis was looming large, and I decided I needed to do something reckless to blow off steam.

"You're new in town," I had said, cocking my hip to the side.

"My uncle's the mayor," he'd replied with a swaggering shrug.

"Good enough for me." I'd trotted out the door behind him, down the steps, and into the beat-up old Buick he'd parked out front.

We started on the strip at Oceanside Beach, where the high-rise condos line the shore like a wall and the tourists block up the sand. Then we had a few beers at the Tuna Tiki, the local beach bar-hangout, before he pulled out a dime bag of weed and we went back to my place to smoke it.

All in all, it was a fun, reckless day, but my buzz is definitely wearing off.

He gives me a boyish grin, and I decide I'm not looking for some *Grease*-inspired Danny and Sandy summer romance.

He walks his hands closer until my boobs smash against his chest. His legs pull my lower half flush against his, and I feel him hard against my panties. It's been a while since I've had a non-solo orgasm, and I'm not opposed to a fling with the town's newest bad boy.

He flashes a cocky grin before tilting his head to the side and kissing my cheek. His lips are soft, and I turn my face, ready to kiss him.

Still, before I do, I issue a warning. "Don't get attached."

His laugh reminds me of a young James Dean, and I'm ready. Our mouths inch closer. Another second, and they'll meet, tongues entwining. The space between my legs grows hotter, and I briefly consider I don't have a condom.

There's no way in hell I'm doing this without protection, when…

FLICK! It's a loud switch, like the throwing of a main breaker.

The entire pool floods with light, and I let go of the diving board, lowering my body into the water.

"What the fuck?" Blade does the same, joining me at the side of the pool.

The water offers little protection, as the lights fully illuminate our half-naked bodies under water. Looking up, I see we're surrounded.

"There she is! I knew I heard her voice." Betty Pepper is on the side of the pool, leaning down. Her lavender bouffant glows around her aged head, and she's wrapped in a peach terry-cloth robe pointing a bony finger in my direction.

"What are you doing in my pool, Tabitha Green?" Her voice is stern as always, the quintessential school marm.

"What does it look like I'm doing?" I snark. "Having a prayer meeting?"

"The pool closes at dark, *Tabitha*. And it's for registered guests only." She says it like I don't know very well we're out here breaking the law. "Who is that with you? Is that Jimmy Rhodes? Jimmy, is that you?"

My eyes flick to Blade. His face is downcast, and if it weren't so dark, I'd be sure his cheeks were red.

"It's me, Mrs. Pepper."

"I told your mamma I'd be looking out for you today. Did you check in with Wyatt at the hardware store? What are you doing running around with Tabitha Green?"

She says my name like it's a bad word.

Like I'm the bad influence.

I hiss at him. "You know Betty Pepper?"

He shrugs, and a male voice cuts through my irritation. "Tabby, did you take Jimmy to the bar at the Tuna Tiki?"

My brows tighten, and I squint up at Sheriff Cole. He towers over us from where he stands at the side of the pool, and his cowboy hat blocks the security light from blinding me. Otherwise, it's pretty much a police interrogation.

I answer truthfully. "I rode down to the strip in his car."

"We need you to get on out of the pool now," Sheriff Cole says, tipping his hat.

I look down at my transparent bra and panties, and there's no way in hell I'm climbing out in front of Sheriff Robbie Cole, Betty Pepper, and what I now see is a tall, quiet guy who's also wearing a khaki uniform.

He's quite a bit younger than Robbie, although he's older than me, and he stretches that polyester in a way I've never seen before.

Muscled arms hang from broad shoulders, leading down to narrow hips. His dark hair is short, and from under his lowered brow, I can see he's observing everything.

"Who's that?" I jerk my chin in his direction. "A storm trooper?"

The big guy's square jaw tightens as a muscle moves in his cheek. He gritted his teeth at me, and the heat in my panties reignites.

"Now's as good a time as any." Sheriff Cole, steps back gesturing to Mr. Tall, Dark, and Sexy. "Chad Tucker's my new deputy sheriff. He'll be working with me until I retire next year."

My lips press together. *No, thank you.* No Sheriffs. I don't care how square his jaw is or how well he fills out that uniform.

"Chad," Robbie continues. "This here is Tabitha Green, Reverend Green's niece, and this young man is Jimmy Rhodes, Mayor Rhodes's seventeen-year-old nephew."

"Seventeen!" The words are like a splash of water in my face, and I jerk off the wall, dog-paddling as fast as I can away from Jail Bait to the shallow end, humiliation burning in my chest.

"You hear that, Tabitha?" Betty shrills after me. "Not only are you breaking and entering, you're contributing to the delinquency of a minor."

Robbie continues introducing the baby wanna-be bad boy. "Jimmy is staying with his uncle until he finishes high school next year."

Every word is a cringing flash of shame, and I stomp up the pool steps, scooping my shirt off the tattered lounge chair and over my shoulders. My tight jeans are next, but it's a challenge getting them up my damp legs.

"What would your uncle say if he saw you?" Betty continues regaling me.

I stomp back to where Sheriff Cole and his new storm trooper stand, not even casting a glance at the kid in the pool. "Are you planning to arrest me?"

Lines form around the sheriff's eyes as he suppresses a grin. "Well, Mrs. Pepper here has listed your potential crimes."

"You're turning into a Jezebel," BP continues nagging. "If you're not careful, you're going to end up just like—"

My eyes flash at her, and her voice dies. She'd better not say my mother. If she knows what's good for her, she'd better not say it.

Instead she tightens her robe. "It's a slippery slope."

"What do you think, Chad?" Robbie exhales, straightening his posture and tugging on his waistband.

Mr. Silent But Deadly's eyes skim the front of my transparent bra before meeting mine. When they do, I realize they're light brown. I also realize they're hot, and chills break out over my skin in the warm night air. It strikes me this sexy future sheriff might be the real bad boy in the group.

His voice is a nice, low vibration. "I think you're playing a dangerous game… Miss?"

"She's single," Betty interrupts, as if not being married is another of my offenses.

Chad's eyebrows twitch ever so slightly. I'm pretty sure he doesn't think my being single is a crime.

My stomach is tight, and I swallow the knot in my throat. *Get a clue, Tabby.* The last thing on God's green earth I have any intention of doing is getting mixed up with a lawman.

"I don't play games, Mr. Tucker." My voice is higher than his, but just as determined. "And I don't check IDs on people I've just met."

"Maybe you should start." I can't tell if Chad Tucker is being a smartass or if he's just naturally cocky.

Seeing as he's a deputy, I'm willing to bet it's the latter.

Robbie's chuckle breaks the tension. "I think we can let you off with a warning this time. Do you need a ride home?"

I've managed to get my feet into my slides, and I see Jimmy standing on the side of the pool, pulling on his jeans and tee. He looks so skinny and young now. I wonder why I ever fell for his counterfeit tattooed bad-boy routine.

My phone is in my hand, and I tap the icons quickly. "No thanks. I just ordered an Uber. Looks like it'll be here in two minutes."

Gripping my shirt closed, I stomp up the sidewalk that leads to the front of the hotel.

Betty Pepper calls after me, getting her final jab in. "Consider your ways, Tabitha!"

I grind my teeth and fight the urge to flip her off as I round the corner. I'm saved by the headlights of a Dodge Dart with a white U in the windshield. It's too late to call my best friend Emberly, but when I get to the bakery tomorrow…

A billboard on the Interstate catches my eye, and I get an idea. Not Robbie Cole, Betty Pepper, or even Mr. Tall, Dark, and Sexy will see this one coming.

Acknowledgments

I'd like to thank **YOU** for reading this book and supporting me as an author.

If you read this book and love it, if you've read more than one or even all of my books and loved them, ***you are my hero.***

This book is for you.

And with all my heart, I thank the following people for supporting, encouraging, loving, and helping me:

God, Mr. TL, and **my girls.**

Ilona Townsel and **Renee McCleary.**

Charlotte, Josette, and all the ladies at **Grey Promotions,** along with **Kylie, Jo** and the awesome gang at **Give Me Books**.

My amazing beta readers, **Jennifer Christy, Amanda Shepard**, and **Maria Black**.

My copy editor **Janice Owen** and eagle-eye proofreader **Jaime Ryter.**

My Mermaid VIPs, **Ana Perez, Clare Fuentes, Sheryl Parent, Cindy Camp, Carla Van Zandt, Jaime Long, Tammi Hart, Tina Morgan**, and **Jacquie Martin**.

Stacey Blake, PB formatting, **Lori Jackson**, cover design, and **Michelle Lancaster**, photography. (*Superstars!*)

My **Mermaids** and to my **Starfish**, and all the **bloggers, bookstagrammers,** and **BookTokers!** who have made an art of book loving. I appreciate your help so much.

I give you all my love,
Stay sexy,
♥ *Tia*

Books by
TIA LOUISE

BOOKS IN KINDLE UNLIMITED

STAND-ALONE ROMANCES

Trouble, 2021

Twist of Fate, 2021

This Much is True, 2020

Reckless Kiss, 2020*

Here with Me, 2020*

Wait for Me, 2019*

Boss of Me, 2019*

Stay, 2019*

Make Me Yours, 2019*

Make You Mine, 2018

When We Kiss, 2018

Save Me, 2018

The Right Stud, 2018

When We Touch, 2017

The Last Guy, 2017*

(*Available on Audiobook.)

THE DIRTY PLAYERS SERIES

PRINCE (#1), 2016*

PLAYER (#2), 2016*

DEALER (#3), 2017

THIEF (#4), 2017

(*Available on Audiobook.)

THE BRIGHT LIGHTS SERIES

Under the Lights (#1), 2018

Under the Stars (#2), 2018

Hit Girl (#3), 2018

PARANORMAL ROMANCES

One Immortal (Derek & Melissa, vampires)

One Insatiable (Stitch & Mercy, shifters)

eBOOKS ON ALL RETAILERS

THE ONE TO HOLD SERIES

One to Hold (#1 - Derek & Melissa)*

One to Keep (#2 - Patrick & Elaine)*

One to Protect (#3 - Derek & Melissa)*

One to Love (#4 - Kenny & Slayde)

One to Leave (#5 - Stuart & Mariska)

One to Save (#6 - Derek & Melissa)*

One to Chase (#7 - Marcus & Amy)*

One to Take (#8 - Stuart & Mariska)

(*Available on Audiobook.)

Descriptions, teasers, excerpts and more are on my website (TiaLouise.com)!

Never miss a new release!

Sign up for my New Release newsletter and get a FREE Tia Louise Story Bundle!

Sign up now! (http://smarturl.it/TLMnews)

About the Author

Tia Louise is the *USA TODAY* bestselling, award-winning author of super hot and sexy romance.

Whether billionaires, Marines, fighters, cowboys, single dads, or CEOs, all her heroes are alphas with hearts of gold, and all her heroines are strong, sassy ladies who love them.

A former teacher, journalist, and book editor, Louise lives in the Midwest USA with her trophy husband and two teenage geniuses.

Signed Copies of all books online at:
http://smarturl.it/SignedPBs

Connect with Tia:

Website: www.authortialouise.com

Pinterest: pinterest.com/AuthorTiaLouise

Instagram (@AuthorTLouise)

Bookbub Author Page: www.bookbub.com/authors/tia-louise

Amazon Author Page: amzn.to/1jm2F2b

Goodreads: www.goodreads.com/author/show/7213961.Tia_Louise

Snapchat: bit.ly/24kDboV

** **On Facebook?** **

Be a Mermaid! Join Tia's **Reader Group** at
"Tia's Books, Babes & Mermaids"!
www.facebook.com/groups/TiasBooksandBabes

www.AuthorTiaLouise.com
allnightreads@gmail.comwww.facebook.com/groups/TiasBooksandBabes

www.AuthorTiaLouise.com
allnightreads@gmail.com

Printed in Great Britain
by Amazon